ESCAPE VELOCITY

VICTORIA ROMANSKI

In association with:

Elite Online Publishing
63 East 11400 South #230
Sandy, UT 84070
EliteOnlinePublishing.com

ISBN: 978-1-956642-55-1 (eBook)
ISBN: 978-1-956642-57-5 (Paperback)

FIC028080

FIC028070

QUANTITY PURCHASES: Schools, companies, professional groups, clubs, and other organizations may qualify for special terms when ordering bulk quantities of this title. For information, email info@eliteonlinepublishing.com.

This book is printed in the United States of America.

PROLOGUE

Night fell over the city, casting the world into darkness. Yet nothing compared to the darkness he felt inside. Shadows crept in, disrupted by flashing red-and-blue lights bouncing off the glass walls of Avion, James Blackwell's research laboratory. The usually empty lobby was crawling with detectives. What started out as a typical workday had ended in tragedy. At the time, he didn't know the story would make headlines in every major news outlet across the country: "Woman Presumed Dead After Experiment Gone Wrong."

James was beside himself, huddled in the corner of the room, head spinning as the chaotic voices and sirens melded into a steady hum. He shut his eyes, trying to slow his breathing. Suddenly, he became aware of himself and how he must look, a grown man in the fetal position. He smoothed out the wrinkles in his Tom Ford suit jacket and glanced around the room with a childlike vulnerability.

The front desk assistant strode over to him, her heels clicking on the floor. She knelt beside him, a blank look in her eyes. "Dr. Blackwell," she said softly. "They want to speak with you."

Her words sounded far in the distance. James grabbed his ear, which wouldn't stop ringing. She was still talking when he spotted the detectives glancing at them from across the room. Unsteadily, he got to his feet and headed toward them.

The coroner walked through Avion's front door, and James stopped to stare at the man who would determine the cause of death—without a body to examine. Suited up with a mask and gloves, he spoke to one of the detectives before stepping into the elevator to descend into the lab. *He'll never find out the truth*, James thought as he twisted his wedding band around his finger.

"Sir."

Louder, "Sir."

It took multiple attempts to pull James out of his trance.

"Dr. Blackwell, we're going to need you to come down to the station and answer a few questions." A large man wearing a suit looked James over as he spoke. "If that's all right," he added.

James knew it was not a request.

The overweight officer had a firm grip on James's arm as he escorted James out of the building. The scientist glanced back through the glass at the entrance to the business he had built over the last decade. *This is it*, James thought, his mind racing through the likely scenario that would play out next.

Three days later he was arrested and charged with the manslaughter of his wife.

1

One year later

Echoing voices bounced off the walls, pulling James from a deep sleep. For a split second each morning, he forgot where he was. He expected to roll over to a still-warm left side of the bed, the aroma of coffee wafting through his nostrils. He imagined warm, yellow sunlight filtering through the windows. But instead, when his eyes flickered open, he saw gray. The uncomfortable gray cot he tossed and turned on each night, the gray cement floor beneath him, and the gray, windowless walls surrounding him. He sat up abruptly and breathed in not the smell of his favorite coffee blend, but the smell of the shared toilet three feet away.

"Shit. I thought you might be dead," Andre said.

James glanced across the narrow room at his cellmate, Andre Wallace, whose large build took up most of the bed he was lying on.

"You were out like a light," Andre continued.

James rubbed the back of his neck and tilted his head side to side. "Wouldn't that be nice?"

"Come on now," Andre said, as he got to his feet. "Are you thinking about leaving me, Doc?"

"Of course not." James lowered his voice. "Tomorrow night will be the most important night of our lives. Make sure you're ready."

"I was born rea—"

"This is serious." James snapped. "Everything has to go exactly as planned. There is no room for error."

"Chill out, man. I know." Andre pulled on his heavily worn prison-issued canvas shoes.

"Do you have a shift?" James asked.

"Yeah, hopefully one of my last," Andre said, smirking at James before he disappeared out the cell door.

James grabbed a book off the table and flipped it open. He devoted most of his waking hours to reading. He wanted to absorb as much knowledge as possible while he was in this place, although the collection of reading material at StormRidge Correctional Facility was an insult to anyone's intelligence. He had been a silent observer over the months he'd spent there. Most of the other men spent their time working out, doing drugs, or bullying the weakest among them. It was in James's best interest to keep to himself.

His anxiety rose each month he was out of work, and he longed to be back in the lab. A small part of him worried his team would make a groundbreaking discovery without him or accomplish nothing at all; he wasn't sure which would be worse. When he was taken into custody, Avion was only beginning to expand their research to human trials.

He sat in his cell, day after day, reflecting on his accomplishments. He'd dedicated his life to physics and unusual astronomical studies. Being the first to patent a new gravitational surveillance system, James and his colleagues were ahead of their time in the study of wormholes. Recognized as a thought leader in his field, James had grown accustomed to a certain kind of treatment. In prison, he quickly learned his days of being idolized were over, and the people there wouldn't take any of his shit.

The cell assignment James received when he arrived at StormRidge was truly a blessing. Good people were hard to come by in prison, but he happened to be living with one.

Andre wasn't like the rest of the inmates. Something was different about him, and it wasn't just his genuine nature and kindness. He would rather stay in his cell reading than be outside during yard time. When he wasn't working his janitorial shift, he was in his bed. James wondered why Andre subjected himself to mopping grimy floors of vomit, urine, and blood when he could've worked in the kitchen, laundry, or any less deplorable job. Andre said cleaning kept his mind occupied. But as James quickly discovered, the janitorial job was also a way to find out information. Andre was always in the know about what went on around the prison, the good and the bad.

James looked at the empty cot across from him and remembered Andre's biggest discovery. One night, Andre returned late from his cleaning shift and woke James.

"What the fuck do you want?" James asked. It was early in his time at StormRidge, and it was rare for him to get any sleep.

"You're not gonna believe what I saw," Andre said with no hint of amusement on his face.

James sighed and sat up. "What is it?"

"So these guards, I saw them acting sketchy as hell, talking quiet to each other. So I waited and watched them."

"I'm sure I don't want to know what happened next."

"Just listen. They were waiting by the door to the tunnel that separates the two sides of the prison. After a few minutes, two more guards showed up, and they had women with them."

"Female guards?"

"No. They were wearing jumpsuits. They gotta be from the women's prison next door."

"What were they bringing them here for?"

"I don't know. Nothing good."

It wasn't long before James discovered the guards were running a trafficking operation. There was no one to stop them from getting away with it. The warden was known for countless cover-ups over the years. He let the guards do as they pleased with no repercussions for their actions.

Now James paced in his empty cell. His mind dwelled on thoughts of the guards' abuse of power, but he couldn't focus on that. For their plan to be a success, James needed to keep a clear mind.

2

James awoke the following day to a crunching sound. Andre was leaning against the wall with a bag of The Whole Shabang potato chips on his lap.

"What time is it?" James asked and shot him an annoyed look.

Andre shrugged. "Hey, it might be my last chance to eat these."

James never understood the fascination among the inmates with this brand of chips. *They're just potato chips for God's sake*, he thought. *They all taste the same.* He grabbed his notebook and tore out a page.

"What are you doing?" Andre asked.

James finished writing and folded up the paper. "When you go down to solitary to clean, I need you to give this to Mason Walker."

Andre took the note. "I might not be cleaning the shoe today, Doc."

"The entire plan depends on this."

"Then why am I just hearing about it now?" Andre shook his head. "Fine. I'll figure something out."

"Thank you."

James had noticed a major shift in Andre's mood since he discovered the plan. When they first met, James immediately picked up on the front Andre put on around people. He would joke around, only to retreat to his bed, his mask coming off. Sometimes he would just lie on his bunk facing the wall, pretending to be asleep. But James knew he wasn't asleep. Something had broken him, and James never asked what it was. After learning about James's plan, Andre became hopeful, looking forward to what would come next.

James walked through the common area to use one of the phones, which were all occupied. He waited patiently, examining his surroundings. He wanted to confirm the most important aspect of his plan was still in motion.

In front of James, a short, unhealthily thin man covered in tattoos slammed the phone down. A guard standing nearby shot the man a look of disgust. James picked up the handset and wiped the mouthpiece on his shirt before dialing.

Chris answered on the second ring. "James, is that you?"

It had been months since James spoke to his closest friend and colleague of twelve years. He wasn't ashamed to admit how much he missed Chris's company. "Yes, I just wanted to check in and see how you were doing."

"Oh, you know, same shit." Chris chuckled.

"The big game is on tonight, right?" James asked.

"Yeah, Patriots versus the Steelers. Right on time too."

James exhaled a sigh of relief. He knew he could count on Chris; he trusted him with his life. Besides, he didn't have a choice. Without Chris's help, he would have no chance of escaping from this horrible place.

3

The court appearance that landed Mason Walker on death row left him condemned to solitude. But he didn't know for how long. He'd heard of a case in Florida where a man had been on death row for nearly forty years. He died of natural causes before they got around to executing him.

Inside the tiny room he was forced to call home, Mason chuckled to himself. *Natural causes. There's nothing natural about keeping a man in a cage.*

In the beginning, he'd served his sentence proudly. For years, he'd replayed that day in his head, that moment of arriving home after a long day of work, only to find the lifeless bodies of the two people he loved the most. At that moment he vowed to avenge his wife and daughter, and he took justice into his own hands. Twenty-five to life was a fair price to pay once he achieved true justice in his heart.

He often wondered if his need for revenge started decades earlier, when he served in the Marine Corps from the impressionable age of eighteen. Back then, he respected the laws of his country and considered himself a true patriot. It wasn't until he was inside that he learned of the abhorrent corruption that plagues not only the nation's prisons, but also its politicians, police forces, and the government itself.

Mason had been unprepared for how bad isolation could be. The boredom. The loneliness. It ate at him from the inside out. It felt like a hunger that could never be satiated. As time went on, he began to feel like a shell of a person. He had nothing else to lose.

Before he was thrown in solitary confinement for a fight his cellmate started, he'd enjoyed the time he spent outside in the yard. Those were the moments when he could imagine he was somewhere else. He reminisced about the years he had with his wife, Jane, and their daughter, Emily. He remembered, so vividly, pushing Emily on her swing set, her first day of kindergarten, and the last family vacation they got to take.

Now Mason leaned his head back against the cold, hard wall and closed his eyes. He thought back to a hot summer day in July, when his shoulders burned as they rubbed against his T-shirt after spending time in the Oahu sun. His wife and daughter wanted to spend their days on the beach, admiring the exceptionally large waves. They even convinced him to hike to the top of Diamond Head, which revealed his cardiovascular health just wasn't what it used to be. But the view from the top of the volcano had been worth the exercise.

He enjoyed every moment spent with his family in Hawaii, but he'd been waiting for one significant excursion. They strode along the dock toward the Pearl Harbor National Memorial. They entered one of the ships, and a strange mix of wonder and resentment filled Mason. His daughter grew bored quickly and was anxious to get back to the hotel, but before leaving the site, he visited the memorial wall. Mason scanned the wall until he found what he was looking for: his great-grandfather's name.

Mason's adoptive parents had expected him to join the armed services, and he would've done anything to please the people who saved him as a child. This made his discharge from the Marines even more difficult. He'd never forget the mistake he made, sending his men on a suicide mission when he was certain the odds were in their favor.

It was the same luck that landed him on death row. One day during the hour he spent in the yard, he opened his eyes from his daydreams and the place was deserted, except for two guards in the distance watching him in anticipation, anxious to see what was going to happen next. The wind made him shiver, and he could feel something wasn't right; something in the air had shifted.

Three men approached him, attempting to corner him against the wall. One of them had a tattoo that ran down the side of his face, one was tall and lanky, and the third had a stockier build. They all wore the same expression. He knew their intention by the look in their eyes. The air suddenly felt thick, and it became difficult to breathe. He made a split-second decision.

Kill or be killed.

The one with the tattoo approached from the right, drawing a small shiv from his waistband, as the other two came from the left. Mason glanced at the two men on the left, but out of the corner of his eye, he saw the one with the face tattoo lunge forward. Mason blocked the man's arm in one swift movement, grabbing his makeshift weapon with ease. A look of shock came over the man's face as Mason's fist connected with it, knocking him to the ground, and leveling the odds to two against one. The two remaining men exchanged a glance before coming at Mason full force.

Then he blacked out.

Mason woke up the following day in the medical room only to find out those two men hadn't made it. He was now facing an additional double-murder charge. Unfortunately for them, they hadn't known he was a trained fighter. He'd kept to himself during the eight years he spent at StormRidge. None of the gangs had bothered him until that day. Someone must have learned of his past. His corrupt friends. His unfortunate ties to the mob. It could be any number of people seeking revenge.

Mason opened his eyes and came back to the present and the reality of his six-by-eight room. Grimy, tan walls towered above his bed—if you could call it that—and constantly felt like they were closing in. He feared his execution date was nearing. He didn't know how close it was, but he felt it coming. After exhausting all possible appeals, he felt like he was watching an invisible clock ticking down, and time was running out.

Mason heard someone shuffling out in the hallway. *That's odd*, he thought. The food delivery wasn't supposed to be there yet.

The shuffling stopped just outside the door.

"Who's there?" Mason asked.

Silence.

Someone shoved a small piece of paper under the door.

"Hey!" He banged on the door. "What is this?"

"Blackwell sent me," a quiet voice replied.

He reached for the paper and unfolded it. All it said were two words: *Riot tonight.*

Mason thought of the peculiar man he'd spoken to in the yard just days before the fight with his cellmate sent him to solitary. *What did he say his name was?* It came to him suddenly. *James, that was it.* An esteemed scientist he'd heard about in the news. He could barely believe it when James approached him with a wildly convincing plan. This man was trustworthy, Mason believed, and after some persuading from James, Mason was in. But after he was blamed for the fight months prior, he thought all hope was lost.

He flipped the paper over in his hands, stood, and leaned against the door. "What am I supposed to do?" he asked quietly.

But the anonymous messenger was gone.

Mason paced around the room. *Maybe the note was meant for someone else?* No, it had to be for him. James had explained the plan to him when they last spoke, in excruciating detail. Mason had an overwhelming urge to get out of his cell. It was like something was calling to him. Every nerve in his body told him to get out of that room. It was a risk, but one he had to take. This was his only chance to see if the scientist was legit.

Mason looked around his filthy solitary cell. Underneath his bed, a part of the metal frame was sharp, most likely filed down by a previous occupant. He'd discovered it one day when he dropped his copy of Hemingway's *The Old Man and the Sea*, which he had read more times than he could count. As he reached down to get the book, he'd sliced his palm.

Now Mason gritted his teeth and, very carefully, ran his wrist horizontally across the metal bar until blood seeped out of the wound and trickled down his arm. All he had to do was alert one of the guards and hope like hell the plan hadn't changed.

4

Wind howled as rain pattered on the roof of the prison. Gently at first, then faster and more violently—as if the skies were growing restless. James imagined the night sky. He pictured clouds giving way to a full moon shining its grace over the earth exactly as he remembered. It felt like ages since he'd seen it. A thunderstorm in the distance was closing in, the sound nearly vibrating the walls. He scrambled for his notebook, frantically tossing aside his belongings until he found it and his pen. He scribbled frantically, words and equations he alone could understand.

Momentarily, James caught Andre's gaze. Andre lay on his bed with his fingers pressed to his temples, likely suffering from one of his headaches. He was looking at James like he was insane. Perhaps Andre wasn't entirely wrong, but James didn't care how he was perceived. Not by Andre. Not by anyone else.

Nothing mattered except the next few minutes.

The sound of thunder roared through his ears again, and he slammed the notebook shut, quickly tucking it into his waistband. James stood with confidence at the front of the cell, resting his hands almost casually on the metal door. He was apprehensive about taking Andre with him. However, the choice was taken away from him when Andre discovered his plan a few months back.

Andre had stormed up to James angrily, showing extreme emotion for the first time since they'd met. "Were you even gonna tell me what you had planned?" Andre had asked.

"What's there to tell?"

Andre let out a sound of annoyance. He reached around James and pulled the piece of paper out of the pillowcase. "When were you gonna tell me about this?"

"So we're going through each other's stuff now, is that it?" James grabbed the paper.

"Don't change the subject." Andre lowered his voice to a whisper. "You're planning to break out of here."

"I was going to tell you."

"You can do me one better. You're taking me with you," Andre said.

"No. It's too dangerous," James started. He thought for a moment, then began again, "Are you really willing to risk everything?"

"Are you?" Andre asked, shaking his head. "You know you're risking a lot with this note in here. What if one of the guards found it during a search?"

James stood and walked to the toilet. He unfolded the paper and read Chris's scribbled handwriting, the date and time he should try to escape. He tore the paper to shreds and flushed it.

Andre stared at James, and something was different about his gaze.

"Are you sure?" James asked.

"I've got nothing else to lose, Doc."

"That's not true. You have your life."

"Which means dog shit in here. Tell me the plan. I'll be the judge if it's worth risking my life or not."

James was filled with the same anticipation he felt back in the lab each time they experimented with his technological creation. He felt the blood coursing through his veins and his heartbeat quickened. Reflecting on his career, he realized being a scientist wasn't just what defined him. It was what made him feel alive.

He'd had a tough decision to make. It would be risky to deviate from his plan and take Andre with him, but they'd developed a bond over the months he'd been at StormRidge. He also had a strong feeling Andre wouldn't take no for an answer. Besides, who knew if Andre would keep his mouth shut if James left without him?

"What exactly is going down tonight in the cafeteria?" Andre asked, bringing James back to the present. "How is this gonna work anyway?"

"You'll see," James said.

"Well, I've been thinking. You said we're supposed to go to the medical wing. But that's where the guards have been bringing the girls."

"Shit," James muttered. "We'll have to hope they're not there tonight."

"Or we can offer the girls help?"

James exhaled loudly. "How do you expect to do that while we're attempting to break out of a maximum-security prison?"

"We can take them with us. They might be able to help. And we have a better chance if we stick together. Power in numbers, right?"

"No!" James exclaimed, louder than he'd intended. "This is something I planned to do on my own. It's too dangerous to bring anyone else along. Even you."

"Oh, I get it. You're the only one that deserves to get out of here. Thanks for clearing that up."

"You know that's not what I mean." James paced around the cell. "It's more complicated than that."

"What's complicated?"

James was silent for a moment. "You wouldn't believe me if I told you," he finally said.

"Cut the bullshit, Doc."

"Now isn't the time for this. If everything goes to plan, you'll see for yourself, okay?"

"Fuck your plan. I won't see shit. I'm sitting my ass right here, and you can have fun getting caught."

James leaned against the wall and listened to the storm pass through as he waited for the signal.

5

Andre had given up hope the instant he heard the jury's verdict: *guilty.* The one word haunted him more than anything else ever had in his life. His fear and confusion slowly turned to rage. *How pitiful it is to turn into a statistic,* he thought. Just another innocent Black man failed by the system.

He'd always been considered the toughest among his friends. Captain of the football team in high school, named MVP in college. Little did he know how broken he would become. Once everyone turned their backs on him and no one believed him, it shattered him to the core. It messed with him so bad he started to question everything, even his own truth.

Only God knows I'm innocent, Andre thought.

But what type of a God would let innocent people suffer at the hands of the system? How many young men's lives would be ruined forever? Years torn away from them, years they'd never get back. What type of a God would let these men be robbed of their youth? Of their innocence? Of their truth?

Now Andre watched as James paced nervously back and forth in the tiny cell they called home. "Can you stop doing that? You're stressing me out."

James stopped and looked him in the eyes. "Sorry. I feel like it should've started by now. What time is it?"

Andre shot him an annoyed look. "I don't know. Maybe you should've had those friends of yours smuggle you in a cell phone."

"They'll come through for us." James took a seat on his bed and tapped his foot on the floor over and over. "They have to."

"Who are you trying to convince?"

"They've never let me down, not in the last decade we've been working together."

"Sounds like there's nothing to worry about then." Andre rummaged through his stuff. "Even if it doesn't happen, we'll be all right." He found the bag of chips he was looking for and tore it open.

James glared at him.

"What?" Andre asked impatiently.

"Now's not the time to be eating your goddamn chips."

"What's your deal, man? I know you want to get out of this place, but come on. You know how risky this is. You don't even have a long sentence."

"You don't understand." James appeared to grow more agitated by the minute, scratching his head.

"You're right, I don't. And you will never understand what I've been through."

"Because you're innocent," James said mockingly.

Andre threw the bag of chips to the side. "Yeah, unlike you, I never killed anyone."

"I never . . . " James started and then grew quiet.

"Exactly." Andre shook his head. "What the fuck do you know?" he added under his breath.

The door to their cell block buzzed open and several guards wandered in.

"It's a random search," Andre said.

James sat up straight on the bed.

The nicer guard spoke. "Stand against the wall, please."

Andre and James did as they were told while the guards looked under their mattresses, through their belongings on a table beside the bed, and even behind the toilet. Andre felt his heart racing. *Why's our cell being searched? Do they know something?*

"Clear," a guard said after a few moments. The guards moved on to the next cell, and Andre let out a sigh of relief.

"I got a look at his watch," James said, breaking the silence. "In twenty minutes, we'll hear our cue."

Andre sat back down on the bed and grabbed his chips, but he was too anxious to eat. All he could think was that he might be making the biggest mistake of his life, following the deranged scientist who'd become his closest friend.

6

Mason's vision started to blur after the third punch the guard threw. He held still and took the beating. He was strong enough, and if he fought back, the consequences would be much greater than the temporary reward.

The guard, a man called Brooks, stationed in solitary for the past few weeks, was notorious for abuse and often targeted Mason. In fact, Mason had heard horror stories of what the man had done to other inmates. It got so bad over at the women's section of the prison the warden decided to move Brooks to the men's side. Why he wasn't terminated, Mason couldn't figure out, but apparently, the number of people pursuing corrections as a career was at an all-time low.

Brooks shoved Mason into the wall, and Mason lost his balance, catching himself with his hands a second before his face connected with the ground. He looked at his wrist, still bleeding steadily.

"Why are you on the floor? Are you disobeying orders?" the guard asked. The corners of Brooks's mouth turned up in a smirk.

Mason grimaced and tried to get to his feet, but the guard kicked him in the stomach with his steel-toed boot, knocking him back to the ground. "Get up, inmate."

Brooks handcuffed Mason, dragged him out of his solitary cell, and brought him to psych, a section of the medical ward where they brought inmates who tried to harm themselves or were having a psychotic break. The stark white room held a single patient bed at the very center. A nurse who appeared to be in her sixties stood by the door. The room smelled of harsh chemicals, likely used to sterilize the miscellaneous medical tools scattered around the room. He eyed the instruments to determine if any of them could be used as weapons, but there was nothing sharp enough.

His ribs ached, and he feared the guard might have cracked one or two. But luck was on his side tonight. The idiot guard had cuffed Mason's bleeding wrist to the bed to temporarily restrain him. To properly dress the wound, the nurse had to remove his handcuffs. He waited for the guard to leave the room so he could make his move. Mason had no intention of staying in there while the riot went down.

Then it happened. The guard received a call on his radio. "Brooks, we need you in Cell Block B immediately. Code red," an urgent voice said on the walkie talkie.

It must have already begun. Mason was brimming with excitement. His heart raced.

"Shit," Brooks said, as he left the keys to the handcuffs on the table and jogged out of the room. Another stupid decision.

"Hello, Mr. Walker. My name is Elaine." The nurse spoke with a hint of a southern accent. Her gray curly hair hung near her eyes. She reminded him of his mother.

Mason nodded and smiled but didn't speak.

Elaine locked eyes with Mason, and he thought he saw fear. Maybe she was trying to determine if he was truly evil. Perhaps she wanted to assess if he deserved his execution.

"All right, hon, I'm gonna uncuff you," she said. "I need you to hold perfectly still while I move the cuffs over to your other wrist so I can put the bandage on. Can you promise me that?"

She was visibly nervous. The guard had left her alone with a death-row inmate, which wasn't standard protocol. Normally, the psych patients were seen by the doctor, but he was nowhere to be found tonight. The nurse was on her own.

"Of course," Mason said calmly.

Elaine approached his arm to remove the handcuffs. She fumbled with the keys and grabbed his hand. Mason felt a twinge of guilt as he slowly lifted the empty metal tray, meant for holding medical supplies, with his free hand and brought it down forcefully over her head.

She fell to the floor without a sound. *It had to be done,* he told himself. She would likely recover with no more than a mild concussion.

He bent down and grabbed the keys, still clutched tightly in the nurse's hand, and removed the handcuffs. He took a bandage off the table and quickly patched up his wound. He then searched the room for anything useful and settled on a small scalpel in an unlocked case, pocketing it as he walked out the door.

Chaos erupted all over the prison. Next to the medical wing were common areas for inmates—those who weren't stuck in solitary—to enjoy. This area was comprised of a rec room, a library, and even a classroom where inmates could study for their GED. These rooms were now filled with men from different cell blocks. Shouts echoed in the hallways.

It was like a switch went off inside everyone's head and told them to fight. There was blood everywhere. The floors showed more red than white. Mason recognized some of the gangs, separated in different rooms. They had guards on the floor, begging for their lives. Some of the inmates were fighting each other to the death. He couldn't believe his eyes. It felt like he was watching a movie.

Mason saw Brooks, the guard who tormented him nearly every day.

Guess he never made it to Cell Block B, Mason thought.

Brooks was slowly backing away from a group of inmates who'd gotten his gun away from him. He had his arms held up to the sky, as if he were innocent. This was an opportunity Mason couldn't pass up.

Mason walked up behind the guard, nodded to the group, and grabbed him. "This one's mine," he said.

The leader of the group hesitated for a moment, glaring at Mason. He raised his eyebrows, causing a tattooed symbol on his forehead to crease into a distorted shape. Then he shrugged, and he and the others went off to find someone else to torment.

Mason withdrew the scalpel from his pocket and held it up to the guard's neck. He could smell his fear, feel the sweat dripping off him. "This is for all the beatings you thought you got away with. And for thinking you're better than us."

"Wait! Please!" The guard's entire body trembled. "I'm sorry. Please don't kill me!"

Mason chuckled. Did he really think begging for his life would work?

"I'll do anything. What do you want?"

"All those times you tortured people, abused your position of power, and thought you could do whatever you wanted, you forgot about one thing."

Brooks turned his head to look Mason in the face, pleading with his eyes. "What?" His voice was barely louder than a whisper.

"We're criminals," Mason said, applying pressure as he dragged the blade across the guard's throat. He threw Brooks on the floor. "And karma's a bitch."

Mason searched the guard's pockets as he coughed and gasped for air, blood trickling down his neck. He found a keycard that would give him access to the control room, and he made his way there quickly, avoiding several deadly encounters.

He waved the card in front of the sensor and a green light appeared.

The control room was spacious with large screens displaying live feeds from the many cameras around the prison. Below the screens was the control panel. Mason pressed the row of release buttons, opening the remaining cell blocks that hadn't joined in the riot yet. He pushed the most important button last, the one that opened Cell Block D, where the scientist was.

As the cell doors unlocked, most of the inmates took their chance and ran. Mason stood back for a moment and watched everything unfold, but only for a moment. He had to complete his task. He disabled all the prison's security cameras and cut the power.

7

Martina Alvarez nervously ran her fingers through her long black hair as she walked through the concrete underground tunnel. She could feel the guard's presence, always just a few steps behind her and her cellmate. Her nerves ran high, but she never dared to show her fear.

She'd learned of the corruption occurring at the prison soon after she arrived. Martina had stayed out of trouble for most of her sentence until a new warden came to StormRidge. Once new guards were hired, it wasn't long before they decided to use the women's side of the prison to their advantage. Women were often brought to the men's side of the prison, willingly or unwillingly, for an exchange of favors, sexual or otherwise.

Tonight would be Martina's third time heading to the other side of the sprawling prison, but it was the first time her cellmate, Hayden Miller, came with her. Martina hadn't planned it this way. What started as an idea to get contraband from the guards turned dangerous. A system of abuse began to form once the guards realized they had free rein to do anything they wanted. She was taking a risk coming here, but it would all be worth it once she got what she'd been waiting for—a cell phone to try to contact her daughter. The foster family caring for her daughter had been dodging her calls for weeks.

Martina looked at her companion, bubbly and carefree with blonde, curly hair bouncing against her shoulders as she walked. This place hadn't worn her down yet, and she had Martina to thank for that. She'd inadvertently assumed the role of a mother figure to the much-tinier Hayden, and being under Martina's protection saved Hayden from a world of problems.

Martina frowned at how casual Hayden seemed. "You need to be careful when we get over there."

Hayden shrugged. "It's not like we're turning tricks. I'm just your standard mule. All I have to do is deliver a package back to our side."

Martina elbowed Hayden in the side. "Don't be stupid. A lot of those men haven't seen a woman in years. Maybe a nurse or a female officer, but we'll be a lot more vulnerable than they ever are."

Hayden giggled and nodded her head at the guard. "We've got private security, so we should be okay."

Martina stopped walking. "You're so naïve, it's no wonder you ended up in this shithole."

Although the two spent an inordinate amount of time together, Hayden usually seemed oblivious to Martina's constant irritation, apparently mistaking the blunt insults for some form of humor. This time, however, Hayden stepped closer, her face just inches from Martina's. "Naïve? At least I'm not a wanna-be bank robber," she said, taunting Martina.

"Move your asses, ladies," the guard barked.

They waited for another guard to buzz open the door leading into the men's section of the prison, and Martina's thoughts went back to the day her life took a turn for the worse. One stupid decision impacted the entire course of her life.

That day, a heat wave washed over California, causing Martina's tiny apartment to feel like a sauna. The air felt thick, and she longed for even a single day with air conditioning. She was sitting in front of the fan when her sister arrived, high and obnoxious, her three children in tow.

"I can't take the kids today," Martina said before her sister even opened her mouth to speak.

"Oh," her sister said, cocking her head to the side. "So it's gonna be like that?"

"Luciana, please."

"Damn, you must be serious, using my full name and all." Luciana pulled a pack of cigarettes and a lighter out of her bag.

"You know you can't smoke in here," Martina said.

"Says who?"

Martina grabbed Luciana's arm and pulled her outside onto the third-floor landing. Luciana leaned against the railing and lit up.

"Look," Luciana said, her voice steady. "I promise this is the last time, okay? I got somethin' really important to do tonight. Can't you just watch them for a few hours?"

Martina sighed and folded her arms. The sun beat down on them unforgivably. She was sick of being the responsible one. It had been that way as long as she could remember. She'd taken on the role of caring for Lucy when they came to the US, while their mother worked two jobs just to get by. Now, as an adult, Martina had a daughter of her own, who she was struggling to feed. She couldn't afford her sister constantly dumping her kids there.

Martina looked at her younger sister. She had always been small, but she looked even more frail than normal. Almost like she was withering away to nothing. "Fine. A few hours," Martina said.

"Thank you." Luciana pulled Martina in for a hug. She smelled of cheap perfume. "You won't regret it."

"Come back early. I mean it. Sofía's got school tomorrow."

"Will do." Luciana winked at her and headed for the stairs, her bag swinging by her side as she hurried away.

That was the last time Martina saw Lucy, whose body was discovered in a lake the following week.

The number of children Martina was responsible for grew from one to four overnight. After losing her waitressing job due to the shifts she missed when she was grieving her sister's death, and an eviction notice on her apartment door, she was prepared to do anything to make fast cash. What seemed like an opportunity to finally be able to provide for the kids ultimately led to her downfall. She'd made peace with her consequences, but not a day went by when she didn't think about the real victims in all this—the four innocent kids forced into the foster care system.

Martina clenched her fists, digging her fingernails into her palms, and it took all her willpower not to mess up Hayden's smug face. Aside from the fact that it would land her in trouble, she'd started to care about Hayden, as much as she hated to admit it.

Hayden saw her reaction and giggled.

"Come on. I'm just kidding." Hayden said. "Don't get your panties in a bunch."

"What makes you think I'm wearing panties?" Martina responded matter-of-factly. It was as close as she could come to a joke. "Look, I'm just trying to do my time quietly without getting into any trouble. I've only got a few years left."

"You lucked out."

"I took a plea." Martina scoffed. "Trust me. Luck had nothing to do with it."

"I'm just saying, you'll get out of here long before me. At the end of the day, that's all that really matters, isn't it?" Hayden suddenly looked like she was going to cry. "I've only been here a year, and I don't think I can do it."

"No talking!" the guard bellowed.

Martina wondered why he spoke as if he was yelling to someone across the room. "Relax, you'll be fine," she said quietly. "You're strong."

The corners of Hayden's mouth twisted up again.

They entered the medical room; its once white walls were tinted yellow. The grimy floors desperately needed cleaning. Patient beds lined the walls, and medical instruments were laid carelessly on metal tables. A stench of chemicals lingered. *At least they seem to be sanitizing something in here*, Martina thought.

"Wait here," the guard said, glaring at the women.

Hayden made a face right back at him. He spit on the ground by their feet and turned to leave.

The door slammed shut behind him and Martina let out a long sigh.

"What a dick!" Hayden said.

They both laughed.

"So how does this work?" Hayden asked. "Is someone gonna bring us what we asked for?"

"They'll bring it to us and ask for something in return," Martina said, lowering her voice.

It was eerily quiet. The medical wing—a generous term for what it actually was—typically was backlogged with patients suffering from a cracked rib or a shiv in the back. What was normally a loud murmur of shouting and swearing voices was now a deafening silence.

"What's taking so long? Let's get this over with, this place is creeping me out," Hayden said.

"I don't know. I've got a bad feeling."

Lights flashed, and the alarm sounded.

"What the actual—?" Hayden said, covering her ears.

Martina froze. In her two years at StormRidge, she'd heard this alarm just once.

8

The lights went out. For a moment, darkness engulfed the prison. James relished it. The darkness felt safe and all-consuming. Like he could close his eyes and cease to exist, and all his problems would go away. James was no longer accustomed to the absence of light, which was one of many things he'd taken for granted before arriving at StormRidge. It had taken him nearly two months to learn to sleep with the lights on.

All the cell doors opened at once.

"Looks like Mason came through," James said.

Andre ignored him and rolled over on his bed to face the wall.

"Come on," James said, his voice barely louder than a whisper.

"How do I know you're not leading me into a shitstorm?"

"You don't." James managed a smile.

Andre sighed.

"Get up. We have to go. Now!" James insisted, grabbing his arm.

"Touch me again, you'll regret it." Andre looked over his shoulder.

James let go of his arm and looked into his eyes, pleading, hoping Andre understood the gravity of their situation. "Do you trust me?"

"No." Andre paused. "But I trust everyone else less."

"This is our chance to get out of here. During the riot. There won't be another one. We must leave right now."

"Okay." Andre got to his feet. "After you," he said mockingly.

James led him out of their cell and down the narrow hallway, a part of him still second-guessing bringing Andre along. He'd initially expected to be alone when he carried out his plan, but he'd soon realized he would need help to pull it off. Besides, he couldn't just leave Andre there. James knew early on that Andre didn't belong in there. This place had taken everything he had, and it was only a matter of time before it took his life. Once Andre discovered the plan, the decision was made for James.

Moments later, the generator kicked in. The lights flickered and returned to their normal state. James's eyes adjusted to the fluorescent bulbs lining the ceiling. The alarm sounded again, and as they approached the end of the hallway leading to the cafeteria, they heard chaos—men shouting and the crashing of tables. James's ears rang from the high-pitched alarm, but he pushed forward, fear rising with each step.

They entered the cafeteria and stopped, staring in shock at the scene unraveling before them. The inmates were fighting each other and fighting guards. Food, plates and cups, and hundreds of pieces of papers from who knew where littered the floor. It reminded James of a food fight he had in sixth grade, although back then, it was just spaghetti and chocolate milk all over the place. Now blood was splattered across the floor of the cafeteria; red puddles formed on the uneven linoleum. Once uniformly arranged tables and chairs had become a tangled mess sprawled across the room. Some tables were flipped on their sides, injured or dead men lying beside them.

Three men ganged up on one of the guards. Two of them held the guard upright while the third wailed on him. The guard's face was sunken in. He'd become no more than an unrecognizable, bloodied mess. His body went limp.

A gunshot went off, causing a deafening ring in James's ears.

"Let's go!" James shouted.

"Stay behind me," Andre yelled back, taking the lead.

Staying close to the far-right wall of the cafeteria, they raced through the madness, barely making it to the other side.

Andre ducked as a shiv was thrust in his direction. His fist connected with the man's jaw, and the would-be assailant collapsed.

Maybe I should've had Andre teach me how to fight, James thought. "Go to medical," James said as Andre made a break for the door.

Andre shoved someone out of the way and pushed the door open. Just before James crossed the threshold, he looked over his shoulder and saw a fire starting in the corner of the room.

9

Martina started to panic and looked around the room for makeshift weapons she and Hayden could use to defend themselves. Anyone could walk through that door, and she felt defenseless. They could take care of themselves, but there in the men's part of the prison, they could easily be outnumbered. The guard was nowhere to be seen.

He must have gone to get the inmates under control, Martina thought. It would be much safer for them on the women's side of the prison, but Martina was betting they were on lockdown. Just as she thought she and Hayden would have to wait it out there, a man burst through the door.

Martina grabbed a pair of medical scissors off the table and held them out, keeping her head high, attempting to conceal her fear. Hayden cowered against the back wall, but the man threw his hands up in surprise, indicating he wasn't a threat. Martina noticed a bandage on his arm, then her gaze traveled upwards, and he locked eyes with her. Martina was taken aback. She felt such an intensity in his stare that she couldn't look away.

"What the hell is going on?" Hayden asked, her back still pressed flat against the wall, as if she was trying to back away but couldn't proceed any farther, her chest rising and falling rapidly.

"There's a riot. Everyone started to go insane during dinner, I guess. I saw a guard get his throat slit," he said with an amused look on his face.

Martina snapped out of her trance. "If all the fun is out there, why are you in here with us?"

"I'm here to meet the scientist. Did you get a note too?" the man asked.

"What note?" Hayden asked.

Still clutching the scissors, Martina walked over to stand close to Hayden. "Who's the scientist?"

"I'm sure he'll be here soon." He glanced at the door with uncertainty. "Anyway, I'm Mason."

"I'm Hayden, and this is Martina," Hayden said, her bubbly personality masking any sign of nerves.

Martina shot Hayden a disapproving look. Martina didn't trust him. Something seemed off about him. She just couldn't put her finger on it.

"On second thought, maybe I should go look for him," Mason said, looking back and forth between the two of them. "You girls better stay in here. Safer that way."

"Worry about yourself." Martina narrowed her eyes at him.

His eyes met hers again and Martina saw a hint of amusement. "I'll do that." Mason opened the door to leave and was nearly knocked to the floor by the two men barging into the room.

10

The metal door shut with a bang. The noise of the riot quieted, and the shouting became no more than muffled voices. James's heartbeat pounded in his ears.

"You made it," Mason said, catching his balance on a metal table.

James backed away from Mason and scanned the room. Behind two tables covered in medical equipment and three empty beds, two women stood against the back wall. One was tall with caramel skin and midnight-black hair that nearly reached her hips. The other was much smaller, but just as intriguing, with angular cheek bones and curly, blonde hair that hung down to her breasts. She looked innocent, naïve almost. James had a sudden urge to talk to her, to get to know her, mind and body. The women exchanged glances and talked quietly with one another.

James couldn't hear what they were saying. He tore his gaze away. He needed to focus, and he turned back to Mason. "The way out should be directly underneath us, here," James said, pointing at the back wall. "There should be an alternative way off the property that no one else knows about."

Andre sat on the bed closest to the two women, and James heard them introduce themselves as Hayden and Martina. He got the feeling Andre and Martina had met before, perhaps during his cleaning shift.

Mason withdrew a utility knife and started cutting into the drywall.

"Where'd you get that?" James asked.

"Took it off a guard," Mason replied as he cut a large rectangle into the wall.

"What are you doing?" Hayden asked.

"We're getting out of here," James said.

Hayden laughed. "Yeah, okay," she said sarcastically.

"There's another wall behind here," Mason said. "Looks pretty flimsy. Get me something heavy, and I'll try to break through."

James searched the room and found a metal IV pole. He handed it to Mason.

"You're not really doing something this stupid," Martina said, looking at Andre.

"Come with us," Andre said.

"And let you add time to both our sentences?" Martina shook her head. "No."

"On our way here, Andre and I passed the cafeteria," James said. "The whole place has gone to hell. Someone even started a fire. Best-case scenario, the SWAT team comes in, they put the fire out, and we end up in solitary for the rest of our sentences. Worst-case scenario . . . Well, I'll let you decide."

"Martina, maybe we should go with them," Hayden said. "How are we going to explain being in this part of the prison?"

"That's the least of our worries right now," Martina said, sitting on a bed and putting her head in her hands.

"Maybe we could just go back the way we came in," Hayden said.

"It's too late for that now," Andre said. "The prison's locked down."

Mason cleared the wall and James handed him a flashlight.

"What do you see?" asked James.

"It's a tunnel," Mason said. "This must be it."

"Let's go," James said, walking toward the hole in the wall.

Andre looked at Martina. "It's now or never."

"I know you don't wanna screw things up," Hayden said to Martina, "but I can't spend my life in here. I mean, if there's even a chance—"

A deafening *boom* somewhere inside the building rattled the walls and shook the floor beneath them. The group ducked and covered their heads as medical trays and instruments were strewn across the room. Martina grabbed Hayden and pulled her to the floor, as they clasped their hands over their ears.

"Sounds like that's our cue," Mason said, heading into the tunnel without hesitation.

James watched the women exchange nervous glances, as if they were still debating what action to take.

He nodded to them and climbed through the hole in the wall and into the dark tunnel. Andre and the women followed close behind.

11

They wandered along the tunnel, their shoes sinking into the dirt floor. It smelled of mold and rot. The air felt damp, and Hayden shivered. She crossed her arms, holding them tightly to her chest, trying to get even farther from the mildew-covered walls surrounding her. The tunnel slanted downwards and seemed to go on forever, as if they were descending into hell.

This is insane, Hayden thought. *Are we really going to be able to pull this off? If we don't, we could be killed—or worse.* She could imagine nothing worse than spending the rest of her life inside a solitary cell. There would be no greater torture for her than to face perpetual loneliness.

The scientist finally came to a stop, pulling out a small notebook and attempting to read it in the dark.

Hayden came up beside him. "Is that thing supposed to tell us how to get out of here? Or do you not know where you're taking us?"

He ignored her.

Hayden turned to Martina. "Can we trust him? It doesn't seem like he even knows what he's doing."

Martina sighed.

"We don't even know his name," Hayden said.

"It's James Blackwell. And I am your only chance of getting out of here. Take it or leave it."

Hayden grimaced. There was something about his confidence she found appealing, but also incredibly annoying. What was it that always caused her to be drawn to arrogant men?

A series of memories flashed through her mind, each one more painful than the last. She always loved deeply, and Jonathan had been no exception. All she had to do was close her eyes, and she could feel him with her again. She could imagine the two of them making love under the stars and talking until the sun came up; it was total bliss.

But then, as always, she remembered what he made her do, and her nostalgia turned into pain.

"How much farther?" Martina asked, interrupting Hayden's thoughts.

They came to a solid metal door covered in rust. James pulled it open, the old metal creaking loudly at its hinges. The open doorway revealed an even darker tunnel.

"Oh, great," Andre said.

"What? Are you scared?" Mason asked Andre, grinning.

"There's something wrong with you if you're not scared to enter a dark tunnel. Especially when none of us knows where it leads."

"Anything's better than my fate if I stay in prison," Mason said, pushing forward, leading the group.

James ignored their conversation and walked faster, a determined look in his eyes. Hayden quickened her pace to keep up with him.

This tunnel looked vastly different than the one Hayden and Martina had come through. The tunnel connecting the men's and women's prisons had a concrete floor and lighting. It was also frequently used by the workers who went back and forth between the two prisons. This tunnel looked like it hadn't been used in years.

The more steps they took, the darker and narrower the tunnel became. Claustrophobia started to creep in. Hayden felt like she was wrapped in a heavy, soaking-wet blanket, unable to stretch out her limbs, and ultimately, unable to breathe. It was dead silent except for the occasional sound of tiny feet scampering across the dirt floor. Martina clutched Hayden's arm, and Hayden smirked. *Who knew such a badass could be afraid of rats?* The group walked in silence for about ten minutes until the tunnel suddenly broke off into two paths.

12

"What's that poem about the yellow wood?" Hayden asked, giggling.

Everyone's eyes shifted between the two tunnels. Andre turned to James and tried to read what he was thinking. This decision could be met with either dire consequences or the greatest reward, but James looked perplexed, his aura of confidence starting to waver. Andre wasn't used to seeing James doubt himself.

Over the past three years at StormRidge, Andre had lived with a handful of cellmates. None of them were as peculiar as James, who arrived less than a year ago. In the months they'd spent together, James had never revealed much about his past. But Andre heard people talk about how he was a privileged scientist who had murdered his wife. In a world such as this one, it was difficult not to be prejudiced, but Andre came to his own conclusions. As time went on, they bonded over similar interests, from professional football to space exploration. Andre never brought up the rumors he heard about James, and James had shown him the same courtesy.

"So should we flip a coin?" Mason asked in a playful tone.

Everything about Mason's demeanor irritated Andre. He didn't understand why James chose him to help them escape. If anything, Mason put the group at greater risk. He was irrational, and Andre knew he was a killer.

"It's this way," James said, after a long pause, extending his arm to the right.

"I like playing follow the leader as much as the next guy, but I'm having a little trouble trusting you. How do you know what's on the other side?" Mason asked.

"Because I've seen the light at the end of the tunnel."

"Okay, enough with the bullshit." Martina said. "We need to get out of here. For all we know, the oxygen down here could be running out." Andre could tell she didn't want to let on how frightened she was. The air was thick, and he noticed she'd been taking shallow breaths ever since they went past the metal door.

"Fine by me," Andre said.

One by one, the group took the tunnel on the right. They followed it until they came to what appeared to be a dead end. James knelt, feeling a small opening in the wall in front of them.

"Looks like we're going to have to crawl through. If my notes are accurate, it shouldn't be more than about thirty feet until we're outside," James said.

"Fuck that," Andre said, starting to turn back. His first instinct was to go back into the prison before ever entering a space that small.

"Yeah, there's no way I'm crawling on the shit-covered ground into that tiny space. What if the tunnel collapses on top of us?" Hayden asked.

"We're almost outside. We can't turn back now," James said. "Just make sure you move through the tunnel quickly. There's rad—I mean, there's limited oxygen in here."

Andre's heart raced. He thought of how claustrophobic he had been ever since he was a child. His fear of small spaces consumed him. A searing pain shot through his head like a knife slicing through his temples, the blade slowly twisting. He clutched the sides of his head with both hands. His anxiety had caused stress headaches for as long as he could remember. *Maybe it's a brain tumor*, he'd once thought. If only.

"This is the only chance we'll get to start over. To have a life that's not behind bars," Mason said. He stepped forward and crouched down, silently volunteering to go first.

"You really believe that?" Hayden asked. "Once we get out of here, we'll be fugitives. We'll have to be on the run forever. When's the last time you heard of escaped prisoners having a happy ending?"

"That's a chance I'm willing to take," Mason said. He looked over his shoulder for a moment and then disappeared into the crawl space.

13

He'd missed the fresh air and sunlight, the sound of wind blowing through the trees. But most of all, Mason had missed looking up at the night sky. His wife, Jane, had studied astrology. She knew the names of all the constellations and how stars and planets affected different people at different times. Mason regretted never taking the time to learn from her. He'd always thought it was a load of crap, but some of his fondest memories were camping with Jane and Emily, sitting by the fire and staring at the sky for hours while Jane pointed out the different constellations.

Then it hit him. This would be his first taste of freedom in seven years.

Mason held his breath and army-crawled through the constricting tunnel, which appeared to be only a few feet wide. *I've been through much worse than this*, he thought. He repeated it to himself until his hands hit a wall. It felt flimsy, like the soft wood of branches or vines. Mason struggled to breathe as he tore at the wall, slowly clearing a path. He forced his way through and fell onto the soft ground.

Unsteadily, he got to his feet and pulled away the rest of the vines so the group could easily pass through. The tunnel was inconspicuous, hidden among massive rocks and plants. It was as if he had stepped into another world. Tree branches stretched to the sky like they were reaching for the stars. The full moon illuminated the forest. The feeling of mist surrounded him. The night was calm, silent except for the sound of the wind. He thought he heard an owl off in the distance.

Mason looked up at the sky now, just as he used to with his family, and he felt their presence. He spotted the Big Dipper and couldn't help but smile.

James emerged from the tunnel behind him and quickly stood, his gaze sweeping from one side to the other, taking in his surroundings.

"Well, looks like I'm finally going to get some peace and quiet," Mason said. "At least for another twenty-four hours, until they come looking for us."

James nodded slowly.

Mason turned to him. "You know, it got to a point where I basically lost all hope in there. Guess I have you to thank for this." He extended his hand to James.

"What happened to your wrist?" James asked.

"What? This?" Mason looked down at the bandage. "I did what I had to do to get out of solitary."

"You'll have to clean the wound, so it doesn't get infected."

"Looks like I made the right move after all." Mason smiled.

"I wasn't sure if you'd follow through," James said. "It's been months since we last spoke."

Mason felt like a weight had been lifted off his chest, one he'd carried with him for close to a decade.

The women, Martina and then Hayden, crawled out of the tunnel, coughing dramatically. Martina stood and looked around, her eyes wide. Then she closed her eyes and inhaled deeply. Hayden sprawled out on the ground as she caught her breath. "Wow," Hayden said, after her exaggerated coughing fit ended. "It's beautiful out here."

They stayed silent for a few moments, listening to nature and fully taking in their surroundings. Shock and relief prevented them from worrying about the consequences of their escape.

"Hey. Where's Andre?" Martina asked James.

14

James turned back to the tunnel exit in one swift movement. "Andre!" he yelled to no avail. "Andre, where are you?"

"Is he stuck in there?" asked Martina. "You have to get him out!"

"Shit!" James dropped to his hands and knees and crawled back into the tunnel.

"He can't go back in," Mason said, his voice muffled and far away.

James started to panic. The tunnel was pitch-black; he was going in blind. He wondered if something had stopped Andre from making it through. He kept crawling despite his extreme discomfort, struggling to maneuver through the restricting tunnel. Finally, his arms came to an abrupt stop, and he felt something solid.

It was Andre, lying still in front of him.

"Andre!"

He was non-responsive.

With little room to maneuver, James did what he could to try to rouse Andre. "Come on, man. Wake up!"

James thought back to his last day at the lab when he put his plan into motion. He and his wife, Isabella, had carpooled to work just like any other day. Avion was conducting a series of trials in a dangerous environment they'd created inside the lab.

While they used their patented technology to study gravitational waves in search of wormholes with negative energy, they also created a simulation in the lab to determine whether a human could safely pass through a tear in the space-time continuum. The experiment had concluded successfully in the previous set of trials, but Isabella wanted to try it for herself. Just like James, his wife was always on a quest for knowledge and brave as hell, which was what he loved about her.

Everything had gone exactly to plan. He was in a meeting on the twentieth floor when two of his lab technicians burst through the door. They explained that Isabella had been exposed to radiation during the experiment. James forced tears out of his eyes and retreated to his office after telling them to call an ambulance.

He shut his office door and walked to the window. Like clockwork, he saw Isabella sneak out the back door and get into a cab. He exhaled a sigh of relief.

After that, all he had to do was get sent to prison. James knew, as founder and CEO of the company, he would be to blame in the eyes of the law. He and his wife had even staged the scene with Isabella's DNA, since her body would never be recovered.

James pushed the memories from his mind. He needed to focus on getting Andre out of the tunnel. It was becoming harder to breathe by the second. Aside from the limited amount of oxygen in the tunnel, he knew there was a great risk of radiation exposure. If this tunnel were, in fact, a tear in space-time, as James believed, it would be extremely unpredictable. His experiments in the lab occurred in a controlled environment. However, there was no way to be certain this tunnel was safe. The wormhole could collapse at any moment if it wasn't stable.

He shimmied backwards and locked his elbow around Andre's. With all his strength, James yanked Andre forward. He repeated this motion over and over, slowly moving toward the exit again. Sweat poured down his face, his breathing getting ragged. It was a nearly impossible task. With Andre's tall muscular build, he had to weigh over two hundred pounds.

I can do this, James repeated to himself. His mind drifted to Isabella again. All he knew was she'd gotten out of the lab safely. But where was she now?

James was about to give up when he felt his feet slide down into the clearing.

"Help!" he yelled to the others as he backed out of the tunnel and fell to the ground, gasping for air.

The group helped pull Andre out and laid him on his back.

"Oh my God! What happened?" Hayden asked. "Is he okay?"

"He's not breathing," said James. "Fuck! He was in the tunnel longer than all of us. He could've had a heart attack." He knelt beside Andre and started giving him CPR.

James wondered if mouth-to-mouth was still the standard practice. He continued the chest compressions, his arms moving on instinct, but fear gripped his mind. He wondered why he felt so terrified about losing Andre. They'd spent the last eight months in a cell together, but they barely knew each other. And they didn't always get along. When they first met, Andre was quiet and intimidating. As time passed, James realized he just liked to keep to himself. People around the prison told him Andre was a cold-blooded killer. But James didn't see it. Maybe it was the way Andre expressed his love for football, once they got to know each other, or the constant sadness in his eyes. James got the impression Andre didn't deserve to be in prison at all. Maybe things do happen for a reason. Maybe it was James's purpose to get him out.

Suddenly, as James was palming his chest, one hand over the other, Andre began to cough. Dirt and saliva erupted from his mouth with such force that the mess hit James in the face. James wiped his face with the back of his hand and stood, finally able to take a deep breath.

"Whoa! Whoa! That's how you thank him for saving your life?" Mason laughed.

Hayden rolled her eyes.

"We should keep moving," James said casually, but he was overwhelmed with relief.

The women helped Andre to his feet.

"Are you okay?" Martina looked concerned.

"I think so," Andre said, still gasping for air, his voice raspy. "We made it?"

James nodded.

"Oh, good." Andre looked at the group crowding around him. "What the hell are we gonna do now?"

15

The forest breathed in as the leaves stirred, only to exhale with a gust of wind swirling around them. *The elements of nature are in total harmony*, Martina thought, watching the leaves sway as she followed the others through the trees. Goosebumps rose on her bare arms, and she longed to change out of her jumpsuit. Her mind was racing, and an array of emotions washed over her. She felt a nervous excitement she hadn't experienced in years. But fear tainted the excitement, the same fear she'd felt the last time the prison alarm brought in a tactical team to stop a riot.

The riot had been justified. Any sane person would see it that way. It happened her first year at StormRidge when a gang of inmates finally banded together to fight back against some of the guards in the women's section of the prison. The guards had been abusing them for months, and some of the women decided to take their revenge. Miraculously, their plan worked. Corruption among the guards didn't start up again until the new warden took over. But the riot didn't go down without casualties.

The prison brought in a team with MP5s to stop the riot. Martina thought the use of submachine guns was overkill. People were shot and killed in the chaos, some of them innocent bystanders. Martina hid under a table and watched her cellmate bleed out. After it was all over, she was stuck in her cell for weeks.

"You okay?" Hayden's voice startled her.

"Fine."

"You don't have to put on a front for me," Hayden said. "None of us are fine."

"Let's just get somewhere safe," Martina said as they wound through the trees, avoiding low-hanging branches.

As Martina took in her surroundings, she tried to figure out where they were. She used to hike through the forest surrounding StormRidge with her friends back when she was in school. The area surrounding the prison was off limits to the public, but the risk of trespassing enticed her teenage mind. The concept of prison was completely foreign to her then, just an abstract picture of danger her mother painted inside her head. They'd spoken less and less in the years since her mother got deported. Martina thought, *she must be so disappointed in how my life turned out.*

The forest seemed different somehow, denser. There were no worn-down walking trails, just overgrown weeds and shrubs nearly as tall as she was. The trees grew closer together, as if the number of them had doubled. That was impossible considering she had hiked here only a decade ago. As they went deeper into the forest, the trees started to look different. The branches weren't just leafless, but they looked almost red. Their bark was peeling, revealing the layers underneath.

Martina pushed her confusion aside and walked forward, hoping to put as much distance between her and StormRidge as physically possible. She had to focus on getting the kids back.

But as a fugitive?

Martina wondered if she'd made another catastrophic mistake. It was bad enough she'd landed herself in prison after the bank job went south, but now she'd increased her problems tenfold. Hayden was right; she would be on the run forever. What type of life could she provide for the kids? Martina sighed.

A branch cracked behind her, and she whipped her head around, her heartbeat quickening. She squinted into the dark forest, but she saw nothing. The others must not have heard it, because no one else stopped. The group was getting farther and farther away from her. A feeling of unease crept in. She shrugged it off and jogged to catch up with the group, her prison sneakers crunching on dead leaves beneath her feet.

Although she had all the odds stacked against her, she couldn't deny it felt good to move. To be outside, to breathe in the crisp fresh air. It was such a relief. Being in prison had taken its toll on her, physically and mentally. She wasn't the same person she'd been when her sentence started, but she felt much stronger now. The hardships she faced in prison allowed her to become a better person, and she learned from her many mistakes.

"James." Hayden's voice carried with the wind. "Maybe we should stop here to rest."

"Don't we need to put more distance between us and StormRidge?" Andre asked.

Martina squinted again through the trees and saw a small single-story building made of stone. Although its foundation was cracking and shingles were missing from the roof, it felt strangely inviting. Maybe it had something to do with living in a cell for the past two years. A barn full of animal feces would probably seem inviting after that.

"We're all exhausted, and this looks like as good a place as we're gonna find," Martina said.

James appeared to think it over. "Okay, just for a few hours," he said, looking at Andre.

Andre shrugged.

"Home sweet home," Mason said. "I'll gather some wood and make a fire."

Martina longed to have her daughter in her arms again. Being out of prison and not being able to see Sofía felt wrong. She'd spent many of her lonely nights in prison thinking about how she failed her sister by losing the kids and how Sofía now faced her night terrors alone. The little girl used to climb in bed with Martina after each one of her nightmares. It tore Martina apart inside to think of how she must have outgrown them by now.

Martina watched as Mason rubbed two sticks together, causing just enough friction to create a spark. He then blew on the pile of wood repeatedly until a large flame appeared. She felt embarrassed that she wouldn't have been able to do it herself. There was something about him that drew her attention; she just couldn't put her finger on it. There was also something off about him, so she steered clear of any interaction. She decided to focus her energy elsewhere and took a seat next to Andre. "Hey. Andre, right? I recognized you back in the medical room."

He nodded. "I saw you during my night shifts."

Their eyes met for a moment before she looked away.

"Thank you," Martina said, "for helping us get out."

He smiled. "So what's the first thing you're gonna do now that you're free?"

"I have a daughter, Sofía. And I got custody of my nieces and nephew after my sister passed." Martina shook her head. "DCFS took them when I got arrested. I guess my priority is figuring out how to get them back."

She wasn't sure why she was being so honest with him, blurting out exactly what she was thinking. But she felt like she could trust him.

"I'm sorry to hear that. It won't be easy."

"Women have been known to lift cars with their bare hands to save their child. Anything's possible for a determined mother," she said, laughing.

Martina saw a smile come across his lips before his expression turned serious again. "What about you?" she asked. "Got any big plans?"

After a few moments of silence, he spoke. "All I've wanted for the past three years is to prove that I'm innocent."

Innocent? Martina thought. That was the last thing she expected to hear. *Was he lying to gain her trust?* If he were telling the truth, she could only imagine the amount of pain he'd endured.

"You were wrongly convicted?" Her voice went up higher than she expected. "I didn't mean to sound so surprised. It's just . . . that's a heavy burden to carry."

"Those are the cards I was dealt. What else can you do when a jury doesn't believe you based off the color of your skin?"

She thought for a moment. "You can fight back."

"My story isn't special. There's a lot of people just like me in prison. People who don't belong there."

"What made them believe you did it?"

Andre paused for a moment and looked down at his hands. "A witness saw someone matching my description, and that was enough. My word against his." He shook his head. "Well, that and my prints were on the murder weapon."

Andre looked up and his eyes met hers. His words sounded genuine to Martina, but she'd met her share of liars in the past.

"So you were there when it happened?"

"I was." He nodded. "If anything, I should've been the witness, not the suspect."

"Shit."

"It's okay if you don't believe me."

"I do believe you. And I don't think you should give up on setting the record straight."

"Once I was locked up, it seemed like there was nothing more I could do. I just wanted to prove them wrong, you know? All I wanted was to show them how wrong they were."

Martina felt sympathy for him. She could think of nothing worse than going down for something she didn't do. She had an overwhelming urge to wrap her arms around him and pull him closer to her. Instead, she placed her hand gently on his arm and said, "Well, it looks like you just might get your chance."

16

She is gorgeous. The thought kept repeating in his mind. James tore his eyes away before she could notice he was staring. Even after he turned away from Hayden, his mind could still see her hazel eyes glowing from the light of the fire, the way her blonde hair framed her face, and how her tiny waist curved into round hips. The way Hayden gracefully crossed her legs reminded him of his wife. Isabella exuded elegance, and she was the most strikingly beautiful woman he had ever met. Simultaneously, the most dangerous. He'd never felt a deeper connection with anyone in his life. Thoughts of Isabella continued to seep into his mind like a poison. He shook his head. It was only natural for him to be hyper-fixating on these things after nearly a year spent in prison.

James stepped outside the tiny stone building nestled in the generous branches of an old oak tree. It was abandoned, but most likely used to be the home of someone who craved privacy; they had their own little sanctuary away from all the societal noise. It felt safe here, almost untouchable. Out of reach from the negativity which consumes the world.

The old house was a decent place for them to spend the night, but James worried about what lay ahead. Traversing through a wormhole was anything but predictable. Despite completing successful trials in a controlled environment inside the lab, this was uncharted territory for James. His research alone couldn't prepare him to make a real time jump. For all he knew, they could be anywhere, at any point in time. James knew they would find out soon enough. He just hoped he hadn't led these people into a disaster.

James thought back to the day in his lab that set the series of events in motion and led him to this point. Avion was located inside a beautiful, twenty-story building they'd bought in the city. The above-ground levels were primarily offices with walls made entirely of glass. There were also five levels below the ground, where many of the experiments were conducted.

He was on level 3B that day, observing a new experiment on rodent brain activity when exposed to conditions of negative energy, when he was pulled out of the room by Tom, the head of his Special Projects team.

"I was right in the middle of overseeing a very important analysis. What could be so urgent you needed to pull me away?"

"I'm sorry, Dr. Blackwell. But you're going to be very pleased."

"With?" James asked, impatiently.

"We finally found another one," Tom said, brimming with excitement. "We've detected another negative mass signature."

James's heart started to race. "I want you to assemble a team to go out into the field and investigate. We need to break ground on this right away," he said firmly, trying to hide his excitement.

"Well, um, that's the problem. I traced the coordinates, and it's not going to be as easy to investigate as we thought."

"Why not? Where is it?"

"It's underneath a prison, sir."

"I don't care if it's at the bottom of the ocean. Get a team on it immediately."

Ever since they'd found the wormhole, James had made it his mission to discover firsthand whether time travel was possible. He had no reservations about turning himself into an experiment, but he hadn't planned to put other lives at risk in the process. His intention had been to go alone, but the harsh realities of the other inmates' lives swayed him to change the plan.

Hayden walked up to James. His heartbeat quickened; he could hear it pounding inside his ears.

"You were quite the lifesaver today," she said.

"Just basic CPR," James said, shrugging.

"That's not what I meant." She smiled. "So how did you know where to go? And, well, *when* to go?"

"I just saw an opportunity, and I took it."

"You mean the riot. Can I take a look at that magic book of yours?"

She meant the notebook. James silently cursed. He knew he shouldn't have allowed these people to come along. It was wrong of him to put them at risk, to lie to them. Although, on the other hand, maybe the unknown was better than the circumstances that led them to end up in prison.

But what if they deserved to be in prison? he thought.

James glanced over at Mason, who was warming his hands by the fire. His blue eyes locked on the flames, like he was in a trance.

"It's private," James finally said.

She rolled her eyes.

"Tell me something about yourself."

"What do you want to know?" she asked.

"Anything you'd like to share."

"Well, I'm twenty-seven. I'm a real estate agent—was a real estate agent. My life was going pretty normal until I fell for someone. You know when you'd be willing to do anything for someone?" Her voice cracked. "Just because you love them that much? When you're completely oblivious to the manipulative power they can have over you?" Hayden's voice rose with each question. She looked down and away from him, and a single tear ran down her cheek.

Wow, she was just waiting to let that out, James thought. He wasn't sure how to respond to her outburst of emotion.

"Anyway, what about you?" she asked, recovering quickly.

"I'm thirty-six. I grew up in Los Angeles. I got my PhD in physics at Berkeley. Then I started my own research laboratory, Avion."

"Well, isn't that impressive?" Mason smiled, clearly eavesdropping on their conversation.

"It is," Hayden said.

James heard a low growling sound in the distance.

"What was that?" Mason asked.

"I'm sure it was just the wind," James said. He was sure it *wasn't* just the wind. It sounded like some kind of animal. He was scared, and reasonably so, but there was no need to get everybody worked up just yet.

Martina appeared from inside the cabin with a bottle in her hand. "Look what I found!"

"Here we go." Mason chuckled as he jogged over to her.

"Weird, I've never heard of this brand before," Martina said.

"Are you an expert on liquor?" Andre asked, joining them.

Martina shoved him playfully. "I'm not an alcoholic if that's what you're implying."

"I've never heard of it either, but vodka's vodka," Mason said, opening the bottle and taking a long swig.

"Come on," Hayden said, gesturing toward James. "I know it's been a while."

"I'm okay. You go ahead though."

She smiled and headed over to the others, who were fighting over the bottle.

James watched her walk away.

He kept to himself while the others drank and danced around the fire. He didn't share their giddiness about the escape because he was wrapped up in his own anxiety. He'd led these people here against their will, and it just wasn't sitting right. The wind picked up, and James poked at the fire, trying to ignore the feeling in his gut that he'd made a huge mistake.

17

The wind whipped through the night so hard it shook the house. The old cabin creaked and groaned like it was finally waking up after being undisturbed for so many years. If it weren't for the noises of the house, the forest would be eerily quiet.

Hayden tossed and turned beside Martina for hours on an old wooden bed, unable to sleep despite the warm fuzzy feeling she got from the booze. Her stomach growled, and she realized finding food might be an issue. They couldn't just wander into a grocery store.

She'd grown accustomed to insomnia. The transition from her California king bed and floral down comforter to the top bunk in her prison cell had been anything but easy. After a while, it got so bad she would stay awake for days. When she couldn't take it anymore, she started to rely on a little pharmaceutical help. Due to the incompetence of the staff at StormRidge, it was easy to steal a few pills from the medical wing. Unfortunately for her, she didn't prepare for a long trip when she left her cell today. Hayden's stash was still tucked away safely in the lining of her extra pair of prison-issued underwear.

She looked over at Martina, who was sleeping peacefully on the bed next to her in the sole bedroom of the cabin. Andre was asleep on the floor, on the other side of the room, wrapped in a mound of blankets. Hayden quietly walked into the living room, keeping her weight on her toes, trying not to wake them.

The living room was empty.

She decided to look around. On one side of the room stood an outdated kitchen, which looked like it hadn't been used in many years. She checked the refrigerator with false hope, but there was no power and it was empty. The other side of the room was lined with crowded bookshelves. She pulled off several books but didn't recognize any of the authors. A worn brown leather couch faced an old TV by the front door, and there was a small desk in the far corner.

Curiosity got the better of her, and she pulled open the desk drawers one by one. She pulled open the bottom drawer and there it was. James's notebook. Hayden was shocked it wasn't still tucked inside his waistband. She carefully picked it up and flipped it open to the first page.

It contained notes pertaining to Einstein's theory of general relativity, but they were above her level of knowledge. It sounded so familiar to her, like a memory she could reach if she went deep inside her mind. But she'd missed her college physics class often for the sorority she rushed. On the next page, she read about gravitational echoes, exotic waves, and negative energy. The difference between black holes and wormholes in the ringdown stage. She became frustrated trying to understand the material. She flipped the page again and came across a series of equations, completely incomprehensible to her. Hayden quickly thumbed through the pages, trying to make sense of any of it. She recognized a series of numbers as coordinates, and she wondered if James knew exactly where they were going.

Muffled voices came from outside the cabin.

Hayden quickly closed the notebook and returned it to the drawer. She walked over to the window and pressed her ear against the glass, her breath creating a fog on the pane.

"Maybe I don't deserve to be out. But do you? Why were you even in there in the first place?" Mason asked.

"At least I wasn't on death row," James said.

"Yeah, I'm sure you're completely innocent."

After a long pause, James said, "It was Avion."

"Your company?"

"We were a legitimate research facility. But some of what we studied was . . . unorthodox." James scratched his head. "We made revolutionary discoveries about the space-time continuum."

"Look, you don't need to bullshit me—"

"We pushed limits no one else dared to," James continued. "I was prepared to prove the existence of wormholes. And not just the existence, but the ability of a human to pass through one."

"What?" Hayden said under her breath.

"Wait a minute. You really expect me to believe you know how to mess around with time?"

"Everything was on track. We just had to gather a more significant amount of data before we presented the theory to our board of top scientists. My team created a new technology that would enable us to identify traversable wormholes. We wanted to get another patent underway, but . . . but then something went wrong in one of the experiments. I lost the love of my life. Her name was Isabella."

Hayden crouched down. She remembered hearing the news story, but something seemed off. There was no emotion in his eyes as James told the story. Could he be lying?

"So you got charged with murder?" Mason asked.

"Manslaughter. Ever since I was arrested, I've been planning how to get out of there."

Mason thought for a moment. "Why did you pick me?"

"What do you mean?" James asked.

"That day in the yard. You came up to me. You sought me out."

"You just seemed like a smart guy."

"Bullshit," Mason said, getting in James's face. "I want to know why."

"I needed help, and I picked you. That's it. There's no deeper reason."

Mason locked eyes with James and Hayden's heart started to race. She lowered herself even farther beneath the window ledge to ensure she wasn't seen.

"I know you're lying," Mason said flatly.

"I'm not lying," James said.

Mason grabbed James by his jumpsuit and slammed him into the house.

"You know I served. You know I've been trained in interrogation. And you know exactly why you picked me," Mason said through gritted teeth.

James was silent, and Mason threw him to the ground.

Hayden wondered if it was the liquor that made him this way or if he truly was a cold-blooded killer like everyone said.

Mason knelt on the ground and cocked his fist back.

"Okay! Okay! I sought you out," James blurted.

"Why?"

"You're family," James uttered.

"What?" Mason lowered his fist. "What the fuck does that mean?"

"You're right, okay?" James said, holding his hands up. "When I found out you were at StormRidge too, I had to take you with me. I couldn't let my half-brother get executed."

Mason fell silent. "I don't even know you," he finally said.

"Well, I know you. Our mother told me about you when I was young."

"I don't know that *bitch* either. All I know is she left me alone with an abusive man as a small child. I grew up in the foster care system before I was finally adopted. So what would I want with her other son?"

"You know it's more complicated than that," James said.

"I don't think it is. You were born with a silver spoon in your mouth, and I got shit on," Mason said, his anger returning.

"No." James shook his head.

"Yet we both ended up here," Mason said, laughing. "Thanks for helping me get out of prison, but I think it's best we go our separate ways."

"I couldn't believe the monstrosity of a coincidence that my brother was doing time in the same prison as me."

Mason seemed to think it over. "Everything that comes out of your mouth sounds like bullshit." He started toward the front door.

Hayden quietly returned to the bedroom and sat on the bed. Her head was spinning. What the hell had she gotten herself into? *This can't be real.*

Hayden wished she had her stash with her. She buried her face in a pillow and thought it over. If what James said was true, that meant he'd planned the escape all along. But how could he have known about the riot? Her heartbeat quickened with terror. She took deep, steady breaths in an attempt to calm herself. She tried to quiet her mind and drift off to sleep, but it was no use.

Heavy footsteps inside the house startled her. She rolled over and faced the wall, pulled the blanket up to her chin, and pretended to be asleep.

Moments later, James and Mason burst into the bedroom breathing heavily. Mason's clothes were disheveled and torn. James had a scratch running down his arm.

"Guys, wake up!" James said.

"There's something out there," Mason said.

Martina sat up beside Hayden and rubbed her eyes. "What do you mean? What's out there?"

"We saw—I don't know." James's expression was hard to read, but Hayden could tell he was truly disturbed.

"Whatever they were, they weren't human," Mason said.

Andre got up and walked toward them. "What the hell are you guys talking about?"

"What were they then? Wild animals?" Martina asked.

"No. At least I don't think so. They walked on two legs, but I didn't get a good look at them in the dark. We were outside talking, and then out of nowhere, they just attacked us. We barely made it inside," Mason said.

"Walked on two legs?" Andre asked. "Sounds like people to me."

Hayden pulled her knees to her chest and shut her eyes. *This can't be happening*, she thought. There was no way she was getting any sleep tonight.

Martina and Andre went into the living room to look out the window by the door.

"I don't see anything," Martina said.

James and Mason looked shaken and confused. Something had frightened them out there. Hayden could only imagine what could be lurking in the dark forest in the middle of the night.

Andre dragged the desk across the room, its legs scratching the floorboards, and placed it in front of the door.

"We should cover the windows too," Mason said, as he looked around the room.

"The windows are locked. Nothing should be able to get in," Martina said.

"You didn't see them," Mason said.

"Okay, let's all just calm down," James said, as he lit a fire in the fireplace.

Hayden risked a glance out the front windows. The moon emerged from behind a cloud and lit up the trees like a spotlight. Everything looked still, almost too still.

"Whatever it was, it's gone now. Are you guys okay?" Hayden asked.

Mason shot her an annoyed look.

"We're fine," James said calmly. "Everything's going to be fine."

Hayden sat in front of the fireplace while James and Mason searched the house for weapons. Something had changed; they were all on edge. James and Mason were trying to play it cool, but she'd seen the look of fear in their eyes when they came into the bedroom. Wherever that tunnel had brought them, something wasn't right about this place. She could feel it in her bones.

18

Their legs tangled between the silk sheets. The sunrise seeped through drawn curtains and caused the bedroom to glow. Jane kissed Mason passionately and rolled on top of him, her hair sweeping over his face. He grabbed her waist and kissed her hard, pulling her closer, as if he could convey how deeply he felt for her with his lips. For a moment, they were no longer two people, but one connected being.

Thud!

Mason jolted awake as the cabin door was forced open. Blinking away his fuzzy vision, he was suddenly torn out of his blissful dream and brought back to reality. Unfamiliar voices murmured all around him, and he opened his eyes wide to see a man standing above him.

"Who are you, and what do you think you're doing in the East woods?" the man asked.

"What?" Mason asked.

The man, who appeared to be in his early twenties, had scraggly brown hair and a beard. He wore a disheveled navy-blue outfit, a uniform of some type. Mason looked around the room to see about a dozen men and women dressed just like him. A thick tension hung in the air.

Who are these people? They don't look like cops.

"What should we do, Jones?" a short older woman who appeared to be of Asian descent asked as she stood by the door with her arms crossed over her chest. "Should we bring them to the Circle?"

"You better back off, *Jones*," Mason said getting to his feet. "You're not taking anybody anywhere."

Two larger uniformed men walked out of the bedroom behind him, dragging Hayden and Martina by their arms. The men's faces were expressionless as the women struggled to break free from their grasp. The women looked scared, and that made Mason angry.

"Get your hands off them," Mason said, blocking their path.

The men stopped and silently exchanged glances. After a moment, they nodded to the group by the door. The man referred to as Jones grabbed Mason by the shoulders. Mason swung around and punched him square in the jaw with such force that it knocked Jones to the floor. Another man in blue got in Mason's face. The wound on Mason's wrist started to sting, but he didn't hold back. As he fought, Mason scanned the room. *Where the hell is James?*

Andre, who had also been grabbed by two uniformed men, followed suit. He elbowed the man on his right in the nose, getting him to release his arm. Then he swung around and punched the man on his left in the stomach. The man toppled over.

Martina kneed the man restraining her in his crotch and made a break for the door, but the men and women by the exit created a wall so she couldn't get through. Mason and Andre exchanged glances and charged at them. Greatly outnumbered, their group of four fought fearlessly. Hayden and Martina were tough fighters, Mason realized, after he saw them get a few good punches in. Together, they had most of the "soldiers" laid out on the floor.

He thought he was handling the situation just fine until a second group arrived. These men and women were armed and not in the mood to waste any time. The last thing Mason remembered was getting slammed in the head with the back of a rifle.

19

We went from one prison to another, Martina thought, as she took in her surroundings. They'd been thrown in the back of an SUV and driven for what felt like an hour while she drifted in and out of consciousness. As she came to in a strange room, her head throbbed, and she struggled to break the thin ropes binding her wrists. She rubbed the material back and forth along the jagged edge of a metal rack containing general supplies from toilet paper to soap. Fragmented memories of a fight with people in blue uniforms came back to her. She felt the sharp metal dig into her skin, but she quickened her pace. Back and forth.

And the rope broke free.

She rubbed her tender wrists and scanned the room. She was surrounded by white. White, windowless walls; an immaculately clean, white tile floor; and a white ceiling. The only furnishings were two peculiar white plastic chairs, like the kind you would have at a family barbecue. Martina thought of her daughter, Sofía, and of her own childhood. Her fondest childhood memories were of the summertime. Her extended family would throw parties on the weekends and invite dozens of people over for barbecues. She remembered playing with her sister and cousins the entire day without a care in the world. They sat on plastic chairs just like these.

The only exit was a stark white door, which appeared to have an electronic locking mechanism.

Hayden and Andre were passed out in the corner of the room, and they began to stir. Martina was immediately flooded with relief. Andre got up first.

"Over here," Martina said, nodding toward the metal rack.

He walked toward her, and Martina showed him the sharp piece of metal. He positioned his tied wrists against the edge and followed her example.

"Where are we?" Martina asked, looking up at him from where she sat cross-legged on the floor. "Who are these people?"

"I don't know. It looks like we're being held in some kind of storeroom."

"Held temporarily? Until they move us somewhere else?" Martina couldn't hide her fear.

"Listen, I promise we're gonna get out of here." Andre quickly broke his hands free and sat next to Martina, so close his shoulder touched hers. Then he looked into her eyes.

She held his gaze for a moment. His brown eyes looked like caramel in the fluorescent lighting. For the first time, she noticed the strong angles of his jaw, his broad muscular shoulders. Without thinking, she leaned in and kissed him. His lips were soft and inviting, like a favorite pillow after a long day.

"I'm sorry," Martina said, pulling away. "I don't know why I did that."

"Either this is your way of coping with a traumatic situation, or you're starting to like me," Andre said, a wide grin plastered on his face.

It was the first time she'd seen his smile touch his eyes and light up his face.

Hayden giggled from the corner of the room. "If you guys are done acting like children, we're in a real predicament here."

"Oh, fuck off," Martina said, unable to keep a straight face.

Hayden crossed the room to free her hands. Once she removed the rope, she rested her head on Martina's shoulder. "You know I couldn't have made it this far without you," Hayden said.

"Lucky for you, it looks like you're stuck with me a little longer."

Hayden sat up straight. "What are we gonna do?" she asked, her tone suddenly serious. "Why aren't we back at StormRidge?"

"And where are James and Mason?" Andre asked.

The mechanism on the door unlatched, and the door swung open. The three of them jumped.

In walked a child who couldn't be more than ten years old. Big brown eyes peered at them under dark bangs. Martina saw her drop what looked like a key fob in her jacket pocket as she approached them. The girl was visibly nervous, but Martina could tell she had a big personality. She reminded Martina of her daughter.

"Hi, I'm Mina," she said shyly.

Martina edged her way toward the girl. "Hi, Mina. My name is Martina."

"You must be hungry." Mina held out her hand and offered what looked like small cookies.

"Thank you," Martina said, accepting the food. "Can you tell us where we are?"

"The East District."

"What does that mean?" Hayden asked.

"At the cabin, I heard them call it the East woods," Andre said.

Mina looked back and forth between them. "The East District is one of the four places where survivors live."

"Survivors? Of what exactly?" Martina asked.

Voices came from the hall, and Mina turned to go.

"Wait!" Martina grabbed the little girl by her jacket. "Tell us who you people are," she demanded. "What is the Circle?"

Mina screamed, broke free from Martina's grasp, and scurried to the door. The little girl stuck her hand in her pocket and came up empty. She punched a code in the keypad, flung the door open, and ran. Andre tried to stick his foot in the door to catch it, but it slammed behind her and he jumped back, defeated.

"Either one of you catch that code?" asked Andre.

"What's wrong with you?" Hayden asked Martina. "We might need her on our side."

Martina turned around slowly to face them. "Pretty good for a wanna-be." She grinned. A small key fob dangled in her hand. "I just got us out of here."

2 0

Blinding pain seared through James's forehead. He struggled to move and realized he was bound to a metal chair. Ropes weaved around his wrists, pinning them to the chairback. His legs were bound to the chair's legs, bending perfectly at right angles, as if his body were trying to mimic the chair's manufactured shape. James rocked back and forth violently, struggling to break free.

Fuck.

It was no use.

Except for him and the chair, the room was completely empty. The ground beneath his feet was solid concrete, and a metal drain on the floor marked the very center of the room. *What's that used for?* He shuddered. Then he squinted up at the bright lights along the ceiling and winced.

Why am I here? Where are the others? His mind was racing. He shifted in the chair and noticed his notebook was no longer pressing against his back. James craned his neck, hoping to see it still tucked in his waistband. But it was gone. He struggled against the ropes again to no avail. His wrists burned as the rough material dug into the top layers of his skin.

James closed his eyes, trying to formulate a plan to escape. But all he could see was Isabella's face. It was like she was drilled into his memory, a beautiful image he could never escape. Why did she always appear during times of trauma? He couldn't get her out of his head. The way her full lips twitched at the corners whenever she tried to hide something from him, the look she gave him when she was waiting for him in the bedroom after a long day at the office. Never in his life had another individual affected him this much. No one had ever held this kind of power over him.

It had been over a year since she slipped out the back door of the lab and he saw her for the last time. He'd been so focused on finding a way into the prison that he'd been blind to his wife's problems. Looking back now, he realized how oblivious he was. He never even questioned why she was so quick to agree to fake her death.

I must have a concussion, James thought.

The door opening tore James from his spiraling thoughts. A man walked in with an over-confident gait, leading James to believe he was in a position of power. He would tower above most men, but James could tell he was very thin by the way his stylish clothing hung on his body. He reminded James of a wealthy Middle Eastern businessman who sat on the board at his company. They had the same strong jaw and straight, long nose. His presence overwhelming, the man stopped just two feet before the chair and stared blankly at James.

After a moment, he spoke. "I want you to tell me everything you know." His voice was calm and low.

He reminded James of a salesperson or a conman, someone who could talk their way out of any situation. He was straight to the point, something James could respect. The man's demeanor was calm and collected, but James felt the tension rising after each passing moment, which made his stomach turn over. He tried to shift uneasily in the chair, only to be reminded he didn't have the freedom to move.

"About what?" James asked. "Your people brought me here. That's all I know."

The man chuckled, but the look in his eyes was anything but amused. "I want you to tell me . . . about this," he said, pulling the notebook from behind his back.

James managed a shrug and said, "That's not mine."

The man narrowed his eyes. "Perhaps. But if it was yours, then you would probably know that this information is extremely valuable to certain groups of people. Some people might even do anything to obtain it." He paced around the chair, slowly, displaying his authority.

Every muscle in James's body screamed, begging to move. His head throbbed, and he noticed the blood dripping on the floor, likely from the source of the pain on his forehead, which was growing increasingly unbearable by the minute. "How about you untie me, and we can have a discussion like gentlemen?" James struggled against the ropes again.

"You are not exactly in a position to give orders," the man said, his voice still so calm it would almost be soothing under different circumstances.

"Where are my friends?"

"Don't worry about them."

"If you hurt them, you'll never find out what the book means."

This time, a look of amusement crossed the man's face. "Over the years, I've realized something about myself. I don't take kindly to threats," he said as he rolled up his sleeves.

James gritted his teeth.

Suddenly, a small blonde woman hurried through the door. She was dressed in business attire, although she wore a top with an extremely revealing neckline. She spoke quietly to the man. "I'm sorry to interrupt. But we're in need of your help."

"I'm busy at the moment," he said, barely acknowledging her.

"They're asking for you, Kendrick." She fidgeted with a delicate necklace hanging between her breasts.

He glared at her and then back at James, as if gauging which was more important. Then he locked eyes with James again and said, "We'll have to finish this later." Kendrick walked swiftly out of the room with the blonde woman following behind, and the door slammed shut.

James was alone with his thoughts once again.

21

Allison led Kendrick to a nearby cell and pulled the door shut behind them.

"Allison, what was so important that it demanded my immediate attention?" he asked.

The harsh lights along the ceiling made her look washed out, and Kendrick questioned what he ever saw in her. She was childish and emotional, just like most women he had the pleasure of knowing.

Allison placed her hands on his chest and stood on her toes, making herself tall enough to kiss him. His lips met hers and he indulged her for an instant, caught in the moment, their brief affair dancing on his mind. Then he grabbed her by her tiny shoulders and pushed her away. The concrete cell surrounding them made this encounter feel even dirtier and more wrong than it already was.

"I can't. And you have no right to come down here and interrupt me, much less during an interrogation. Am I even needed upstairs?"

"Marc's looking for you."

Kendrick sighed.

"I'm sorry. I missed you. I was hoping we could spend some more time together."

"Don't count on it," he said, turning to leave.

"Wait!" Allison grabbed his arm.

"This has to stop." He ripped his arm free. "What happened between us was a mistake. It won't happen again."

Allison was one of his assistants. Kendrick knew he shouldn't have let things go as far as they had. Now she followed him around relentlessly, like a dog follows its owner.

"You can't just shut me out like this." She crossed her arms and pouted.

Her lips looked inviting. Kendrick was simultaneously attracted to her and repulsed by her. He wondered how that could be possible. He scowled at her. "Watch me."

"Don't forget it was my idea that found those people." Allison smirked.

About a month earlier, Kendrick's assistants had come to him with an idea to have the guards do sweeps of the surrounding area. It turned out to be a fruitful plan. They were able to gather more valuable items, find people living on the outside, and track the dangers lurking around the district. Within the last week, they'd extended their sweeps all the way to the perimeter of the East District.

He was sure one of the other more intelligent individuals came up with the idea, not Allison. "Don't kid yourself into believing you have the ability to form a single independent thought inside your head," Kendrick said as he stormed out of the room. He walked down the hallway with Allison close behind and came face to face with Marc, his number two.

Marc shot him a look of disapproval that amplified Kendrick's anger.

"What do you want?" Kendrick barked at him.

"Board meeting. Ten minutes." Marc shook his head and walked toward the stairwell.

Allison walked away from Kendrick with tears running down her face. Once Kendrick was alone, he drove his fist into the wall.

<h1 style="text-align:center">22</h1>

ndre held his breath as he waited patiently for someone to walk by. His back was flat against the wall, keeping him out of sight. He watched the still-cracked door. He didn't have a clue where they were, but he had every intention of leaving. He needed a weapon.

"We need to get out of here," Hayden said, "while we have the chance."

Andre held up his hand to her.

Hayden scoffed.

"Wait," Andre said.

"Wait for what?" Hayden asked. "The door is open. We gotta fucking run before someone comes back and locks us in here again!"

Andre put his finger to his lips. The sound of footsteps carried down the hall, and as an armed man wearing a blue uniform walked past the doorway, Andre lunged and grabbed him. He locked an elbow around the man's neck and dragged him backwards into the room before he could make a sound, a little trick he'd learned from his older brother. Memories of his childhood, usually a source of pain, flashed through his mind. But for the first time, there was no pain along with them.

Andre squeezed hard with his forearm until the guard passed out and his body fell limp.

"Or we could do that," Hayden said, walking up to him and grabbing the gun out of the man's holster. She looked it over with an expression on her face that was hard for Andre to read. Then she released the magazine to reveal it was full of bullets.

"You know how to use it?" Andre asked.

Hayden nodded. After checking if there was a bullet in the chamber, she put the magazine back in and pulled the slide. "What's our plan? How are we gonna get out of here?"

"We're gonna find James and Mason and run like hell," Martina said.

"Sounds easy enough," Hayden said, rolling her eyes.

They cautiously exited the room and made their way down a narrow white hallway.

"What if someone sees us?" Hayden asked.

"If we stay *quiet*, maybe we can get out of here undetected," Andre mumbled.

"I don't see any security cameras, so they can't get the jump on us that way," Martina said.

They turned down another hallway.

And another.

Right, then left, then right.

Andre attempted to map the place out in his mind. *It's like a maze,* he thought. *A carefully designed labyrinth with no chance of escape.*

They searched countless rooms and found no one in sight. Where were all the people who brought them here? Finally, they reached a stairwell. An incomprehensible murmur of voices came from the room below. They crept quietly down the stairs and waited, watching through an open door on the next level down. They stuck to the shadows to avoid being seen.

Andre squinted, looking into a factory-like room filled with people. But these weren't the soldiers who'd taken them out of the cabin in the woods. These people weren't in uniform. Men, women, and even children worked machines in assembly lines on the far side of the room. A group of them, closer to the door, walked in a line and carried heavy objects that Andre couldn't quite make out. They wore tattered clothing and moved like zombies, dutifully following orders from armed guards standing against the wall. Many of the workers appeared to be in poor health, possibly even starving, moving sluggishly along with blank stares on their faces.

Were these people being forced to work? Andre exchanged glances with Martina and Hayden. He watched as some of the guards in blue uniforms walked around the room to ensure everyone was doing their jobs efficiently. They barked orders and insults at many of the women.

"Are you guys seeing this?" Andre asked, blinking rapidly.

One of the women stopped what she was doing and looked straight in their direction, locking eyes with Andre. She'd heard him.

"Shit. Come on," said Andre. "We gotta go."

One of the guards told the woman to get back to work as the trio ran up the stairs, exiting the stairwell multiple floors above where they'd begun. They turned left and came to a dimly lit corridor. It looked like a row of futuristic prison cells with solid metal doors. There was a small keypad on each door.

What the hell is this place? Fear took over Andre's thoughts.

Martina tried to use the key fob she'd taken off the little girl on each door, one by one. She was able to get some of the doors open, but the rooms were all empty.

"What I wanna know is why they separated us," Hayden said to Andre. "Why are the three of us together? Do you think James and Mason are in a room together too?"

"No idea." Andre shrugged. "Maybe they saw them as a bigger threat."

"Guys." Martina was standing in front of a cell she'd just unlocked.

"Is it James?" Hayden asked as she approached the cell.

Andre came up behind them and saw a man curled up in the fetal position against the back wall. "Hey, you okay?" Andre asked.

"That's not James," Hayden said, snatching the fob from Martina's hand and proceeding to try the doors to the rest of the cells.

Andre and Martina approached the man cautiously. He was shaking and breathing heavily, but he didn't look up. The cell was covered in dirt and filth. A strong musty odor washed over them.

Andre offered his hand to prove he wasn't a threat. "Let us help you."

"Who are you?" the man asked, his voice hoarse.

Andre imagined it had been a long time since this man had received a drink or a proper meal.

"It's okay. We'll get you out of here," Martina said.

They helped the man to his feet and headed out of the cell.

"I can walk," the man said. He freed himself from their grip and placed a hand on the wall to steady himself. He used his other hand to push strands of long, greasy, blonde hair from his eyes.

Andre noticed his loose-fitting clothing, a few sizes too big. "How often do they feed you?"

The man stared back at him with bloodshot eyes.

"Over here," Hayden called out, unlocking the last door at the end of the hall. She pushed the door open, and inside, they found James tied to a chair. Hayden freed James's hands, and he flexed his fingers. Andre helped her free James's legs, and the scientist groaned as he was finally able to stretch.

"You have no idea how happy I am to see you guys," James said.

Andre extended a hand, pulled James to his feet, and gave him a pat on the back. "You good?" Andre asked.

"Where's Mason?" James replied.

"We don't know," Martina said. "They kept the three of us together, but we haven't seen him."

"He's not in any of the cells," Hayden said as concern spread across James's face.

"I don't understand why they split us up," James said.

"I don't know, but we'll find your brother," Hayden said quietly so no one else could hear. "Don't worry."

James looked at her with wide eyes.

"There's something fucked up going on here," Andre said.

"Why haven't they sent us back to StormRidge?" Martina asked.

"We're not ever going back there," James said. "Who's he?" He asked, noticing the stranger standing just outside the cell.

"I'm Noah." His voice cracked as he spoke. Noah's lips were white and chapped with dryness. He looked incredibly weak, and he appeared to have a hard time standing.

"He was in one of these cells," Andre told James.

James looked the stranger over. "Well then," he said, "I guess he's coming with us. Let's get out of here."

23

Their footsteps echoed in the sparse hallways. The white linoleum floors and white paint on the walls gave Hayden a futuristic insane asylum vibe. Every hallway was lined with doors on both sides, and nothing hung on the walls. *This building must be huge*, Hayden thought. They might've bought themselves some time, but she knew it wouldn't be long before someone discovered they were gone.

She held her breath as she walked, trying to make as little noise as possible, still clutching the gun tightly against her right thigh. Noah followed her. He seemed so lost; his gaze remained off in the distance. He hadn't made eye contact with any of them. Hayden wondered how long he'd been in that cell.

They found a second stairway at the other end of the corridor. After descending ten flights of stairs, they got to the bottom where a "1" was painted near the exit door. They quickened their pace as they went through more hallways, zigzagging in different directions. Architecturally, it was senseless. It seemed like they were going in circles. They must've walked a mile by now, down one narrow hallway after another.

It was eerily quiet, and Hayden couldn't shake what they'd witnessed. The hopeless looks on those people's faces would haunt her, as would knowing she couldn't do anything about their situation. She longed for even one of her pills right now. What she wouldn't give to close her eyes and fall into oblivion. She clutched the gun more tightly and focused on walking one step at a time. One foot after the other.

Fifteen minutes must've passed before they came to a large, deserted room that looked like a cafeteria.

"You think the food here is any better than at StormRidge?" Hayden asked.

"Based on the cookies the little girl gave us, I'd say the people here are a lot better off than we were," Martina said.

"What's StormRidge?" Noah asked.

"Maybe there's a way out through the kitchen," James said, ignoring Noah's question.

They walked past rows of tables, each perfectly in line like books on a shelf, to the back of the cafeteria and through the kitchen door.

"There." James pointed at an exit door.

"Are we really going to leave without Mason?" Hayden asked.

"Who's Mason?" Noah asked.

"Our friend," Hayden muttered.

"We looked as hard as we could," said Andre. "This building could have a hundred floors for all we know. And we were already seen once."

"We shouldn't just leave him here," Martina said.

"We're not leaving him. We'll come back for him," James said. "We need to get our bearings, get supplies. We'll come back once we know more."

"Come back? I'm not risking my life for him. For all we know, he's already dead," Andre said.

Hayden glanced at James and saw him clench his fist.

Just then, a loud voice startled them. "Hey! What are you doing in here?"

Hayden spun around. An overweight man with a disheveled beard stood behind them with his hands on his hips. He wore a stained white outfit that reminded her of a chef's uniform. As he stared them down, his demeanor shifted.

Hayden saw something in the look in his eyes. She froze.

"Let's go," Andre said, grabbing Martina's hand and making a run for the door.

Noah took off in a full sprint after them.

The bearded man reached behind his back, and Hayden, almost instinctively, raised the gun and fired. Her ears rang. Her vision blurred. Hayden shut her eyes, and she was taken back to the worst day of her life.

Two years ago, she'd held a different gun. But she'd felt the same pain. She could still see the surprised look in the man's eyes when she shot him. With perfect precision, right between the eyes, just as she was taught. She'd watched the life drain out of him as he lay there on the sidewalk. Hayden was frozen in fear then. She felt like she'd finally snapped out of a trance, and the realization that she'd been coerced to commit murder washed over her. As she looked down at the man's lifeless body that day, she understood the gravity of taking a life. She'd erased his existence from this world, and there was no going back.

"Hayden, we have to go *now!*" Martina yelled back to her.

But it was just a distant sound to Hayden's ears, as she was lost inside a memory.

"Come on! What're you doing?" James grabbed her by the shoulders and pulled her out the exit door.

24

James led the group once again. Outside the building, Hayden came back to reality, and they followed James as he ran, leading them deeper into the city. There was no time to make sure Hayden was okay. James hadn't expected to run outside and see the thick forest they were taken from, but he wasn't prepared for the horrific sight in front of him either.

Deteriorating buildings, cracked pavement, and torn-up sidewalks surrounded them. It was eerily quiet. As his feet pounded against the pavement, James tried to get his bearings, but there was nothing of significance to guide him. The crumbled structures were identical. What were once skyscrapers standing tall and solid had been reduced to nothing more than piles of rubble. The air smelled of death and devastation. They were lost somewhere in the middle of a broken city.

James looked back over his shoulder at the building they'd come out of and stopped in his tracks. It was as wide as it was tall, a spherical building with a polished white exterior. It was one of the few buildings still intact as far as the eye could see. As if hell had rained down all around it in a perfect circle, never to breach its reinforced walls. This must be what the soldiers referred to as the Circle. The building certainly appeared to protect whatever was inside.

At least now James knew one thing for certain. It was no longer 2025.

"What the hell?" Martina and Andre mumbled. Their whole group stared up at the massive structure. Based on the looks on their faces, James thought their confidence had started to deteriorate.

"What are you guys doing?" Noah asked, managing to raise his voice. "We have to keep moving. It's not safe!"

The group exchanged nervous glances.

"Come on," James said, following Noah.

They moved at a fast pace for nearly a mile before they stopped to catch their breath. James rested his hands on the side of an abandoned house. Cracked plaster walls towered above him. Moss and vines grew up the side, winding their intricate designs along the building. It was the first sign of life he'd seen since they left the Circle.

"I know a place where we can get some food," Noah said, breaking the silence.

"Take us there," James said.

"No, better if we split up and look for supplies. I'll meet you back here at dusk." Noah took off running down the street.

"And just like that, our new friend is gone," Martina said.

The wind picked up, and James went inside the old house. His head throbbed, and he shut his eyes, wishing he hadn't come here. Why couldn't they have ended up somewhere peaceful?

Maybe none of us deserve peace, James thought. He hadn't felt any since his wife's disappearance, or her "death" as the rest of the world believed. And now he'd dragged these people along with him. A small part of him still believed this was their destiny. He hadn't planned to take the women along, but they were in the medical room at the perfect time last night. James didn't believe in coincidences. It felt like he was destined to take them away from a place they didn't belong. But they certainly didn't belong here either.

Hayden's voice tore James away from his thoughts. He sensed the group approaching as they entered the deteriorating living room.

"James, what the hell is going on?" Hayden asked again, louder this time. James looked up to see her and the others surrounding him. "I think it's time for you to tell us the truth."

Martina and Andre exchanged a confused glance.

Dammit. How could he tell them he'd lied? It wasn't really lying, just withholding the truth. A truth they wouldn't understand.

"We have to make a plan and go back for Mason," James said.

"Don't change the subject!" Hayden shouted, but she backed off by a few feet at the same time. "I heard you and Mason at the cabin."

"What's this have to do with Mason?" Martina asked.

"Okay, fine," James said. "I knew the tunnel was more than just a way out. It's why I planned the whole thing." James bit his nails, a nervous habit that reappeared from time to time, ever since he was young. "And I knew damn well the outcome would be unpredictable."

"Where are we?" Martina asked.

James remained silent, unsure how to answer.

"Come on, Doc. We know you're hiding something," Andre said.

"Just tell us where we are," said Martina.

"I believe we're still geographically close to StormRidge," James said, shaking his head. "The question you should be asking is when."

"What the hell are you talking about?"

"I'm sorry I put you all in danger. I never should have brought you with me. This was a mistake." James paced around the room.

"What are you not telling us?"

"You're lying," Martina said. "Oh, God. How am I ever gonna get the kids back?"

"When the hell is it then?" Andre asked, growing more frustrated by the minute.

"I don't know," James answered quietly.

"Stop bullshitting us." Andre stepped closer to James.

"I don't know!" James yelled.

A look of disgust washed over Andre's face. "You got us into this mess. Now you're gonna get us out. And you can start by filling us in on everything you know about what's happening to us."

James sighed. "If I had to guess, based on my studies, I would say the time jump is around a hundred years. So it's probably around the year 2125."

"What?" Andre shook his head.

"How is that possible?" Martina asked.

James grabbed his head at the source of the pain. "StormRidge is located on a wormhole."

The group stared blankly at James, and he realized he needed to elaborate.

"A wormhole is basically a tear in the space-time continuum. It can only be traversed when very specific conditions have been met. My research led me to that prison, and when I pleaded guilty to manslaughter, my colleagues helped ensure StormRidge was the prison I was sent to. They have friends in high places."

"I don't believe any of this," Martina said, storming out the front door.

James turned to Hayden and Andre. "Look. Frankly, I don't care if you guys believe me or not. I'm sorry I got you into this, but we're all stuck here right now, and we have a problem."

Hayden rolled her eyes and Andre grimaced, but James knew he had their attention.

"Someone came in to interrogate me back there. I think he's their leader. They called him Kendrick, and he seemed to know something about how we got here. I don't know what's happening to Mason right now, but whatever it is, it can't be good."

"Let's go back and get him then," Hayden said.

Andre shot her a disapproving look. "Are you crazy?"

"What choice do we have?" Hayden asked.

Suddenly, Martina's scream ripped through the shell of a house they were standing in, echoing off the bare walls.

25

Andre was the first to run outside. His thoughts were unraveling after the bomb James just dropped on them, but he pushed them all aside and focused on her.

Four men surrounded Martina and grabbed her. They were covered in dirt and grime; Andre could smell their stench from fifteen feet away. Tattered clothing hung from their thin bodies. They appeared to have been living on the streets for years. Andre got closer and saw what looked like burn scars on their skin. They reminded him of a kid from his neighborhood who ran inside a burning house to save his dog and came out permanently damaged.

"Let her go," Hayden said, raising the gun to meet them at eye level.

The group laughed high-pitched disturbing laughs, like a pack of hyenas. Andre took another step toward them, and the one standing closest to Martina withdrew a rusted blade from his pocket and held it to her neck.

Andre got a good look at him. Most of his hair had fallen out, and the gash down the side of his face looked infected. He opened his mouth and most of his teeth were missing.

"Easy, hero," said one of the men, his hands buried deep in the pockets of his red jacket.

"Stay back, or she gets cut," said the man holding the blade.

"What do you want?" James asked.

"We're taking the girl. Lower your weapon and no one gets hurt."

"Never gonna happen," Martina said through gritted teeth.

She took them by surprise. Martina angled her head down, causing the knife to cut into the skin on her neck, and she bit the man's arm as hard as she could. He yelled as her teeth tore into his flesh, and he faltered enough for Martina to get the knife away from him. She ripped it from his hand and spun around in one swift movement. She placed one hand on his shoulder and jammed the knife into his stomach with the other.

"No! You stupid bitch!" the man with the red jacket yelled.

Before the group could react, Andre charged forward, taking down another man. He pinned the man to the ground and his fist connected with the man's jaw. Martina held the knife out toward the remaining two just as James and Hayden descended upon them. One of the men grinned and picked up something from the street. He exchanged a glance with his friend, and they took off running down the street.

"Andre, that's enough," James said.

Andre was still on top of the man, beating him with his fists. The man's face was becoming nothing more than a puddle of blood.

"Stop!" Martina grabbed Andre's shoulder, and James helped her pull him away.

The man, clearly disoriented, took the opportunity to drag himself to his feet and limp away. He didn't look back.

"Piece of shit," Andre muttered under his breath as he walked back toward the broken house.

"Are you okay?" Hayden put her arm around Martina.

"I'm fine. Just when I thought this day couldn't get any worse." Martina patted the pockets of her jumpsuit, gently at first and then with frantic motions. She pulled away from Hayden and searched the ground around them. "It's gone!" she cried.

"What's gone?" asked Hayden. "What are you talking about?"

Martina held her head in her hands and let her hair fall over her face. "The key fob I took from Mina," she said. "It's gone. I saw one of those guys pick something up before they ran away. It must've fallen out of my pocket. How are we going to get Mason out of there now?"

"Another reason not to go back to that place," said Andre, and Hayden shot him a look to shut him up.

"Everything's going to be fine." James tried to comfort her. "Don't worry. I'm going to come up with a plan."

"You keep saying that, but it's not fine," said Hayden. "None of us are. And it's all because of you." She glared at James as she and Martina walked back inside.

Martina took a seat on the couch and looked up at James. "How could you bring us here without telling us where we were really going?"

"I never planned to take you with me. But you were there in the room." He glanced at Hayden. "No one was supposed to be there. I didn't know what to do. Andre wanted you to come with us."

"I'm not taking the blame for this one, Doc." Andre shook his head.

"Are we gonna be able to get out of here?" Hayden asked.

"Once we find our way back to the wormhole in the woods, we can go back the way we came in. But I don't know what will be there to greet us on the other side."

"Okay, so all we need to do is locate that exact spot in the woods where we came through," Hayden said.

James nodded. "I had a map and the exact coordinates for the wormhole in my notebook. Kendrick has it now. But we'll figure this out together."

"They drove us out here," Martina said. "I have no idea where we are."

"Maybe Noah can help us get our bearings. He must know where that forest is," Andre said.

"Exactly," James said. "Rest up for a bit, and when you're ready, we'll go look for supplies and find Noah. Plan our next move."

26

Lights flickered and water dripped onto the cold, hard cement floor from metal pipes running along the ceiling.

Mason jolted awake. His body twisted uncomfortably with his arms behind his back and his legs bent underneath him, he tried desperately to move. His hands were bound to a pipe behind him, restricting his upper body from moving at all. He stretched his legs and got some relief. But it was nothing compared to the growing agony and stress in his shoulders, the tension building in his neck and back.

What is this place? Where are the others? A fuzzy memory came back to him. A fight in the cabin. With a man named Jones. Then they knocked him out.

Cowards.

His head throbbed, and rage burned deep inside him. He tried repeatedly to free his wrists to no avail.

Shit!

He thought back to his time spent in prison and the many similarities between his solitary cell and the room he was being held prisoner in now. The size of the room was about right. But the lack of furnishings and growing pain shooting up his back was starting to make his old cell look like the Four Seasons.

In this moment, more than any other, he longed for his wife and daughter. He would give anything to spend just one more day with them. This wasn't how his life was supposed to turn out. He was supposed to grow old with Jane and attend Emily's graduation and walk her down the aisle at her wedding. He could still see them clearly in his mind, even though he no longer had a photo of either of them. People told him their faces would eventually fade away and he wouldn't be able to remember them. But he'd drilled their beautiful faces into his mind. He would never forget, not as long as he lived. And he would never forget the face of the man who took them away from him.

That man was gone, but even though Mason had exacted the revenge he needed, it would never bring them back. It would never undo what had already been done. Mason's life was over the day they were killed.

Tears streamed down his face. He couldn't remember the last time he'd cried. He struggled against his restraints and cried out until he'd exerted all his energy. Mason let his body collapse, and his head met the solid concrete floor, his arms twisting behind his back, creating a sharp pain in his shoulders. He closed his eyes and tried to shut out the world forever.

Thoughts of the scientist seeped into his mind. Was he full of shit, or could James really be his half-brother? *It's possible*, Mason thought. Growing up in the foster system, he often wondered if he had any other biological siblings out there. But the last thing he'd expected was the slap in the face that was James. Privileged, entitled, successful. And seriously messed up in the head. After the secret James revealed to him at the cabin, Mason had no clue where they were. Any hope of escaping this place seemed dim. *What about all that "time travel" nonsense?* Mason thought. *There's no chance in hell that tunnel we crawled through was a wormhole, right?*

Mason suddenly felt nauseous, bile threatening to rise in his throat. *It didn't last long*, he thought. What were the odds? He finally got a taste of freedom, and not twenty-four hours later, he ended up back in a tiny, windowless room, hopeless and utterly alone.

27

The familiar sound of jazz caressed his ears as he walked through the door to his penthouse apartment at the top of the Circle. It was the same track Kendrick's wife played every night when she was preparing dinner. Recorded music had become a delicacy only the wealthy could afford. This was one of only twelve records they owned, along with a beaten-up ancient record player. And he never got sick of hearing a single one of them.

"Honey, I'm home," he said playfully, as he walked through the sleek marble foyer.

"It's about time." His wife, Zara, emerged from the kitchen, wearing an apron, and threw her arms around his neck, pulling him in toward her. Bare faced with her hair pulled back into a small ponytail, Zara still looked beautiful. There was something about her performing her wifely duties that increased his attraction.

He kissed her hard. This woman had been by his side through everything, and he belonged only to her. He wouldn't allow some frivolous girl to destroy his marriage over one mistake. He'd once believed he achieved fulfillment in life when he became Commander of the East District at such a young age. But once he met Zara, everything changed. She provided him with things he never knew he was missing.

"Daddy!" His son, Ethan, and daughter, Jasmina, sprinted to him, grabbing at his side. He wrapped his arms around them and embraced his family. He wished moments like this could last forever. What he wouldn't give for a pause button, to be able to cherish these moments for just a little longer.

"How was school today?" he asked the kids as he sat in his favorite chair.

"Ethan learned how to multiply." Jasmina giggled. "He thinks he can do math faster than me now."

"That's because you're slow." Ethan taunted his sister and started playing with a toy car.

"Even I can't do math faster than you," Kendrick said to his daughter with admiration. She excelled in every subject his wife taught her, and Kendrick couldn't be prouder. "You know, you can learn a few things from your sister," Kendrick said to Ethan. "She's very smart."

Ethan stuck out his tongue and ran his toy car along the chair, tracing its curved back and making the car do a flip in the air.

"Come on. Help your mother set the table."

The kids did as they were told, and Zara handed them each a full plate as they sat down to eat. Because he held the highest rank in the district, as commander, Kendrick's family was very fortunate. He had done everything in his power to shelter his children from the extreme poverty many people faced in the East District, and in the other districts, he assumed, though he never traveled far from his jurisdiction, beyond the safety of the walls.

It was just the way things were and always had been. The rich members of society increased their wealth exponentially. The working class did all the hard work; they kept everything in motion, and they were allowed a roof over their heads as payment. *They should be grateful*, he thought.

After dinner, the kids went to play while Kendrick helped Zara clean up.

"Something on your mind?" she asked.

"The usual." He shrugged. "It's getting worse and worse down there. The people resent me."

"Nothing else?" She stopped cleaning the dinner plates and turned toward him, raising an eyebrow.

"Such as?"

"You think I don't hear people talk? I know about those people you brought in this morning."

Kendrick sighed. "I didn't want to worry you."

"You didn't think it was important to keep me in the loop? I mean, who are these people? Are they a threat?" She glanced over at the kids playing their made-up game.

Kendrick took her hands in his. "Of course not, my love. I'm going to share something with you that I trust you'll keep in confidence."

Her eyes widened. She stared at him eagerly now, and he enjoyed having this power over her. Kendrick led his wife to the bedroom, where he hesitated for a moment and then, reluctantly, handed her James's notebook.

She flipped through the pages for a few moments. "What is this?"

"Zara, I know it seems unbelievable. But I believe these people may have come here from . . . another time."

"That's impossible," she said dismissively.

"Take a look at this book. They know of some advanced technology that allows them to do this. I don't know how yet, but I have every intention of finding out." He became frustrated. "The only problem is they seemed to have slipped away without anyone noticing, and they took one of our prisoners with them. Honestly, what does it take to employ sufficient guards around here?" He slammed his hand down on the bedside table and Zara winced.

"Maybe we need to take more people in from the outside," she said quietly.

Kendrick walked over to the closet to change his clothes.

"That's a great idea, my love." He climbed onto the bed beside her. "But I fear there isn't anyone left."

2 8

Rain poured like buckets dumped from the skies. Andre never minded the rain. Some of his fondest memories were out on the field during a downpour, his cleats digging into the softened ground and sliding into the end zone. He loved watching his girlfriend dancing in the rain in her cheerleading uniform. She hated when it rained during games, but he always told her how beautiful she looked with her soaking wet hair and smeared makeup.

Despite the rain persisting through the evening, the group split up to search for food, weapons, and supplies.

"Martina and I can search the houses on the next street over," Andre said.

"I think it's best if you and I stick together," James said, contradicting him.

Andre caught Martina's gaze, which flickered back and forth between him and Hayden. He found himself wanting to spend more time with her. It would've been safer for each of them to go with one of the women, but James was stubborn.

"I better stay with Hayden. I've had her back since the day we met. That's not gonna stop now," Martina said.

"Uh, hello? I'm standing right here. Don't I get a say in this?" Hayden stepped between them.

"Come on." Martina grabbed Hayden's arm, practically dragging her in the opposite direction.

Andre watched them walk down the street as Hayden protested. Then he and James searched the row of identical houses leading away from their hideout. They weren't really buildings anymore. All that remained were piles of cement, some far worse than others. A few homes were relatively intact, the interiors full of stuff. They contained little of value; Andre assumed all the buildings had already been looted.

Cautiously, they went inside one of the houses. Andre entered what appeared to have once been a kid's bedroom. The furniture was in shambles on the floor, and he noticed several shiny objects underneath a collapsed set of shelves. He dug through the rubble only to realize they were trophies for a series of sports championships. Underneath the pile of them, he found an old football, its brown leather tearing at the seams, preserved below the debris. He picked it up and smiled, turning it over in his hands.

He thought back to when his college team made the playoffs, all the way to the semifinals. He could still feel how torn up inside he was when they lost. He didn't know it at the time, but he had it easy then. He could get any girl he wanted, every weekend was filled with parties, and he didn't have to work hard at anything except football. Life was simple back then; he went about his days without a care in the world. Sometimes he wondered if that carefree boy was still deep inside him somewhere or if he was lost forever after the conclusion of his trial.

James appeared in the doorway, looking out a hole in the house where a window used to be. "I wonder who's out there."

"I don't know. Seems like something wiped out most of the population," Andre said, tossing James the football. "What I don't get is why all those people are living at the Circle. I'd rather take my chances out here than live in that place of oppression."

James caught the football with a surprised look on his face, and a slight smile crossed his lips. "Maybe they thought they were doing what was right for their families, and then they got stuck there. The guards don't let them leave." James tossed the football back to Andre in what would've been a perfect spiral if the football hadn't been damaged.

"I didn't see much security when we left." Andre hurled the ball at James, hitting him square in the chest.

James caught it at the last moment. "You're right. We were able to get through the building without being seen." He tossed the ball back. "It's getting dark. We should head back to the meeting point."

"Good idea, considering we don't have a flashlight." Andre stared at the football, debating whether to keep it, before exiting the bedroom. He decided to hold on to it. "Let's check one more room."

James struggled to open the next door down the hall until he gave it a shove with his shoulder. As Andre approached James, he saw the scientist's eyes widen.

A growl erupted from the mouth of a creature barely resembling a human as it lunged out of the bathroom and at James. The skin on its face was peeling away from the bone, and open wounds covered its body, revealed under tattered clothing. James was frozen in fear, but Andre reacted quickly, putting himself between James and the creature.

The creature reached for Andre, and he held the football up, blocking his face. He felt the football pop, air hissing out of it, as the creature's bony hand closed around it.

"Shit!" James yelled. He helped Andre shove the creature back into the bathroom. Despite its decaying appearance, it was strong. The two men finally pushed it over the threshold, and Andre quickly shut the door.

"What the fuck was that?" Andre headed for the front door.

"I don't know." James followed quickly behind.

Andre heard the creature clawing at the bathroom door, trying to get to them as they exited the house.

Andre and James carried the supplies back to their hideout. Their most useful finds amounted to a change of clothes: a mixture of T-shirts, jeans, and sweatpants. Andre was grateful to change out of his jumpsuit. It felt symbolic, like he could put that part of his life behind him. Only now, he had to deal with this world James had brought them to. The rain poured even harder as the sun dipped below the horizon, and Andre blinked, trying to see where they were going.

"You gotta know it's a big risk," Andre said, looking at James. "Going back for Mason."

"It's not just about Mason." James sighed. "They have my book."

"Your book?"

"I need to get my notebook back. It has all my research in it."

"Are you really worried about those people looking at your research?" Andre asked. "If what you said is true, I don't think any of that matters anymore. And we need to get the fuck out of here before it's too late."

"It contains my equations, coordinates, a map, information we'll need if we want to get out of this place. I don't even know where we are right now."

"You wanted to come here in the first place. You said it yourself. Why the sudden change of heart? Is the future not everything you hoped it would be?"

Andre walked faster, trying to put some distance between him and James. He couldn't stand to be near him right now. He was starting to realize the guy was an asshole. He'd put them in this dangerous situation against their will, especially the women. They didn't deserve this.

"I told you. I knew it was unpredictable. I had my assumptions. But I didn't know exactly where it would take us. There wasn't supposed to be an *us*! It was just supposed to be me." James jogged to keep up.

They moved in silence for a moment until James spoke again. "I know you were wrongly convicted, and I'm sorry about that."

Oh, now he thinks I'm innocent, Andre thought. "What would you know? You're blinded by your own privilege."

"Come on, man. That's not true," James said. "I worked for everything I have. What? You think every white scientist was born with a silver spoon in his mouth?"

Andre stopped and turned, blocking James's path. Their faces were just inches from each other, so close he could feel James's ragged breathing. "Remind me again what you did to go to prison? Oh, that's right. You killed your girlfriend."

"I didn't kill her. And she was my wife!"

"Do you know what I did to go to prison? I was born Black. And in the wrong place at the wrong time," Andre said, fighting to keep his composure. "Privilege doesn't just mean money, James. It means opportunity. It means justice. It means being believed by the police, by the fucking court system! When all you're doing is telling the truth!"

James ran his fingers through his wet brown hair as the rain beat down on their faces. "I'm sorry for what happened to you. No one deserves that." He looked down. "None of us were meant to be in there. I truly believe that."

Give me a break, Andre thought. "I guess you did us all a favor. Especially Mason." He still felt a fire burning deep inside him, but he realized his anger was misdirected at James. "I mean you saved the guy's life."

"Yeah, now it looks like we have to do it again," James said, shaking his head.

Andre nodded. "Why do you believe I'm innocent now?"

"Because you're a good man," James said without hesitation.

Suddenly, the rain let up. For a moment, it was dead silent. Then Andre heard a sound that sent a chill down his spine. Ominous gusts of wind swirled around them. The night felt angry, like the elements were out of whack. The sound of footsteps came from down the street, growing closer by the second.

Silhouettes emerged from the darkness, and a low growling sound erupted from them.

What the hell? Andre locked eyes with James, and as if they'd made a silent pact, they began to run.

29

After the twelfth house Martina and Hayden searched, they started to grow restless. They'd barely found anything worthwhile, except a few cans of beans that looked like they had expired many years ago and what appeared to be a modern lantern. It was made of white plastic and seemed to be solar powered. Whatever it was, it gave off light, which was all that mattered.

"Do you think we're gonna die out here?" Hayden asked.

"We'll be fine. We just need to eat something and change out of these clothes."

Hayden frowned. "Let's check one more house before we head back."

Martina followed Hayden up the eroding staircase of a quaint two-story home. Tattered wallpaper hung off the walls and the ceiling had caved in. Nevertheless, Martina could tell it was once a beautiful house. She imagined that before the destruction, this had been one of the houses with a white picket fence and a dog that ran joyously around the yard. She wondered what the family was like that lived here and if any of them were still alive.

"I would've liked to live in a place like this, start a family," Hayden said, trying a light switch to no avail in the upstairs hallway.

"Hey. This door's locked," Martina called from the last door on the left.

Hayden appeared at her side. She knelt and looked under the door. "I don't think it's locked. There's something blocking the door."

"Maybe there's another way in." Martina thought for a moment. She looked out the adjacent window. "Watch my back." She climbed out the window and onto a narrow ledge that ran along the side of the house.

"Are you crazy?" Hayden called after her.

Martina steadied her breathing and inched along the ledge until she reached the cracked bedroom window. She kicked out the remaining glass and carefully climbed inside.

Moments later, she opened the bedroom door and Hayden let out a sigh of relief.

A canopy bed sitting in the center of the room and elegant chairs and dressers were somehow left unscathed. The bedroom had a huge master bathroom attached, equipped with two walk-in closets.

"I miss my daughter more than anything," Martina said.

"You'll get back to her, one way or another."

"I'm not so sure about that anymore."

"Don't say that." Hayden turned to face her. "The minute you give up, all my hope will be lost."

"I can't be here for you forever, Hayden. You need to be strong without me. I'm just as scared as everyone else."

"I know, I just . . . I don't know. Without you, I probably wouldn't have made it through the last year, and I'm grateful for that."

She did get lucky, Martina thought. *If I hadn't taken her under my wing, she would've been an easy target in prison.*

"Oh my God!" Hayden said from inside the closet.

"What? Did you find something?"

Hayden emerged from the closet holding a ball gown, somehow still in perfect condition. It had a black, strapless, corseted top, a flowing train of black silk, and little embellished rhinestones that looked like a galaxy of stars.

Martina rolled her eyes, but even she could admit the dress was undeniably beautiful. She went to search the other closet and she knew without looking that Hayden was trying on the dress. She'd gotten to know Hayden well during their time spent together in prison. She knew underneath the shallow, dramatic outer shell, Hayden was just a girl with some deep-rooted, unresolved problems. Maybe that was why Martina felt the need to protect her like an older sister, or maybe it was because it filled the void she'd felt ever since she lost her own.

She opened the door to the other closet and froze, staring into the empty eye sockets of a skeleton leaning against the shelving unit. She stepped carefully over the body and perused the shelves. Aside from human remains, the closet was filled with expensive-looking suits. A tie for every day of the month. Some cash was stuffed in the sock drawer, and Martina wondered whether it was still of any use. She pocketed it anyway. She looked through all the drawers and shelves, coming up with nothing useful. Then she noticed a gap behind the row of shelves. Everything was in such perfect order it looked out of place. She reached her hand into the open space.

Bingo!

A small revolver and a box of ammo had been tucked between the closet shelf and the wall. *Two guns are better than one*, she thought.

She pulled the cylinder latch and was relieved to find all six bullets remaining in their chambers. As she turned it over in her hands, she felt a nauseating feeling in the pit of her stomach. The revolver looked almost identical to the one Gabriel, her boyfriend at the time, gave her the day she got arrested. He handed it to her just moments before she, Gabriel, and her best friend, David, slipped masks over their heads and entered the bank. It was the first time she'd handled a revolver; she was used to her semi-automatic nine-millimeter. The revolver reminded her of an old movie.

Images flashed through her mind and bile rose in her throat. They'd been so sure they'd picked the right bank. They took every precaution, so the possibility of getting caught wasn't even on her radar. She'd never forget the look on the old woman's face when David held the gun to her head. Or the way the young female teller, who couldn't have been more than eighteen, trembled with fear, loading her bag with cash as Gabriel knocked out the security guard. If it hadn't been for the record-breaking police response time, maybe they could have gotten away. They could have avoided the crash that ended fatally for her best friend in the back seat. She never would have woken up in the hospital, handcuffed to the bed, only to learn David was dead and she and Gabriel were going down for armed robbery.

Tears dripped down her cheeks, and she wiped her face dry before exiting the closet. Back in the bedroom, she saw Hayden looking at herself in a cracked mirror, a broken expression strewn across her face. "You're not really gonna wear that, are you?" Martina asked.

Hayden tried to hide it, but Martina could see a tear running down Hayden's cheek. Martina's throat ached, and tears threatened to break through her tough exterior again.

"No. I haven't completely lost my mind. Yet."

"Come look at this." Martina gestured toward the closet.

Hayden walked over and gasped at the sight of the skeleton.

"Guess we can thank whoever that is for keeping this stuff barricaded in here."

Hayden nodded. "We better start heading back."

They changed into jeans and T-shirts and left their jumpsuits on the floor of the elegant bedroom. It was such a relief to wear normal clothes again.

As they stepped outside, a gust of wind gave Martina chills, and she heard a low growling in the distance.

"Do you hear that?" Hayden asked.

Martina nodded. "It sounds like something's coming toward us."

Suddenly, James and Andre came barreling down the street.

"James? What's going on?" Hayden yelled.

Then something emerged from the darkness. The creatures approaching them resembled humans. They walked on two legs with an unsteady limp. Their faces were skeletal, decaying. Their skin was peeling off, revealing rotting flesh underneath. Some of them had no skin left, and others were missing limbs. They smelled like death, and they dragged themselves forward slowly. Tattered moldy clothes clung to their maggot-ridden bodies. Martina instinctively covered her face with her hands.

She could tell they were dangerous, and they all had one thing in common: their intent to kill.

Hayden screamed.

They were getting closer by the second. One approached Martina ahead of the rest, and she could clearly see its face. It hissed through its decaying teeth; its mouth pooled with blood. Martina realized it was salivating over its next meal.

"Martina, the knife," Andre said calmly.

She handed the knife to Andre and withdrew the revolver, cocking the hammer.

"Give me that and run!" James said, his hand outstretched toward her.

She gave him the gun without hesitation, almost relieved to have it taken off her hands, and she took off running in the opposite direction.

Glancing back, Martina saw Andre stab the creature closest to them in the head, and the creature collapsed on the uneven pavement.

"Head shots!" he shouted to James.

They took down the first few with ease, but more and more kept coming.

"Help!"

Martina stopped and turned around. It was Hayden. One of the creatures had knocked her to the ground. "Shit," Martina muttered under her breath, and she sprinted back to her friend.

James was at Hayden's side in a second, pulling the creature off her. But it was strong; it overpowered James and knocked him on his back.

Andre acted quickly, shoving the knife clean into the creature's skull before helping James to his feet.

"Hayden, are you okay?" asked Martina.

Her shirt had been sliced open, and a shallow cut across the width of her chest had started to bleed. "I think so," Hayden said, struggling to breathe.

More creatures were headed their way, but they were taking their time, slowly dragging their limbs down the street.

"Let's get her back to the house," Martina said.

The four of them took off in a sprint, hoping to put as much distance between them and the creatures as possible.

30

Mason drifted in and out of sleep, trying to disappear from his dismal reality. Each time he closed his eyes, he dreamed of his family—the way things were before his life was ruined. Looking back, he realized he could pinpoint the exact moment his life turned into chaos. An old military buddy got into contact with him after Mason had long separated himself from his old life. He didn't realize it then, but he was the one who put his family in danger.

At first, Mason didn't want any part of his friend's scheme to rob shipping containers at the port. But his buddy was always very convincing. After considering the risk versus reward, Mason agreed to help. He never officially learned how the owners of the shipping containers found out his name and address, but his friend must've given him up.

After his family was murdered, Mason was never the same. He found the man who was sent to kill his family, and he tracked him for weeks, watching his every move. Mason followed him to the port, to the coffee shop, and to his home. A small house on a quiet street. One day, Mason broke into the man's house and waited. He'd picked up on the assassin's schedule by then and knew the exact time the man would be arriving home. Mason tortured the man until he grew bored and put a bullet in his head. He believed it had to be done, but it didn't make him feel any better. All he could feel was an emptiness inside his chest, a space that never stopped expanding.

Suddenly, the door creaked open, and adrenaline surged through Mason's veins. He struggled to sit upright as a man walked toward him, stopping a foot in front of him.

Mason spit at the man, successfully hitting one of his shoes. The man didn't flinch.

"Who are you?" Mason asked, his voice raspy, desperately needing water.

"My name is Kendrick. You and your friends were found in my district, so we brought you in," he said.

"What did you do to them?"

"I'm afraid they've escaped. They left you behind." His voice was irritatingly calm.

"You're lying." Mason shook his head.

"But don't worry. I expect them to come back."

"What do you want from me?" Mason twisted uncomfortably. "Just let me go."

"I would let you go. But that would greatly decrease the likelihood of your friends coming back. Don't you think?"

Mason glared at Kendrick under heavy eyelids.

"I'm going to figure out how you people got here," Kendrick said. "I know you came from another time."

"I'm not telling you shit." Mason tried to spit again, but his mouth was too dry.

"You don't need to tell me anything," Kendrick said before turning to leave. "You're just bait."

31

Fluorescent lights flickered over the long glass table and the twenty chairs surrounding it. Each seat was filled by a member of the richest families in the Circle. Kendrick took a seat at the head of the table, next to his wife, Zara. He didn't usually take her to meetings. The board met once per week, as they had earlier today. They'd discussed plans for the district and the status of all ongoing efforts. But this was no ordinary meeting. It was an emergency meeting Kendrick called after his second-in-command, Marc, showed up at his door, disrupting his evening.

"First order of business," Kendrick said to the room, hiding his annoyance at being dragged down to the conference room when he should be home relaxing. They grew quiet, all eyes locked on him. "Everything needs to be perfect. We need to make every effort in preparation for the gathering. We have less than forty-eight hours to get everything in order."

"Sir, surely you must place some level of importance on the intruders who escaped right out our doors," Marc said.

People around the room whispered, and Kendrick turned his steely gaze to Marc.

"*Surely*, you're not trying to undermine me, Marc?" He kept his voice low, but he felt Zara's eyes burning a hole in the back of his head, and he regretted bringing her along.

"I can assure you I've taken this matter under careful consideration," Kendrick said to the room. "We have something they want. Perhaps something they *need*. They will come back for it."

"And when they do?" Zara asked quietly.

"And when they do, we'll force their leader to comply and show us how to use this technology," he said, not missing a beat and carefully setting the notebook on the table.

How humiliating, his wife and his second-in-command undermining his authority in front of the board on the same night. Kendrick struggled to maintain his composure.

"Our main priority is still to ensure everything goes as planned at the gathering. There will be leading members from all four districts in attendance. We must be ready."

"As previously discussed, we do have a very important assignment for all of you," Marc said.

"That's right." Kendrick nodded. "First, I want you all to attempt to secure a closer relationship with the North District. Their food resources are plentiful compared to ours, and I intend to establish a new trade agreement. But most importantly, we need to focus on the South District. Over the past few years, their wealth has grown exponentially, and we need to figure out why.

Ever since the formation of the districts, they have been the lowest rung on the ladder. But now, the tables have turned. They must have increased their production dramatically and started selling new items to the other two districts. I've heard rumors of weapons and cannabis being sent to the North and

West. We've been excluded from some sort of deal, and I want you all to investigate during the gathering. Get to know the members from the South and see what you can find out."

Board members around the room nodded.

"That will be all for tonight," Kendrick said.

Zara stood and placed her hand on Kendrick's arm.

"I'm going to my office. I'll meet you upstairs," Kendrick said quietly to Zara before she could speak.

He left the room swiftly, Marc following close behind. They walked along the narrow, stark-white hallway until they reached Kendrick's office. The room had a bulletproof metal door and tall ceilings. Its walls and floor were made of white marble. A huge modern desk made entirely of glass sat in the center of the room. The rear wall was also glass, a window looking out over the Circle and beyond to what used to be the city skyline.

"I'm sorry I interrupted back there. I just have a bad feeling about this whole thing," Marc said. "What are the chances of them showing up now? Do you think it's a coincidence?"

"It's of no worry," Kendrick said dismissively. *Why do I have such incompetents working for me?* "We have one of them. The guards said he was the toughest fighter, so we separated him from the rest and put him in a secure room on the twelfth floor. If they don't come back for the book, they'll come back for him."

"Well, that's reassuring." Marc picked up the notebook and flipped it back and forth in his hands. "Are you thinking of putting this up for auction too?"

Kendrick looked at Marc like he was insane and then proceeded to go through files on his desk, ignoring his outrageous question. Every year at the gathering, they held an auction for some of the valuables they'd collected over the years. Many of the guests donated their own valuables to add to the auction, fighting over who had the highest status based on the worth of their donations. They reveled in the idea of contributing something more elaborate or rarer than everyone else. It was an entertaining way to make a huge profit off drunk, rich idiots. Last year they took in a whopping thirty million dollars, far more than the items put up for auction were worth.

The profits were distributed evenly among the board members after Kendrick skimmed fifty percent for himself. These families were considered the one percent, the elite. With each year that passed, they grew richer as the poor in the district became poorer. The lower class worked for food and shelter, and they were given nothing more than their daily rations and small sleeping quarters. This meant the work done both on the lower levels of the Circle and outside the walls was done at little or no cost to the board. This way, the upper class was able to stay comfortable on the top floors of the building. The top of the food chain, so to speak.

"It's imperative that they return to try and save their friend," Kendrick said, gesturing toward the notebook. "This is science from another time. All records of it were destroyed during the Incident, and this depth of knowledge was lost. We need them to translate this into terms we'll understand."

"I'm sure they'll be back. That's what concerns me. But hear me out," Marc said nervously. "About the auction, we can start the bidding for the notebook so high only the wealthiest among them can participate. We don't let them know what the item is until they're already in a private room with just a handful of others. And then of course, the highest bidder, well, he doesn't make it out of here alive."

"There's no guarantee they will bid if they don't even know what the item is."

"These people have more money than they know what to do with." Marc said. "Just the enticement of having something so exclusive is enough to reel a few of them in. I'm sure of it."

"You'll need to get one of our most discreet employees to take care of the winner. We can't risk this getting out."

"Of course." Marc nodded.

"Someone will come looking for the winner."

"We can make it look like an accident."

Kendrick thought it over for a moment. This just might work. It could be a way to double or even triple their profits from the auction.

He smiled and said, "And out of nowhere, I remember why you're my number two."

32

Zara walked into the public restroom next to the conference room, placed her hands on the sink, and stared at herself in the mirror. Fine lines creased her face, her skin sagging just enough to remind her of her dwindling youth. She pulled gently on the skin by her eyebrow and cheek in an upward motion and sighed. She hardly recognized the face staring back at her. The face of a pathetic, powerless woman. Known as nothing more than the commander's wife, as if she herself held no value without him.

There was a time when she dreamt of becoming someone powerful. After she settled into life at the Circle, monotony slowly dulled her aspirations. She thought she'd found purpose once she started a family. But even the love and joy she experienced when she became a wife and mother were not enough.

Zara had been slowly drifting away from her husband for some time now. But she knew she couldn't leave him. Not just because of the kids but also because, sometimes, she feared him. She'd been putting on an act, hoping she could figure out a plan, but weeks and months had passed, and nothing had changed.

The situation was only getting worse in the Circle. The people were oppressed now more than ever. Kendrick increased work hours, lowered the working age, and decreased rations. He was trying to propel their district forward because he felt like the other three were starting to surpass him. It hadn't been like this a few years ago, but since the board always agreed with everything Kendrick said, it seemed like nothing would ever change.

Those people who showed up in the East woods disrupted the natural order of things, and she could tell it was deeply affecting Kendrick even if he didn't show it. He feared them, or at least the idea of them. She could see it through his tough exterior.

"Everything okay?" Kristal, the only board member Zara considered a friend, exited a stall behind her.

"Yeah, I'm fine."

Kristal washed her hands at the sink next to Zara, appearing to accept her answer. Zara hesitated to speak her mind, but she figured Kristal might be the only person in the Circle she could trust.

"Actually, I've been a little stressed lately. It's just that he never allows for my involvement in politics. I was grateful to come to the meeting tonight, but I have my own opinions about the way things are being run, and I'd like to be able to express them." She hoped she hadn't said too much.

"We can't question the commander's decisions. You know we have to trust his word."

Zara nodded. Obviously, Kristal wasn't the right person to talk to about this.

Then Kristal checked the stalls to make sure they were alone and lowered her voice. "You're not the only one who doesn't agree with everything that's been going on."

Surprised, Zara leaned in closer. "Who else doesn't agree? And why hasn't anyone on the board tried to discuss topics they don't agree with? They need to speak up."

"Some of us have been talking. But honestly, I think everyone fears your husband. He is our leader after all. He's meant to decide our fate."

"What about the fate of the people downstairs? Who decided for them? I mean, I remember a time when we had some semblance of equality. The new rules implemented over the past few years have really dragged us down."

Kristal opened her mouth to speak, but the bathroom door swung open and another board member walked in. "It was great to see you." She gently touched Zara's arm and hurried out of the bathroom.

Great, Zara thought. She didn't get many chances to talk to anyone besides her husband. Most days she was cooped up in the penthouse, cooking, cleaning, and homeschooling the kids. She figured Kendrick preferred it that way. He liked to keep her quiet and submissive. If it weren't for the kids, she probably would have gone crazy by now and risked leaving him.

She pulled herself together and headed for the stairs that led to her beautiful penthouse, her own personal hell, silently vowing to herself that soon things would be different.

3 3

It was pitch-black outside by the time they reached the house. As they approached, James thought he saw a shadowy figure standing outside. He turned to Andre and realized he saw it too, as Andre slowed down his pace and withdrew the bloody knife from his pocket. Andre crept up to the house quietly, the others following behind. He grabbed the figure and slammed it against the wall of the house, holding the knife to its throat.

"Hey! It's just me!" a raspy voice said into the darkness.

Martina raised her lantern, illuminating the front of the house.

"It's Noah," James said, grabbing Andre's arm.

Andre backed off.

No one said a word as they walked into the house, their energy depleted from the peril they'd faced. Once safely inside, Martina helped Hayden clean her wound, and Hayden changed out of her ripped T-shirt. Andre and Noah went through the supplies they had gathered.

James felt the need to break the silence. "I'm sorry." It came out more pathetic than he'd intended.

Andre scoffed. "You knew something like this could happen."

"No. You think I would've come here if I'd known? All I wanted was to finish my research. There was no way to know we'd be in this type of danger."

Noah perked up, listening to the conversation, but kept quiet.

"Your research might cost us all our lives," Andre said. "Why would you risk everything?"

"I told you," James said. "I needed to see if time travel was possible."

"I'm not buying it." Andre shook his head. "There's gotta be more to it than that."

"You should've told us what we were getting ourselves into. None of us signed up for this," Martina said.

"Yeah," Hayden said as she approached the group. "What was that back there?"

"Survivors of nuclear war or something like it, I'd guess," James said, shrugging. "The ones not lucky enough to get safely inside the Circle."

Noah chuckled to himself.

What's this guy's deal? James thought.

"Where did you people come from?" Noah asked.

The group exchanged glances.

"You know this place," said Andre, moving closer to Noah and lowering his voice. "You must have some idea where the East woods are."

Noah looked up, as if visualizing a map of the city on the ceiling. Then he shook his head. "It's been too long. If there are woods nearby, I don't remember them."

"What can you tell us about those creatures?" James asked.

Noah was silent for a moment, lost in thought. "So you encountered the lost ones?" he finally said. "The poor souls who lost who they once were and are now trapped here, damned to spend eternity as monsters."

"They seemed pretty soulless to me," James said.

"The East District calls them Remnants. Because they're what's left over after the war, to remind us of what we've done," Noah said. He crossed the room and crouched in front of the fireplace. He slowly stacked small pieces of wood and pulled a lighter out of his back pocket.

"What war? I mean, who was fighting it?" James asked.

Noah lit a fire and stared at James.

"How many people died?" Hayden blurted.

"No one knows the real numbers, but they wiped out over ninety percent of the population. I figure by now it's more like ninety-eight percent."

"How long ago?" Andre asked.

Noah scratched his head. "Honestly, I don't know. Maybe fifteen years ago? I sort of lost track of time, being at the Circle."

"What created the Remnants?" James asked. "They appear to suffer from radiation damage, but it must be more than that."

"During the war, each country involved had their own method of destroying their enemies. Some had their nukes. And we were prepared for it. But then . . . a biological weapon was unleashed."

"What was it?" asked James.

"I don't know exactly. But my guess is that a mutation caused the Remnants." Noah shrugged.

"How do we know if it's safe for us to be out here?" Martina asked.

"It's not," Noah said coldly. "But as far as I know, enough time has passed so the bioweapon shouldn't affect us. But we have the Remnants to deal with, among other things."

Hayden sat on the couch and covered her face with her hands. "I wanna go home."

"We all do," Andre said.

James sat beside Hayden and put his arm around her. "Everything's going to be okay. We'll figure this out. Together."

They huddled around the fireplace to keep warm and ate some of the canned food they'd gathered. Everyone was on edge. After a while, their anger toward James appeared to subside.

Andre and James did what they could to board up the exposed side of the house. An old two-story with a spacious living room, it had strong bones and most of the house was still standing.

James wondered why Noah had hardly spoken since they got him out of his cell. He took a seat beside the stranger next to the fire. "So what's your story?" James asked, figuring bluntness was the only way to get him to talk.

Noah stared into the fire for a while. Just when James thought he wasn't going to share anything, Noah said, "They took everything from me."

"What happened?" Martina asked.

He hesitated before he said, "My wife and I lived in Sacramento when it all happened. Then we traveled down to the area that's now the North District."

"Can you tell us about the districts? I mean, what are they?" asked Hayden.

"In the times of mass devastation, there was a large group of people here in North America that were prepared for it all to happen. They were rich, political types. They had four indestructible facilities built, all here in what used to be California, and they just waited to step in and take their place as leaders when the people needed it most."

"Like the Circle?" Andre asked.

"Yes. The Circle is one of the four."

James asked, "If you're from the North, how did you end up down here?"

"My wife and I sought shelter at the facility in the North. Everything seemed fine at first. But then we started to notice . . . things just weren't right. There were rumors that the other districts were different. Better. And then my son was born. So we did the only thing we thought was right. We escaped." Noah shoveled beans into his mouth from an unmarked can. "We traveled Southeast, toward the city we're in now, but it took a very long time to get here. We lived out there on the road for years, not sure how to find this place. This so-called sanctuary. I had my doubts about it all along, but I was aware of the dangers out here."

"The Remnants?" Hayden asked.

"We came across them from time to time. After a while, I realized I couldn't guarantee my family's safety anymore. Then we found the Circle." His voice cracked. "It felt like we'd finally found our salvation. To have a roof over our heads was the most important thing. But then we realized it wasn't just as bad as the North District. It was worse."

"Because of Kendrick," James guessed.

"He made us work for food. All of us. My son was just six years old. It was cruel and senseless. Name one six-year-old you know who's an efficient worker." Noah started to break down.

"It's okay." James reached out to pat Noah on the back, but Noah pulled away.

"So of course, I protested. I fought back. That's not the type of life I promised to provide for my family. We were better off on the road. We tried to leave, and they wouldn't let us. So we waited. And then one night, in the middle of the night, we tried to escape again." Tears streamed down Noah's face. "But they caught us. My wife was shot by one of the guards. They beat me and locked me up in that cell. I never saw my son again."

"Oh my God," Hayden muttered.

"I assumed they were both dead."

They comforted Noah as much as they could until he fell asleep on the couch. Then the others tried to get some rest. With the house boarded up and no sign the creatures had followed them, it was the first time in a long while that any of them could relax. Outside the confines of their prison cells, they were free. And even though James had put everyone in a terrible situation, he believed they preferred anything over being locked up, even this.

Images of Mason's face flashed in James's mind. Mason had been locked up much longer than any of them, and he could be in agony right now for all James knew. All those years when James imagined meeting his older brother, he never could've guessed it would end up like this. He thought he was helping Mason escape his state-sanctioned execution. But he'd led him into another terrible fate. Saving Mason had to be his top priority going forward. Despite landing himself on death row, he didn't deserve what was happening to him now. James pushed the thoughts out of his mind and finally tried to get some sleep.

<h1 style="text-align:center">3 4</h1>

Sunlight poured through the cracks in the side of the house and tore James out of his sleep. What time was it? How long had he slept? It was the best night's sleep he'd had in months. James tried to get up and discovered Hayden lying next to him, her head pressed against his chest. He realized this was the first time he'd had contact with a woman in well over a year. It had been, by far, the loneliest year of his life. He remained still for a while, savoring the moment.

James remembered the last morning he woke up beside Isabella. Whenever he opened his eyes and she was the first thing he saw, he knew his day would be great. It didn't matter what happened at work; if he didn't see her during the day at the lab, just knowing he would be with her when he got home was enough to make him truly happy.

He'd spent most of his time in prison, at least for the first couple of months, replaying their last day together in his head. They had everything planned. Isabella would fake an accident in the lab and sneak out the back, meeting James at their house later. But when James got home that night, Isabella was gone, along with a couple of suitcases and most of her stuff.

He wondered what he could have done differently. How he had missed the signs that she was in trouble. He would've known if she wanted out of the marriage. Their relationship was as close to perfect as it gets, but in the early days when they first met in college, he'd caught glimpses of her troubled past. She never went into detail with him, but he knew she suffered from childhood trauma. *But who doesn't?* Maybe that's what they saw in each other, why they became inseparable from their first date.

In the time leading up to her disappearance, he was fully consumed with his research and the idea of studying the wormhole under the prison. Maybe he should have questioned why his wife, an esteemed scientist herself, would agree to fake her death in the first place. In hindsight, his mistakes were clear. He spent his days thinking of all the things he could've done to stop her from leaving. But none of it mattered now because James feared he would never see her again. What he regretted most was not being there for her.

Finally, James got up, trying unsuccessfully not to wake Hayden. It appeared the only person already up was Noah. He was eating out of another can, and James wondered what they had fed him at the Circle.

"I want to head back over there now," James said to the group once everyone was awake. "I'm going to check the perimeter of the building and figure out our best way in."

"I'll come with you," Hayden said.

"No, I'll take Andre."

Hayden rolled her eyes at him but didn't protest. James could tell she didn't really want to go, but she was worried about him going. It was nice to have someone care about his well-being again.

"You people are insane," Noah said as he finished off his breakfast.

"Shouldn't we be working on finding a way back to the woods?" Andre asked. "We need to leave this place."

"Right now, our priority is scoping out the Circle, finding a way back in," James said.

"We're not leaving here without Mason," Hayden said.

"Agreed." Martina nodded.

"Mason's probably dead," Andre said harshly. "We need to start thinking about saving ourselves."

Noah got to his feet and walked toward the door.

"Where are you going?" James asked.

"To get more food. You got a problem with that?"

"No." James put his hands up. "None of my business."

Noah looked back over his shoulder and said, "There's some kind of underground tunnel system between the districts. It's like a train."

"You mean the subway?" Andre asked.

Noah shrugged. "I heard about it when I was at the Circle. It's been here since before it all happened. Apparently, they worked with the other districts to restore it. That could be your way out of here." He disappeared out the door.

"Maybe we should check it out," Andre said.

"I don't know. Could the subway really bring us back to the woods? It only runs underneath the city," Martina said.

"Who knows what could've happened over the last century? The woods could be in the heart of Los Angeles," Hayden said.

James grabbed the revolver off the table and tucked it in his waistband.

"Okay. If we find it, we'll check it out and see where it leads. Stay safe in here until we get back," James said as he and Andre headed outside.

James and Andre walked along the cracked pavement back toward the Circle, their eyes alert for anything out of the ordinary. The sun shone high in the sky, and it felt good against James's skin. If they weren't surrounded by utter devastation, he'd go as far as to say it was a beautiful day out. His mind was clear, and he was determined to put an end to this mistake he'd made and get them back to the tunnel in the woods.

"Hey. How's your head?" James asked.

"Now that you mention it, it's been fine ever since we got here."

"Well, at least something good came out of this," James said. He knew his attempt at humor was weak, but he had to try something to lighten the mood.

"What are we gonna do, Doc?" Andre asked after a few moments of silence.

"We're going to gather some intelligence, break in, and take back what they took from us."

"You think it's gonna be that easy?"

"Do you have a better plan? We have to at least try to find Mason and get my notebook. Let's go check out the Circle, and then we'll find the subway."

"I've just been thinking, what if he's expecting us to come back? What if we're walking right into a trap?"

"I prefer to be an optimist. We just have to—" James stopped.

A group of men walked in the distance, determinedly, like they had somewhere to be. They wore hard hats and carried bags full of tools.

"What if they're like the others?" Andre asked.

"I don't think so. They look . . . they look like they're going to work," James said, confused.

"For Kendrick?"

"Only one way to find out."

3 5

"Where do you think he's going?" Hayden asked.

"What do you mean?" Martina got to her feet and approached Hayden.

"Noah. He's disappeared twice now to go get food. Don't you think it's a little unusual?"

"Unusual?" Martina shook her head. "We just rescued him from a cell he's been in for God knows how long in this creepy future society. I've had about all the unusual I can take."

"I'm just saying we should see what he's up to."

Martina thought it over. She couldn't bear sitting in this house all day, doing nothing, while Andre and James were off investigating. "We better hurry if we wanna catch up to him."

"I think he went this way," Hayden said, leading Martina out of the house.

They wandered along the debris-covered cement and Martina began to feel uneasy. Hayden had the Glock on her, but Martina was unarmed and terrified of running into those things again, especially with no way to protect herself. She scanned the street for a makeshift weapon and settled on an old broken pipe.

"Do you think they only come out at night?" Martina asked.

"What?"

"Those things. The Remnants."

"I don't know. Let's just keep our eyes open."

Although it was the middle of a bright, sunny day, and they didn't appear to be in imminent danger, Martina felt as fearful as ever. The city was quiet, which made her footsteps sound even louder. A splash startled her as she stepped in a puddle soaking through her right shoe and sock. She shuddered at the feeling of the wet sock clinging to her toes but kept moving. As the ground became more uneven, puddles filled much of the narrow street. A musty smell lingered in the air.

Hayden quickened her pace and turned right at the end of the street. "There he is!" she whispered, pointing straight ahead.

"Okay. Now what?"

Noah was walking along the street about thirty feet ahead of them. He looked like he knew exactly where he was going. The women followed him, keeping a good distance. Finally, Noah stopped and gazed up at an old two-story brick house still in reasonably good condition. There was nothing remarkable about it, Martina thought, but Noah took a deep breath and walked through the door, slamming it shut behind him.

Martina and Hayden exchanged glances.

"Should we go in after him?" Hayden asked.

Martina nodded.

They walked closer to the house but stopped when they heard the back door slam. From the road, they saw Noah walk into the backyard, carrying a bottle in his hand. He sat on the ground, took a long swig from the bottle, and rubbed his hand over the dirt, caressing it.

"What's he doing?" Martina whispered.

He took another drink and set the bottle down. Then he lay on the ground, his chest rising and falling rapidly, and sobbed.

They watched for a few minutes, unsure how to react.

"I think we better go over there," Hayden said. She took the lead as they approached him slowly, trying not to startle him. He had curled into the fetal position, and Martina felt like she was intruding on a private moment.

"Noah," Martina said softly, as she and Hayden sat a few feet away from him.

There were four slightly raised areas in the dirt, like they had been dug up and filled back in. *Are those graves?*

Noah sat up, his face flushed red. "What are you doing here? You followed me?" His tears stopped flowing and a flash of anger crossed his face.

"We just wanted to make sure you were okay," Hayden said.

He stared at them, and his anger subsided. Noah took another long sip from the bottle and handed it to them. Martina took a sip and then passed it to Hayden.

"I buried them here," Noah said, a tear streaming down his face.

"Your family?" Martina asked.

"No."

"Then who?" asked Hayden.

"I didn't tell you before, but we were traveling in a group. It helped us stay alive for a time." He took the bottle back. "By the time we got to the East District, it was just me, my wife and son, and another couple with their two kids. We stayed in this house before we found the Circle."

"What happened to them?" Hayden asked.

"They were so strong. Always looking out for us. I don't think I would've made it this far if it wasn't for them." Tears slowly rolled down his cheeks again. "I didn't see it happen. They must have gotten overrun."

"You really have been through hell, haven't you?" Martina felt sorry for him.

"I found them. I buried them. And the next morning, we set off to find the Circle. I wasn't going to have this happen to my family," he said, looking at the ground.

Hayden put her arms around him and pulled him into a hug.

"You didn't. You did right by them," Martina said.

"No. It's my fault. I was supposed to protect them."

"You did everything you could. I honestly believe that," said Hayden.

"It wasn't enough." Noah slumped back down and laid his head on the pile of dirt.

"Crying won't bring them back," Martina said, getting to her feet. "You can't change the past, but what you can do is put a stop to your enemies. We can make Kendrick pay for everything he's done. Now, come on. Andre and James might be back at the house by now. Get up and bring that bottle with you."

3 6

James and Andre followed the group of men, for what seemed like miles, toward the outskirts of the city. The woods were nowhere in sight, and James started to worry they'd never find their way back to the wormhole. As they approached what looked like a clearing, out of nowhere the ground gave way to an open pit that stretched as far as the eye could see. The concrete of the city stopped abruptly, turning to dirt and rock. The men wandered, single file, down a treacherous dirt path along the side of the cliff.

Andre took a step back and held his arm out in front of James. "Holy shit!"

"I think they're mining," James said.

They cautiously stepped closer to the drop-off, trying to see what was going on down there. James inched his sneakers forward until he reached the edge of the cliff, which sent small rocks tumbling over the edge. He made the mistake of looking down into the dark abyss that could swallow them whole.

Andre started to walk down the path.

"What are you doing?" James asked.

"Don't you wanna find out what they're doing down there? Or did we walk all this way for our health?"

James let out an exaggerated sigh. "Fine."

He followed Andre down the narrow path, his hands gripping the wall of rock to his left side. They walked single file. His mind was racing. If he took a wrong step to his right, he'd tumble into oblivion just like the rocks had. James didn't realize he was holding his breath until he started to get light-headed. He exhaled and then took a deep breath, forcing air into his lungs. Seconds felt like minutes as James avoided looking down and to his right. The path widened about a third of the way down the massive pit. He quickened his pace as he followed Andre into the entrance of the mine.

James's eyes adjusted to the dim lighting inside what looked like a giant cave. It smelled of must and it felt damp, although he didn't see any running water nearby. Workers wearing hard hats shoveled dirt and talked amongst themselves. Tables were set up around the large open space with miscellaneous tools scattered on them. Many of the men carried buckets. He spotted an old, rusted elevator meant for carrying the men deeper into the mine.

They watched from a distance, crouched beside an empty table by the entrance of the mine, as the men worked. Groups of ten or more piled onto the elevator, tools and buckets in hand. It slowly descended, the metal creaking treacherously, until it disappeared out of sight.

They didn't realize one of the men had noticed them until it was too late, and he was now heading straight in their direction.

"Hey!" The man hurried toward them with an unsteady gait.

Shit. James's instinct was to run, but it was too late. They had already been seen, they were in unfamiliar territory, and they were greatly outnumbered. "Hey," James said, standing his ground, prepared for just about anything to happen.

"You have to wear a hard hat in here," the man said.

"Safety first." James nodded. "That's great, but we don't work here."

A look of confusion came over the man's face.

"You work for Kendrick, right?" Andre asked boldly.

The man shifted uncomfortably in his work boots.

"I'm sorry. My name is James. Your boss has something that belongs to me, and I intend to get it back. But I'd like to find out more about what's going on around here. What's your name?"

"I better get back," the man said, pointing behind him.

"Wait. Please." James looked into his eyes. "We're not from around here. We just found this place."

"You can talk to us," said Andre.

"We need someone on our side. Our friend is in danger," James said.

The man eyed them suspiciously. "I'm Carlos," he said after a moment of hesitation.

James exhaled a sigh of relief. "It's nice to meet you, Carlos. Can you tell me a little bit about what you guys are doing?"

Carlos seemed anxious, but he was willing to talk to them. "We work in the mine every day, searching for valuables, in exchange for food and shelter."

"What kind of valuables?" James asked, intrigued.

"Gold, gemstones, metal, any type of ore." Carlos shrugged.

Andre shook his head. "That doesn't sound like a fair deal."

"I have four kids. At least at the Circle, they're safe."

"Have you seen them too?" Andre asked.

"Seen who?"

Andre looked around the pit as if the creatures might be there. "The Remnants."

"I don't know what you're talking about." Carlos scoffed and turned to walk away.

James got in front of him and held his hand up. "Hold on. I'm trying to help."

Carlos sighed. "Not all of us chose this, you know?"

James took a step back, giving Carlos room to leave if he wanted. "Please, tell us what happened."

Carlos still looked confused, but he didn't question James. "After the Incident, we were all just fending for ourselves, trying to survive out here. But then we learned about the districts. It's like they were formed before everything happened."

"By whom?" James asked, wanting a second opinion. He wasn't sure how much he trusted Noah's sanity. There was no telling how long he'd been imprisoned or how his mental state had been affected by all he'd experienced.

"I don't know. Rich people. Powerful people. They offered all of us sanctuary in exchange for work. My brother knew it was too good to be true." Carlos looked down at his calloused and filthy hands. "I would bring him and his wife rations when I could. On my way to the mine, I'd stop at the house they were staying in. Then, one day . . . I'll never forget. I was bringing them food just like any other day. But when I got there, they were dead. Not just dead, it was like something tore them to shreds. They were barely recognizable. I only knew it was him because he was still wearing the cross our grandmother gave him around his neck."

"I'm sorry," James said.

"Listen, it's not safe out here. You should go," Carlos said.

"It's not safe in the Circle either," Andre said.

"I have to get back to work."

James backed off. He was about to wish Carlos luck when he heard a deep rumbling noise and the ground started to shake. Men shouted and ran in all directions, nearly trampling James and Andre. Then dirt and rocks fell all around them, the ceiling crumbling. Dust filled the cave so James couldn't see a foot in front of him.

"Come on!" James grabbed Andre and pulled him in the direction the men were running. As they ran, a cracking noise directly above them spurred James to dive out of the way as a pile of rocks tumbled down.

"Andre!" James yelled, squinting through the dust. He scrambled to his feet to look around. There was Andre, pinned underneath a pile of rock.

37

Andre felt like someone had flattened out his lungs. He tried to take a deep breath, but his lungs had no room to fill with air. It felt like he was breathing through a straw. The weight of the rocks made it impossible to move. Each time he strained against them, the pain grew worse. He thought he might die in there, and for the first time, he realized he wasn't ready to die.

James appeared at his side. He tried to lift the rocks off Andre's torso, but it was no use. He wasn't strong enough to do it alone. "Carlos! Carlos!" James yelled.

The ground shook again, causing more rocks and dust to break free. It was as if the entire mine was about to cave in.

"It's okay. Just go," Andre said.

"Be quiet. I'm going to get you out of here. Carlos!"

Carlos appeared in Andre's foggy vision.

"Help me get these rocks off of him," James said.

James and Carlos pulled and pushed at the rocks as Andre gritted his teeth. Each time one rock shifted, the others dug into Andre's flesh a little bit more. He knew his clothes must be torn to shreds.

Andre heard the creak of the elevator as it ascended to the top, and he realized some of the men below must have been able to get back to it. He thought about how meaningless it all was for his life to end in this place after all he had endured over the last few years. Maybe he wasn't meant to live any longer. He was meant to rot in his cell until the day he died.

Another man came over to help. They struggled to move the rocks for what felt like ages as Andre cried out in agony. Finally, the three of them were able to lift the rocks off Andre's chest, revealing a red stain forming on his tattered shirt. James pulled him to his feet, and he, Andre, and Carlos exited the mine and walked single file up the dirt path.

Once safely above ground, Andre collapsed. James helped him sit up, and Carlos brought him a bottle of water.

"Thank you," Andre said to Carlos.

"No problem."

Andre felt the wound on his abdomen and winced. Then he looked back at Carlos and said, "It's not worth it, you know."

Carlos was silent for a moment. "I have to keep my family safe. At all costs."

Andre was finally able to catch his breath and steady himself. "All I'm trying to say is maybe there's a better life than this."

Carlos smiled. "If not this one, then the next one."

3 8

As James and Andre walked back toward the Circle, luck fell into their laps. On the street corner, across from several still-standing commercial buildings, there it was. A random staircase in the middle of the city, descending into the unknown. A structure that once covered the subway entrance had collapsed, making the steps difficult to climb down.

"I'm guessing you weren't the type to ever take the subway," Andre said as he climbed over piles of debris, wincing and clutching his side.

"I've taken the subway in cities all over the world," James said, annoyed. He stared at Andre's chest and stomach, where blood was seeping through his torn shirt. "Let me see that."

Andre stopped and leaned against a metal pole that lay across the width of the staircase and reluctantly lifted his shirt.

"I'm shocked the cuts don't look very deep," James said. "Are you okay?"

"Fine. I had worse in just my first year playing football." Andre shrugged it off. "Come on. We've already wasted half the day."

They reached the bottom of the stairs and an awful stench washed over James. He covered his nose and mouth. The subway was grimy as he'd expected, but it was left untouched by whatever devastated the city. To his surprise, there was electricity still running. Dim lights flickered along the ceiling. They walked cautiously toward an empty subway track.

"This looks like it hasn't been used in ages," Andre said.

James heard disappointment in his voice. "You're right. But maybe just this specific station is never used. I mean we are in the middle of nowhere."

"If that's true, what makes you think it will even stop at this station?"

"Let's just wait it out."

They waited for what seemed like an hour, so long that the stench eventually went away, or James got used to it.

"Let's just go," Andre finally said. He headed back toward the stairway.

James followed him, feeling defeated. Their last hope would be to get the notebook back and find the coordinates of the tunnel.

Near the top of the stairs, Andre suddenly stopped. "Do you hear that?"

James did. A distinct screeching off in the distance.

They sprinted back down toward the landing. Sure enough, a subway car came along the tracks and ground to a stop right in front of them, brakes squealing. The doors slid open, and they stared at each other. Pushing aside his fear, James walked onto the subway and took a seat. It was relatively clean, and there was no one else on board. He wondered who was driving this thing—or if anyone was. The doors slid shut and they moved along down the track.

"How do we know what stop to get off at?" Andre asked.

Puzzled, James looked at the route map on the wall. "I have no clue. I think we're heading west."

The subway skidded to a stop, and Andre and James exchanged nervous glances as an older woman shuffled on and took a seat across from them.

She broke the silence. "Are y'all headed to the West District?"

"Yes," James lied. "You?"

She nodded slowly, seeming to take in their appearances for the first time. They were dressed in casual clothes, but Andre's shirt was badly torn and covered in dark red stains. "Trouble on the road?" she asked.

"I'm fine," Andre said. "What were you doing so far from home?"

James was shocked at his bluntness. He wanted to avoid confrontation if possible, but Andre had opened a can of worms that might be hard to close.

She sighed. "I could ask you the same thing."

Dammit, Andre.

The three of them stared at one another, the only sound the screech of the subway car.

Finally, she spoke. "I had business in the South. Not that it concerns either of you."

"They let you leave?" Andre asked.

She scoffed. "At my own risk." She narrowed her eyes. "You must be from the East District. Don't tell me you've escaped."

"We're not from around here. But we do have a problem with the East District. They took one of our people."

"Andre!" James shouted. He didn't think they should trust this woman. She could be working for Kendrick for all they knew.

"So what're you coming to the West for?" she asked.

"For answers," James said abruptly.

The subway skidded to a halt again.

A computerized voice came through speakers James hadn't noticed were there: "Final stop."

The woman got up and slung her bag over her shoulder. "Follow me."

They followed her out of the subway car and onto the platform.

3 9

The woman led them out of the subway station and down a city street. The devastation was the same, but Andre had a different feeling here than in the East District. There were actually a few people in sight, walking quickly to their destination. He could already tell this place wasn't a prison like the Circle. People were free here.

"Here we are," she said as they rounded a corner.

Andre couldn't believe his eyes. A bunker in the shape of a perfect cube, much smaller than the Circle, sat on a cliff. Beyond it, he could see the ocean. It was violent, waves relentlessly crashing against the rocks. Mist hung in the air.

"Wow," James said. "It's beautiful here."

They approached the bunker and Andre remembered visiting the beach as a kid. He thought back to when he used to tell his college friends that once he went pro, he'd buy a house on the beach for his whole family.

"I'm afraid I can't be of much more help to you, but if you want answers, this is probably the best place to try. Many brilliant minds live here, and unlike the other districts, they're good people."

"Thank you," James said.

The woman turned to leave and then paused. "If you want to get your friend back, tomorrow evening is your best bet."

"What makes you say that?" Andre asked.

"The gathering is tomorrow." She smiled and walked away.

They exchanged puzzled looks as they entered the small, crowded bunker. Andre realized the bulk of it was actually underground, embedded in the cliff.

"How are we going about this?" James asked.

"We'll have to ask around, find out who's in charge."

They piled onto a large steel elevator packed with people. The elevator plummeted twenty floors downward in one swift motion, and Andre used the wall to steady himself. After tireless questioning and searching, it turned out there was no commander in the West District. In fact, they weren't certain there was any leader at all. Most of the people seemed busy and wouldn't give them the time of day. They settled on one final person to ask, a young man sitting at a table, minding his own business.

James asked him, "Can you bring us to someone in charge around here?"

"Who are you?"

"We're in some trouble," James explained, "and we need to talk to someone who can help."

The young man looked doubtful. "What kind of trouble?"

"Shit, Andre! I give up," James said. "Let's just get out of here. We'll go back to the Circle and gather intel like we originally planned."

"The Circle?" The man perked up.

"Yeah. Do you know anything about it?"

"No, I've never been out that way."

James sighed loudly and turned to walk away.

"But I have the next best thing," the young man said. "I know someone who used to live there."

"Can you take us to them?" James asked.

"Sure, I'll bring you down to the technology director's office."

Andre let out a sigh of relief. "After you." He motioned with his hand.

"Why was that so hard?" James mumbled to Andre.

The man led them back into the crowded elevator, and they descended even farther into the bunker.

40

They were led into an office to wait for the technology director. James had no idea what to expect. He could only hope whoever they were meeting would be able to help them get back home. When the door opened, his jaw nearly dropped.

A woman with long dark hair, thick eyebrows, and full lips strode through the door. She was wearing business attire, and her hips swung as she walked. She took a seat behind a large desk and looked them over. "Pleasure to meet you. I'm Camilla."

"It's nice to meet you too. I'm James."

"Andre." He raised his hand slightly.

"So I hear you came from the Circle." Camilla looked at them inquisitively.

James stared at her for a moment. She was straight to the point, which he liked.

"I apologize for my bluntness," she said. "But I'm extremely busy, and well, I'm very protective of my time."

James decided to be blunt as well. "Thanks for seeing us. We didn't exactly come from the Circle. Could you tell us about your time there?"

She looked down. "What exactly is it you want from me?" she asked.

James could tell his question made her uncomfortable. "Any information that could help us," James said. "They have a friend of ours, and they took something of mine. We intend to get them back."

She seemed to think it over. "Walk with me." She got to her feet.

James and Andre followed Camilla into a long hallway that reminded James of the interior of the Circle. She led them into a laboratory, and his interest piqued tenfold. The room was large, open, and stark white. White cabinets lined the walls, and the place was filled with equipment. A few lab technicians were working in a far corner of the room.

"Like you, I escaped the Circle," she said quietly. "My time there was anything but pleasant. But I am a scientist, and I tend to make the best of every situation."

"I'm a scientist too." James didn't realize how weak his words sounded until after they had left his mouth, his voice a higher pitch than he'd intended.

Camilla held back a laugh. "I came here before the tunnel system was refurbished, so you can imagine how difficult my journey was."

"I bet it was really challenging," Andre said. "We didn't have an easy time getting here either."

She led them over to a table. "We've been working on this technology for years now, and it's almost finished." They gathered around a large computer screen as she presented them with a new computer program and prototype robotic equipment. "We've built artificial intelligence, which I believe could eliminate the type of work people are forced to do at the Circle. These assembly-line jobs can all be replaced by intelligent machines."

"That's very ambitious of you. But what makes you think the commander would want to buy your machines when he already has a free labor force?" James asked.

"That's been my dilemma all along. We've been trying to find a way to put our plan into action, but I don't have a way in. And even if I did, I clearly wouldn't have any influence there." A look of sadness washed over her. "My family is still at the Circle," she said quietly. "I knew if I tried to get them out, I'd likely be killed. So I've spent my time trying to figure out another way to help them. And now you two fell into my lap."

"What do you want *us* to do?" Andre asked.

"I know you have your own objectives, but if you're serious about going back there, I could use your help."

"Camilla, do you know what the gathering is?" James asked. "I hear it's tomorrow night."

She smiled. "It's something I'll never attend, a lavish party thrown by the East District. It's a money grab. Everyone of importance will be in attendance."

"Do you think it's a big enough distraction for us to slip in unnoticed?" James asked.

Her eyes lit up. "Absolutely."

"That's when we'll go in," James said, filled with confidence. "They won't even know what hit them."

"Many of the people here attend the gathering. In fact, my partner will be in attendance for the sole purpose of putting up some of our creations at the auction."

"There's an auction?" Andre raised his eyebrows.

"Yes, it's a total rip-off. But all the people there are too rich to care."

"I don't want to be a letdown," James said, "but I'm not sure how we can be of any assistance to you. I don't know anything about your technology, and I have a feeling we'll be preoccupied trying to get back what they took from us."

"You can help my partner. We need to ensure the commander wins my technology at the auction. He must be convinced that it would be beneficial to him in some way. And I'll have my partner help you in return. He'll have your back there, in case things go south."

"We'll do what we can," James said.

"Yeah, as long as your partner can find us there, we'll do whatever we can to help," Andre said.

"Thank you so much." She squeezed James's hand and then Andre's. "I'll be forever grateful to you."

41

A soft tapping on the door startled Kendrick, breaking his concentration from the book he was reading, a love story, one from his wife's collection. He'd started making his way through her trivial books once he'd exhausted his own collection several times over.

He pushed his chair back from his desk and stood. It had to be Marc at the door, coming to bother him about something insignificant. Kendrick didn't typically stay in his office this late, but his nerves were on edge. The gathering would start in less than twenty-four hours, and he couldn't go home to his penthouse until he was sure everything was in order. He was getting burnt out and had turned to the book to clear his mind.

He pulled open the door and let out a sigh of disappointment as Allison pushed past him into the office. Kendrick shut the door behind her. "What are you doing here?" he asked. His patience was wearing thin.

"I had to see you." Allison paced back and forth.

"What you have to do is stop harassing me. Forget about what happened and move on with your life."

"Forget about us?"

"There is no *us*! I will not repeat myself again."

Allison grimaced. "You can't just use me and then toss me aside like I mean nothing."

"You are my assistant. You will do as you're told, or you will no longer be in my employ."

"Now you're firing me?"

"You should be grateful. If you prefer, I would be happy to send you back to work on level three."

She closed the distance between them, and the tension in the air thickened. "What would your wife think if she found out?"

"Leave her out of this." Kendrick was growing tired.

"Maybe she should know." Allison looked up at him with her big, blue, innocent eyes, only now they contained a hint of malice.

"There's nothing for her to know," Kendrick said dismissively.

"We can let her be the judge of that." Allison turned to leave the room.

Kendrick grabbed Allison's arm, pulling her close to him, twisting her wrist hard. "You would be wise to rethink that decision."

Allison ripped her arm away. "You're not going to do anything to me. You're nothing but a coward. You hide behind your guards and your money. Always getting somebody else to do your dirty work."

Kendrick's temper flared. He saw red.

"And now I'm going to let your wife in on a little secret. She's married to a monster," Allison said as she walked to the door and reached for the handle.

Kendrick grabbed the back of her head, his fingers woven into her blonde hair. He yanked her backwards, and Allison let out a cry. Without stopping to think, he used all his force to drive her head forward again, straight into the solid metal door.

The sound of her skull cracking against the metal was so loud Kendrick was sure someone must have heard it. Her body fell in a heap on the floor, and a steady pool of blood poured out of a gash on her forehead, spreading in all directions, a vibrant red against the sleek white marble.

Kendrick's mouth dropped open as he slowly became aware of what he'd done. His breath grew ragged, and he sank to the floor. He stared at her lifeless body for what felt like hours. When he came back to reality, he radioed the head of the guards to come clean up his office and dispose of the body. Once he was sure the office was clean and all proof of their encounter was destroyed, he returned to his penthouse.

Kendrick climbed into bed beside Zara, who was already asleep. He stared up at the ceiling, replaying the last hour in his head, his heart racing inside his chest. Tomorrow was going to be the biggest day of the year, and somehow, he had to try to get some sleep.

4 2

The night was dark and unnerving by the time they left the West District. All they had to light their way was the moon and a few weak streetlights by the subway station. James had learned from Camilla that some of the tech gurus were able to get the subway working on an automated system. Without the former masses of passengers, there was much less risk involved should the subway not operate properly. There were only two tracks, one east to west and one north to south.

"I didn't want to say anything back there," James told Andre, "but I think we're trying to do the impossible."

"We should at least try to help her," Andre said. "I saw those people at the Circle. They looked so hopeless. Empty. Kind of the way I used to feel."

"Used to?"

"Being out of StormRidge has given me a new sense of purpose. I can finally move forward. Now it's just a matter of surviving long enough to get back home."

James smiled.

They rode the eerie subway back to the East District, the train screeching along the tracks the entire way. Before long, James realized they should've already reached a stop.

"This train's not stopping," Andre said, as if reading his mind.

James got to his feet. "Maybe this is the express."

"Well, at least we'll get back faster."

James looked at a map on the wall. "Why are you so calm?"

"Sit down and relax. There's nothing we can do but wait."

James sat, biting his fingernails.

"Okay, now you're making me nervous," Andre said.

"Final stop." The computerized voice echoed in the small subway car.

They walked through the subway station, which looked nearly identical to the one they'd entered earlier. James hoped they were closer to the house. It was late, and he wanted to get back. The others were likely wondering where they'd been all this time.

The familiar stench wafted through his nostrils again. This time, James recognized it. It smelled like rotting flesh, a scent he remembered all too well from the lab. The lights flickered above them as they walked toward the exit stairway. James felt a chill run through him, and the hair stood up on the back of his neck as a deep growling came from behind them. He fumbled for his gun.

"Look out!" Andre yelled.

One of the creatures descended upon James, its arms flailing. The skin on its face was deteriorating, and blood covered its mouth. Soulless, red, bloodshot eyes looked past him rather than at him as the creature lunged.

James ducked and flung himself to the side, nearly tripping on the bottom step. Then he whipped around and held his arm stiff, knowing full well he couldn't miss. James fired at close range. The sound was deafening, and his ears rang.

The creature's forehead blew apart, and it fell to the ground.

"What the fuck?" Andre muttered, putting his hands on his head.

James grabbed the grimy railing and tried to catch his breath.

Growling and hissing enveloped his ears again. Three more creatures were headed straight for them.

The flickering lights in the subway alternated between illuminating the creatures for a moment and hiding them in darkness. When the lights shone over them, James recognized radiation burns covering their skin. He'd seen pictures of what nuclear radiation could do to the human body, but he'd never seen anything like this. Their skin had peeled away, exposing insect-ridden wounds. His stomach turned.

The Remnants quickened their pace.

"Run!" James yelled, and he and Andre both took the stairs two at a time. As they exited the subway, James tried to get his bearings, but he didn't recognize anything. "Where are we?"

"I don't know, but we have to keep moving."

The Remnants were right behind them. As James ran down the street, he could hear them gaining. He risked looking back and fired a shot at the one closest to him.

He missed.

Now there were a dozen of the creatures chasing them.

James's heartbeat pounded, and adrenaline surged through his veins, the only thing keeping him in stride with

Andre. His eyes darted frantically from side to side, but he recognized nothing. It was all the same, one pile of cement after another.

"Doc," Andre said, looking back over his shoulder.

James looked back, and it was as if the Remnants were multiplying. The dozen he saw before had turned into a hundred barreling straight toward them. "In there!" he shouted. He pointed at a sturdy brick building, one of the only ones still standing on this street. It appeared to be a commercial building. A solid metal door stood centered between two boarded-up windows. James hoped it wouldn't be locked. As they approached the building, the growling became louder, and James had a feeling more and more of them were joining the horde.

Suddenly, a Remnant appeared between them and the door. James looked into its eye sockets, just two gaping holes. The slowly deteriorating skin on its face revealed all its teeth and the bones around its mouth.

Hundreds of footsteps pounded behind them, closing the gap.

Andre shouted something, but James couldn't hear him. He was frozen in fear.

As the creature leaned forward, its skeletal mouth open just inches from James's face, a blade was driven into its empty eye socket. The creature dropped and James looked at Andre, who was holding the knife.

Yanking the knife free, Andre grabbed James by the arm, pushed the door open, and pulled him inside. He slammed the door shut and threw the bolt just as a group of Remnants was about to cross the threshold. Their rotting bodies slammed into the metal as they tirelessly tried to get inside. After ensuring the doors and windows were sealed and they were safe, Andre dropped to the ground and lay on his side, his chest rising and falling rapidly.

"Are you okay?" James's voice was no more than a raspy whisper.

Andre nodded. "I think so."

James caught his breath and decided to look around. They were in what used to be a hardware store. Most of the items were gone. The place had clearly already been looted. But James found a handy flashlight and a few spare tools that could be used as weapons. There were three sleeping bags and an empty backpack collecting dust on the ground against the rear wall. "Looks like someone's been living here."

Andre walked over and examined the space. "I hope they don't mind, but it looks like we're gonna have to crash here tonight."

Outside the door, the growling was louder than ever. They were drastically outnumbered. They wouldn't be able to leave the safety of the store until the Remnants lost interest in them.

"I don't think they're coming back," said James. "Looks like they left and took everything with them."

Andre nodded and took a seat on a sleeping bag.

James walked back over to one of the boarded-up windows and peered through the cracks. It was just as he'd feared. Hundreds of them were out there, trying everything they could to get inside. He and Andre were sitting ducks inside the store. It was only a matter of time before the Remnants broke through the reinforced windows or knocked down the door.

4 3

Martina woke with a start. Dripping in sweat and gasping for air, she couldn't for the life of her remember where she was. She blinked into the darkness and waited for the memories of the terrible nightmare she'd just experienced to drift away. Her eyes adjusted, and she saw Hayden lying on the couch across from her and Noah beneath her on the floor, still asleep. Her fear started to subside. She managed to stand and look around the house. The floor felt cold beneath her bare feet. Hunger pains nagged at her stomach, and she tried to push them aside.

Where are James and Andre? They can't still be out investigating. Something must have happened to them. Her fear kicked up a notch again, but Martina realized she couldn't ignore the pain in her stomach. She fumbled in the darkness for one of Noah's cans of food.

Martina walked outside and sat in front of the house to eat. Dawn was creeping in, and first light gave the city a soft glow.

"Stealing my food? That's not a good look," Noah said.

Martina jumped, but Noah sat beside her and smiled. Her shoulders relaxed. They sat in silence and watched the sun rise. The sky looked like an oil painting. Shades of yellow and orange melted together until the sun was high enough that all they saw was blue.

"They're not back yet," Hayden said, stepping outside to join them.

"Yeah. Something's wrong," Martina said. "I can feel it."

"Don't assume that. Those two? I'm sure they're fine. They're tough," Noah said.

"We have to go look for them," said Hayden.

Noah gazed into the distance as if he might see them coming at any moment. "I don't know if that's a good idea."

Martina stood. "You don't have to come with us," she told Noah, "but we have to go. They'd do it for us. Besides, we're not doing any good sitting around here."

After gathering their weapons, Martina and Hayden started walking down the street. Noah sighed and got up to follow them. Alert, they walked along the broken sidewalk. The city was silent except for the sound of their footsteps. They searched countless streets, but there was no one in sight.

"What exactly did you expect to find?" Noah asked.

Martina pushed her hair out of her face and came to a stop on a street corner. "I don't know. I just felt like they needed our help."

"Let's head back to the house and wait," said Noah. "It's not safe out here."

Martina looked around at the devastated city, her eyes peeled, expecting to see James and Andre giving them some sign of distress.

"Fine," she said, after a moment, but a loud screeching, like metal against metal, caused her to throw her hands over her ears. "What was that?"

"Let's get back to the house," Noah said again, a sense of urgency in his voice.

Martina ignored him and ran in the direction of the noise.

"Shit," Hayden muttered. She ran after Martina. "Where are you going?"

The screeching came to a halt, and the familiar growling filled the streets.

Hayden rounded a corner and her eyes widened. She held back a scream and grabbed Martina by the shoulder, pulling her behind the building.

Noah caught up to them, and they all peered around the corner of the building. Hundreds of the creatures were wandering the street, their stench overwhelming. They must have been attracted to the screeching noise. But what was it?

"They're going toward the underground train," Noah whispered.

"Shit! What if James and Andre are on it?" Hayden failed to hide the fear in her voice.

"We need to go," Noah said. "Now!"

A few creatures straggling behind the rest of the group noticed their presence. One turned around and stared straight at them. It growled, which signaled the others.

Martina finally came to her senses.

"Go! Run!" she shouted, and the three of them sprinted back the way they'd come.

44

The sound of the subway tore James out of a deep sleep. The car screeched along the tracks and came to a halt at the nearest station. Andre was already up, circling the room and looking out the windows. Every joint in James's body ached, but he forced himself to stand. The fear James had felt last night still lingered, and he wondered how he'd gotten any sleep. He could still hear the Remnants outside, but they sounded distant.

"They're being drawn away," Andre said quietly, "by whatever poor soul is riding the subway this morning."

James joined him at the window and looked through the crack between the boards. Andre was right. They were headed toward the subway station where James and Andre got off the train last night.

"This is our chance to get out of here. Let's go before the subway leaves and they turn back around," James said. He gathered the flashlight and tools and stuffed them into the backpack.

Andre peered through the window. "Wait a minute! Some of them are coming back."

"We have to go. It's now or never."

Andre said, "They'll see us if we go out the front door."

"Follow me." James led Andre to the back of the store, where he'd spotted an emergency exit. It was blocked off, but it was safer than going out the front.

They hauled crates, cardboard boxes, and old packing materials to the side. Whoever was living in here had barricaded the rear exit with as much stuff as they could find.

Outside, the growling grew louder.

"We gotta hurry up, Doc."

James's fear kicked up a notch, but he didn't let it show. The Remnants sounded so close. It was like they were right outside the building. James was suddenly filled with doubt. "I don't know what to do. If we—"

"Listen!" Andre cut him off and pressed his ear against the door.

James shut up and leaned in close.

"It sounds like they're going right past us."

James nodded.

They waited until the creatures had quieted down, somewhere far off in the distance.

"Now," James whispered.

They snuck out the back door and broke into a sprint.

James's lungs were still not used to this level of activity. "Finally," James said, grinning as he fought for his next breath.

"What?" Andre shot him an odd look.

"I know where we are."

They were almost back to the house. He recognized the road they'd walked along when they fled the Circle. Half a mile down the road, there it was. The house covered in vines. Andre let out a sigh of relief and sprinted ahead. James took his time, trying to process everything he'd seen over the past couple of days. As he approached the front door, Andre came back outside with a puzzled look on his face.

"What is it?" James asked.

"The house is empty."

4 5

Clutching a map of the districts in his hand, Kendrick climbed the final set of steps to the rooftop. He was going to the roof to meditate, as he did whenever he felt overwhelmed. Kendrick had learned the practice from his father, who often said, "Good energy has been within us all along, and we simply must access it."

Kendrick sat on the smooth cement of the rooftop above his penthouse. He felt on top of the world, and he pushed lingering thoughts of Allison and his troubles aside. He closed his eyes and breathed deeply.

In and out.

Focusing on each breath.

How the inhale expanded his chest and the exhale collapsed it.

He listened to the sounds all around him. The wind whooshed past his ears, and he heard the slight hum of power running through the building, but otherwise, all was quiet. Until the stairwell door opened.

"What are you doing up here?" Zara asked.

Kendrick kept his eyes closed and continued to focus on his breathing, but he felt her presence as she sat beside him.

The paper map crinkled as Zara opened it and laid it out flat in front of them. It was his father's. He had it drawn up after he became leader of the East District.

"Are you worried the board won't follow your commands for tonight?"

Kenrick opened his eyes and scanned the map in front of him. "I would like to develop a stronger working relationship with the North. Some of our more . . . friendly members would do well to secure that tonight. Once I set up a new trade route, they won't have a choice in the matter."

Zara's eyes met his, and she looked uncertain.

"There is something I've been meaning to tell you," Kendrick said, as if reading her thoughts.

"What is it?"

"We've struck gold in the mines," he said, grinning.

"That's great," Zara said quietly.

Each of the districts was known for something, either their strengths or their weaknesses. The East District was known for mining. They traded gemstones, iron, coal, and other minerals found in the mine. The North District was known for its abundance of food. They'd created an indoor farm in their compound, where they grew a large variety of fresh food. The other three districts were heavily reliant on trade with the North to feed their people. The West was known for its advanced technology; the leading members had conserved some tech from the previous era, before the war. The South was known for being full of degenerates, the lowest class of people. Their district was filthy, unorganized, and without a real leader. They excelled at nothing and rarely traded or communicated with the other three districts. Until recently.

"What worries me is the South District," Kendrick said.

"I trust we'll find out everything tonight."

"I expect your help with the matter."

"Of course." Zara fidgeted uncomfortably. "Kendrick, since we've come into such good fortune, perhaps we could reward the working class?"

"Reward the working class?" Kendrick scoffed. "What would you have me do next? Pay them equal wages and educate their children?"

"Actually, I've been wanting to voice my opinion about that. The children have no place working in the factory on level three. They deserve a proper education."

"You don't have a voice here," Kendrick said coldly. "I am the commander and, therefore, the law." His concentration was diminishing. His thoughts drifted to things he would rather keep buried.

Zara got to her feet. "As your wife, I expect to be treated with respect and to have my voice heard."

Kendrick's rage welled up inside him again. It felt like everyone was testing him, trying to see how far they could push until he really went over the edge. He stood, towering above her. "Go on. Yell. Say all you want. No one can hear your *voice*."

He moved closer to her, causing her to step backwards, inch by inch. He kept walking, forcing her back, until she was against the low railing that surrounded the perimeter of the rooftop.

Zara looked over her shoulder and imagined what it would be like to fall hundreds of feet into the courtyard below to a certain death.

Kendrick stared into her eyes until she shut them, fearing for her life.

"It's time to get ready for the party," Kendrick said. Then he stepped back from her, turned, and walked to the stairwell.

Zara sunk to the ground, catching her breath. Once she was sure Kendrick had already descended the stairs, she hurried to the door, wanting nothing more than to get back inside.

4 6

They ran as far as they could before Hayden dared to look over her shoulder. Once they were sure the Remnants were no longer following them, they decided to go scope out the Circle. Noah led the way there, and Hayden was thankful to have him around. Things would have been much more difficult without him.

The sun had started to descend on the horizon by the time they reached the Circle. The building, at least twenty stories tall, was windowless on the side from which they'd escaped. They were carefully circling the perimeter, looking for entry points, when suddenly, loud mechanical noises, like shifting metal, erupted from the building. Hayden, Martina, and Noah dove for cover behind what remained of a cinder block wall directly across from the Circle.

When Hayden dared to look over the edge, she couldn't believe what she saw. The spherical walls of the building were opening, retracting along the curve of the building, resulting in a large U-shaped perimeter. With the exterior walls open, this side of the building had windows, an entire wall of glass. Now it looked like there was a part missing from the sphere, an indentation that contained a giant courtyard filled with flowers and benches. The wall of glass curved beautifully into a semi-circle bend. It truly was magnificent architecture.

"What the hell?" Martina's voice tore Hayden from her admiration of the building.

"That's incredible," Hayden said.

"Not sure that's the word I'd use for it," Noah said.

"All they have to do is flip a switch, and they can close themselves in. Safe from the radiation and safe from whatever is lurking out here." Hayden shook her head. "It's genius."

"Genius? Instead of admiring the building, we need to figure out how we're gonna break in," said Martina. "What's the plan?"

"I don't know. We need to get in undetected and when they least expect it." Hayden turned to Noah. "Maybe you can be our advantage. You know your way around."

Noah said, "I'll tell you what I know."

Hayden turned to Martina. "What about you? How much do you remember from walking through it?"

"I remember enough," Martina said confidently. "I think I can find my way around."

"Good. I just don't know how we're going to find Mason. We searched so many hallways until we found James and Noah. I don't understand why they would keep him in a different part of the building."

"What makes you so sure he's still alive?" Noah asked quietly, reiterating what Andre had said before.

"I'm not," said Martina. "But I'm not giving up on him yet. He deserves to be free, just like the rest of us. And as for James's notebook, I bet it will be with Kendrick. He probably hasn't let it out of his sight if he thinks it's so valuable."

"What does he want with the notebook anyway? Does he understand what's in it?" Noah asked.

"James said Kendrick claimed to know it was valuable information, but I have a feeling he doesn't truly understand it. I certainly don't," Hayden said.

"If you're right, maybe they're keeping Mason as collateral," Martina said. "Maybe they're waiting for us to come back."

Suddenly, a familiar sound roared in the distance. The three of them crouched behind the wall again and looked over the edge at a clear view of the courtyard.

"Is that a car?" Martina asked.

Before Hayden had time to respond, the lifted, blacked-out, military-grade Humvee sped past them, straight into the courtyard. It was moving too fast to be sure, but it looked like it had spikes along the grill, which were stained red.

The Humvee stopped abruptly in front of two twenty-foot-tall doors, likely the Circle's main entrance. Two men and a woman got out of the vehicle. They were dressed like they were about to walk a red carpet. Apparently, chivalry was still alive, even in this era. One of the men did an awkward jog to get in front of the woman and open the door for her. Her heels clicked against the pavement as she took her time walking into the building, completely unbothered.

Hayden caught the look of annoyance on the face of the other man who arrived with them. "What's going on?" she asked.

"I completely forgot," Noah said. "The gathering must be tonight. Come on. Let's get out of here."

"All I know is we need to find a way back to the woods. And fast," Martina said.

"We will. And you're coming with us," Hayden said, looking at Noah.

"I don't know. If there's any chance my son is still alive—"

"I understand," Hayden said. "But if things go wrong, we're not gonna leave you behind."

They waited and watched as a half dozen more vehicles showed up, each of their occupants dressed in formal clothing. Many of them carried briefcases, purses, or bags filled with large objects. Hayden was dying to know what was inside.

"Think we're invited to the black-tie affair?" Noah asked sarcastically.

"We are now," Hayden said, getting to her feet. "Let's get back to the house."

47

Kendrick descended the staircase on his way to the gathering. He smoothed out a crease in his suit jacket and grimaced. Unwanted thoughts of Allison started to creep in, but he pushed them away. This was neither the time nor the place to dwell.

Suddenly, thoughts of the past flooded his mind. He remembered, so vividly, the day the world ended. Well, the world as he knew it. He was just a boy when it happened. When the nations' leaders in different parts of the world were busy trying to kill each other, many of the wealthy families went into hiding to wait out the worst of the storm. Kendrick's parents, the most earnest and kind-hearted people he'd ever known, got him and his younger brother to safety at the Circle. It had been constructed in the years prior, along with three other bunkers, in preparation for the Incident.

After some time, the districts were formed, and Kendrick's father was appointed leader of the East District. Everything went smoothly for a while. The leaders of the four districts met periodically at a central location to discuss policies. One time, after their incessant begging to experience the outdoors beyond the Circle's rooftop, Kendrick's parents let him and his younger brother, Ethan, come along to a meeting. It was rumored that the world wasn't safe anymore, but Kendrick's parents were anything but fearful. They hadn't experienced any danger firsthand since the districts were formed, and three years had already passed since the Incident.

It was a day just like any other, except he finally got to go outside. The sun greeted him like an old friend. Kendrick looked skyward and felt its warmth against his face. The other three leaders were waiting under a canopy of trees in the center of what used to be a park. Kendrick was told to watch Ethan play nearby while the grownups talked. At eighteen, he thought he was old enough to be involved in the adult conversation, but Ethan looked up to him, and Kendrick would have done anything for his brother. He went back to the SUV to retrieve a toy Ethan had left in the back seat.

When Kendrick was safely inside the vehicle, they came. Creatures that looked like people with burned skin peeling off their bodies and a desire to kill. They descended upon the group, tearing them to shreds in moments. Ethan was caught in the middle of it. The guards who accompanied them to this meeting fired their weapons at the creatures, but it was too late. Kendrick watched from the back seat of the SUV in horror as they tore into his mother's flesh, ripping her open. The last guard standing was able to get away. He hopped into the driver's seat and sped off before Kendrick could see anything else. Ethan's death was the hardest on Kendrick. He named his son after Ethan to carry on his brother's legacy. Based on the pure fear in everyone's eyes, Kendrick believed that was the first time the leaders learned of the Remnants. He was certain it was the first time for his parents, or they would never have taken Ethan and him along.

Kendrick entered the ballroom, his painful memories quickly subsiding as he took in his surroundings. Everything was perfect. The ballroom was exquisitely decorated, just as he'd imagined. Sheer black curtains hung from the tall ceilings, creating private rooms around the dance floor. The music was impeccable, from a private collection which had been stored away for special occasions such as this, containing everything from slow jazz to classic rock. Soft candlelight glowed around the room, creating a relaxing environment where people could let their guards down and pretend, even if just for an evening, things were the way they used to be.

The team Kendrick had assembled to prepare for tonight had followed through on every meticulous detail, from the entertainers wandering the room to the glass centerpieces on the tables. Servers from the working class tended bar and waited on tables. They'd been promised extra rations if they displayed their utmost professionalism during the event. Many had jumped at the opportunity.

Kendrick pushed all the remaining negative thoughts from his mind and grinned, brimming with satisfaction. He took a long sip from his glass, relishing the burn of the liquid sliding down his throat. He didn't indulge very often, but whenever he did, it reminded him how much he missed the warm feeling in his chest, the softening of his surroundings, and his increased appetite for conversation.

Many of the guests had already arrived, slowly filling up the room over the last couple of hours. Marc had made all the necessary arrangements for the auction, which would take place in a separate area from the party, and Kendrick sensed there were some big spenders in the building tonight. He would not be disappointed.

This would be the seventh annual gathering of the four districts. Everyone of importance was invited, and he expected a few hundred in attendance. Each year they created a more extravagant gathering than the last. From what he could tell, the guests were enjoying the party as much as he was.

Zara appeared at his side along with his two remaining assistants. She looked beautiful in her little black dress. How could something so simple be such an eye-catcher? He was still aggravated with her for crossing a line in the meeting the night before. He'd wanted her to feel included out of courtesy, but it was not her place to speak during his meeting. Then she'd spoken against him once again on the roof. He decided it was in everyone's best interest to put all that aside, for now, and enjoy the evening. He wrapped his left arm around her waist and took another sip with his right hand. Everything was falling into place.

The assistants hovered nearby. "Can I get you anything?" Nicole, his tall, brunette assistant, asked.

"No. Why don't you both take the night off? Go enjoy the party."

Kendrick's assistants grinned. "Thank you," they said in unison before racing to the bar.

"Where's Allison?" Zara asked, startling Kendrick.

He maintained his composure and took another sip of his drink. "I hear she's feeling under the weather."

"Oh, that's too bad." Zara looked concerned. "Especially on our big night. It must be serious. I hope she feels better."

Kendrick plastered a fake smile on his face. "Come on, my love. Let's enjoy the party."

He led her by the hand onto the dance floor.

48

As Hayden, Martina, and Noah approached the house, James and Andre came outside. The sun was setting, casting an orange glow on the walls.

"Where were you guys?" James asked.

"Looking for you!" Hayden said, shivering as the wind whipped around them.

"Let's get inside. We lit a fire," James said, escorting Hayden.

"There's some kind of party going on tonight at the Circle," Hayden said to the group.

"Yeah, the gathering," Andre said.

Hayden raised her eyebrows at him. "How do you know about it?"

"We learned about it from an ally we made in the West District. This event is a huge deal with hundreds in attendance. It's a perfect chance to get inside unnoticed," James said with an intense look in his eyes, which Hayden was starting to notice was extremely common for him. The man could be talking about toilet paper and still make you feel like you were discussing something with dire consequences.

"Yeah, if only I carried around a tux with me at all times," Andre said.

Hayden and Martina exchanged a glance and started to laugh. "Actually, one of the houses we went through did have some pretty nice stuff," Martina said.

"Take us there," James said. "We'll disguise ourselves, and then we'll make our move." He turned to Noah. "Listen. We could really use your help tonight. You know your way around a whole lot better than we do."

"I don't know," Noah said, an anxious look on his face.

"We need your help." James moved closer to Noah, staring directly into his eyes.

"I'm sorry. I'll tell you what I remember, but I don't think I can stomach going back there."

"How are we going to find our way around in there without your guidance?" James asked.

"You'll figure it out."

"What if your son is still alive?" James raised his voice and gestured in the direction of the Circle.

"James, come on. Leave him alone," Hayden said.

Andre tapped James on the arm. "We don't need his help."

Noah chugged the bottle.

"How about after you get a little more liquid courage into you, you come to your senses and help us? We freed you from your cell. Now you owe us," said James.

"Okay, that's enough. He said he doesn't wanna go, so he's not going. End of story." Martina grabbed the knife off the table and went to stand by the door.

"No, it's fine." Noah sighed. "I'll come with you. It's worth a try. But I might not be as much of an asset as you think. What if someone recognizes me?"

"We're going to be with you the whole time," James said. "It'll be fine. Besides, if Kendrick notices you, then we can kick his ass together."

"I don't like this," Hayden said. "We could use his help, but we're not going to force him into something he doesn't wanna do."

"It's not doing me any good sitting out here. I know I have to face that awful place again," Noah said.

"We just have to get my notebook and find our friend," said James. "We'll be in and out of there. And we'll have someone there who can help us, someone from the West District."

"I'll help with whatever you need. But if I'm going back in there, I need to try to find my son," Noah said.

"Sounds like we all have the same goal," Andre said. "With everyone distracted at the party, we'll split up and tear the place apart until we find our people."

"Agreed." James clasped Noah's shoulder. "We got your back."

All five of them walked in silence to the abandoned house where Hayden and Martina had found formal clothes. Hayden was terrified, she had a bad feeling in the pit of her stomach. She didn't know what she feared more, whatever was lurking out there in the dark or attending the party at the Circle. Any number of things could go wrong in there. If they were recognized, it'd be over, and Hayden would rather die than be thrown back in a cell. Since they didn't find Mason last time, she had very little hope of finding him this time.

They turned a corner and Hayden recognized the row of houses.

"This way," Martina said, walking ahead of the group. She led the way, illuminating their path with her lantern in one hand and her knife in the other. Andre carried the flashlight they'd found at the hardware store.

It was so quiet, Hayden almost didn't hear it at first, until it slowly became more distinct. The low growling sound. "No," she said, barely louder than a whisper.

"What's wrong?" Noah asked her.

"You don't hear it?" Hayden asked.

Out of nowhere, one of the creatures lurched forward, knocking Martina to the ground. Its putrid stench overwhelmed Hayden, who screamed and froze in fear.

The creature bit down on Martina's shoulder, the wound gushing blood, and she cried out.

James acted fast and shot the creature in the head.

Martina pushed the body off her and got to her feet, holding her hand over the wound. She pulled her hand away and looked down at all the blood. "Fuck!"

Hayden took off down the street in the direction of their destination. "Come on! We're almost there!" she yelled back.

But it was too late. Dozens of Remnants were approaching them, and they were closing in. The group slowly backed away.

"Just a few more houses up on the left!" Hayden called.

Noah gently took the knife out of Martina's hand. "Run. Get inside."

"What? No—"

Noah charged forward, killing the creatures one by one, drawing all their attention to him. He stabbed some in the head and some in the heart, and they dropped like flies. Hayden watched in awe. By now, James and Andre had caught up with her, and Martina was trailing behind, still clutching her shoulder.

"Get inside," James said to Martina.

"No," Martina said. "Not without Noah."

The creatures came from all directions, as if they were being summoned. Hayden heard some of them coming up from behind. Martina ran to the front door of the house, and Andre followed her. Noah was fearlessly fighting them off, as if he had been doing this for years.

Hayden thought he had it under control until some of the Remnants cut through the middle of the street and came up behind him. "Noah, look out!" she screamed.

James fired two more shots at the creatures approaching Noah from behind, and then his gun clicked. "Shit," James muttered as he tried to pull the trigger again.

Noah swung around and stabbed the creature directly behind him in the eye. But the horde pushed him forward, causing him to lose his balance. He looked up at Hayden from the ground, locked eyes with her, and gave a slight nod as if to tell her it was okay.

"No!" she screamed again, and she started to run toward him.

James caught Hayden by the arm and dragged her to the front steps, where Martina and Andre stood, wide-eyed. Taking one last look at Noah as the creatures ripped him open and tore out his insides, Hayden collapsed.

4 9

James scooped Hayden up in his arms and carried her into the house. She was dead weight, but he carried her alone. Inside, he set her on the floor of the living room. Then he, Andre, and Martina barricaded the front door with furniture.

Hayden lay flat on the floor and shut her eyes, trying to un-see what she'd just seen. Once the entrance was blocked, James sat beside her and ran his fingers over her hair. Then he pulled her close, and she leaned against him, burying her face in his chest.

"Why would he sacrifice himself like that?" Hayden asked.

"He saved us," James said.

Hayden sobbed. "Maybe we could have saved him. If we had just—"

"There was nothing we could have done," said James. "We'd all be dead if it weren't for him."

Tears streamed down Hayden's face, soaking James's T-shirt.

"Let me take a look at your shoulder," Andre said to Martina.

Martina removed her shirt, revealing a deep wound by her collarbone. "Will I turn into one of those things?"

"No." Andre put his arm around her. "You're gonna be fine."

"How can you be so sure?" Martina looked at him with fearful eyes.

James looked at Martina over the top of Hayden's head, which was still pressed against him. "We've seen no evidence that the condition of these creatures can spread that way."

Martina nodded.

"We have to stop the bleeding. I'll go look for a towel," James said.

Hayden felt a stab of guilt. "I'm so sorry." She started to sob again. "I froze up. I should have acted faster."

"This isn't your fault," Martina said, kneeling beside Hayden. "He did it for us, so we could get away. I don't know about you, but that's the bravest thing anyone's ever done for me."

Hayden rested her head on Martina's lap and cried until she couldn't anymore. Once Hayden calmed down and Martina bandaged her shoulder by wrapping a torn piece of a T-shirt tightly around the wound, everyone got ready for the gathering, the men in one walk-in closet and the women in the other.

"Come on. You know you want to." Martina gestured toward the stunning black dress hanging gracefully at the front of the closet while she rifled through the rest of the garments on the rack.

"None of it matters anymore. It's all superficial."

"What do you mean?"

"I'm sick of always pretending everything is fine. None of this is okay. And I don't know how to deal with it anymore," Hayden said, as tears threatened to drip down her face again. "How can life mean anything if it can be taken away so easily?"

"I don't know. But you gotta pull yourself together. We need to do this for Mason. Don't you want us all to make it back home?"

"Of course I do," Hayden said, annoyed. "I feel so stupid. When I first saw this dress, despite everything we've gone through, I imagined wearing it to an event. I thought about how it would feel to be someone important, to have all eyes on me. What kind of person does that make me?"

"You're a good person even if you don't know it," Martina said. "You have a big heart."

"It seems so meaningless now. I just wish Noah were still here. And I want to go home."

"Me too. More than you know."

Hayden got dressed and tried to regain her composure. Tears threatened the corners of her eyes, but she held them back. She slammed her fist into the shelving unit, which rattled against the wall, shaking free a small object and sending it tumbling to the floor. She winced and looked at her red knuckles, and then she crouched down. A small box containing a pair of diamond earrings had been hidden behind the shelves. She stared at them for a moment. She hadn't worn earrings since before she went to prison. They reminded her of her mother. She smiled and put them in her ears. Hayden exited the closet at the same moment James was exiting his.

He stopped. His eyes widened and his mouth opened as if he had something to say but couldn't find the words. Hayden stared into his green eyes for what seemed like an eternity. She felt like she was going to cry again, but she held it back.

"You look incredible," James finally said.

"Thanks," she said softly. "I mean if you consider red puffy eyes, no makeup, and prison hair incredible."

"You look great just the way you are," Martina said, stepping out of the closet. She'd chosen a dark blue gown with long sleeves made of delicate lace. It looked stunning with her skin tone and raven-colored hair, Hayden thought. Martina was one of those women who could look beautiful without even trying. Hayden envied that.

"I can't believe all this stuff is so well preserved." Andre stepped out of the closet containing the men's clothes. He and James wore similar crisp black suits with black ties to match.

"You both clean up nice," Martina said, her eyes lingering on Andre.

"We better get going. The sun's gone down. I bet the party's started." James reloaded the revolver and tucked it inside his jacket.

Hayden counted as he tucked three more bullets in his jacket pocket. She knew it wouldn't be enough. She looked out the window, fearing the Remnants were still there, lurking in the dark, waiting for them. But they were nowhere to be seen.

James went outside first, carefully checking the perimeter. The coast was clear, so he led them out the back door in the direction of the Circle.

5 0

The waning moon floated in between the clouds and distant music pulsed through James's ears. It took him back to his youth. Before he dedicated his life to his work, he and his closest friends had gone out nearly every night, searching for the place with the loudest music, the most booze, and the best-looking girls.

The group walked in silence from the house they'd raided to the Circle. Hayden was still visibly shaken by what happened to Noah. *It wasn't right*, James thought. *He didn't deserve to die, not like that.* And now they didn't have anyone to guide them into the building, though James didn't dare complain about it to Hayden.

James's nerves ran high, and his heart pounded faster than normal. Everything had to go smoothly tonight, and it was a long shot even without their commitment to try to help Camilla. There was no telling what Kendrick would do if they were seen. Now that the party was in full swing, James knew Kendrick would be there. But where would he keep the notebook? James wished they still had Noah's help.

"Can someone tell me how there's music playing right now? During the goddamn apocalypse," Andre said, sounding irritated as usual.

"Maybe they have some new tech for playing music," Hayden said, struggling to keep up in her high heels. "I mean, what comes next after streaming services?"

James was pleased she was trying to be in a better mood. Her grief over Noah could blow everything tonight.

Martina scoffed. "Maybe they hired a live band."

"I'll bet they have an older way of playing music. Maybe record players. Definitely something predating the Internet," James said, turning to Hayden. "Why did you wear those shoes?"

"Yeah, that's why I grabbed these flat, comfortable-looking sandals. Try not to fall on your ass," Martina said playfully.

"No, you wore those shoes because you're an Amazon," Hayden said angrily, but she still had sadness in her eyes.

"Shh! Wait a minute." James held up his hand.

They leaned against the wall of the building, near the entrance to the courtyard. Two vehicles were dropping people off by the door. James watched as two parties of four hurried inside, as if trying to escape some nonexistent cold.

"Don't forget the plan," James said. "Once we're inside, we split up to get the lay of the land. Then Martina and Andre slip away unnoticed to find Mason. Hayden and I will go get my notebook."

"What if someone notices us?" Martina asked.

"Do you have the gun?" asked James.

"I got it." Andre opened his jacket to show James the Glock in his waistband.

James nodded. "Use it."

Once the vehicles cleared out, the group moved quickly toward the entrance. James attempted to act naturally as he glanced around, ensuring no one recognized them. He put his arm around Hayden and forced himself to smile.

A petite blonde woman greeted them at the door. "Welcome. Where are you coming from?" she asked cheerfully.

The music was louder now, and the smell of booze was in the air.

"The West District," James said.

"Great! You can find your tables toward the right side of the ballroom. Enjoy!" Her high-pitched tone didn't falter on a single word.

They proceeded into the ballroom and walked into a total anachronism. The mass devastation right outside the walls made this party feel more out of place than a highly educated physicist in a state penitentiary. The room was packed. They were surrounded by beautiful people, entranced in conversation and buzzing from the alcohol. Decadent buffet tables lined the far wall, and James felt his stomach rumble. People laughed loudly and danced to the music, sipping their alcohol like it was a delicacy. James felt like he'd just stepped inside a speakeasy during the Prohibition era.

"Let's split up," James said.

Everyone headed in different directions.

51

James made his way to the bar. He was on edge and figured he could use a drink. He tried to make out what they were serving, but all he saw was a line of unmarked bottles and canisters behind the bar. The bartender was a young man, probably in his mid-twenties, with dark hair and deep-set eyes. He filled a glass about halfway with a dark amber liquid. Whiskey, perhaps?

James accepted the glass gratefully and took a long swig. It burned, but not like whiskey.

"Your first gathering," the man said casually.

"Is it that obvious?" James asked, trying to act normal.

The man chuckled. "It's just that you're not letting loose like the rest of them. You seem tense."

Shit! James instinctively grabbed at the back of his neck.

"Don't worry," the bartender continued. "It may seem like a lot at first, but it's really a great thing. A chance for all of us to forget about this shitty world we live in now. Well, at least for the *important* people." He said the word like it tasted vile on his tongue.

James thought he saw the bartender clench his hands into fists.

An older couple, perhaps in their late sixties, approached the bar. They wore gold watches and diamonds, and the woman dropped her designer bag on the wet, sticky bar like it was nothing. The bartender tried to hide his disgust, regained his composure, and put a smile on his face.

James took this as an opportunity to leave and raised his glass, nodding a "thank you" to the young man for the drink.

How could material items still hold such value after everything that happened? These people must be so sheltered. James bet they never stepped foot outside. They wouldn't last a day out there now. He gulped his drink. Thoughts of Noah and their encounter on the way here swirled around his mind. James tried to focus on the burn of the alcohol.

The music vibrated the floor beneath his feet. More people gathered on the dance floor, raising their drinks and moving their bodies. They all seemed so carefree, and for a moment, James envied them. He couldn't remember the last time he felt that way. It was as if the people here didn't mind that this event was simply to benefit Kendrick's greed. Maybe they didn't know.

James scanned the room and noticed, in the very back corner, a group of older gentlemen being ushered out a back door that led to a dark corridor. Then he remembered the auction Camilla mentioned. He started to head in their direction, but he suddenly stopped in his tracks.

There he was. Kendrick.

A mere twenty feet away, standing beside a table, chatting with a group of people who seemed to hang on his every word. His suit was crisp with perfect lines. He was dressed in all black:

a black jacket, black dress shirt, black vest, and black tie. His eyes were as menacing as James remembered, but a smile danced across his lips. He was truly enjoying himself.

James caught himself biting his nail. He quickly turned on his heels and walked in the other direction, but the room was starting to fill, and it became more difficult to navigate through the crowd.

James had to admit the party wasn't half bad, and the place was set up beautifully. Black silk curtains billowed in a slight breeze. Each turn he made around a curtain revealed another otherworldly sight. Acrobats hung from the ceiling, dancing and moving among ropes and giant rings. The men and women wore almost nothing, the fine line between art and sensuality starting to blur. He stopped and watched for a moment.

Two beautiful women with long curly hair, clad in only body paint, moved together on a giant ring suspended ten feet in the air. Their synchronization was impeccable. They wrapped their legs around each other, taking turns hanging upside down, holding on with just the strength of a thigh or a single arm. One woman climbed up to the very top of the rope that attached the ring to the ceiling, while the other dangled her body gracefully from the bottom of the ring, slowly spinning in a full circle.

It was mesmerizing, but James tore his eyes away, wondering how many minutes had passed. He continued walking and found himself inside a black silk tent full of books, crystals, and small statues of animals. In the center of the tent, a table sported a giant crystal ball. One of the two chairs at the table was empty. The other was filled by a woman.

Dark curls hung loosely out of her head wrap, and a gold chain embellishment dangled across her forehead. She had large, perfectly shaped lips painted red to match the red-painted claws on her hands. She tapped her long nails on the table and gestured for him to sit down.

James obeyed as if on impulse. And only then, face to face with her, did he realize her eyes were as black as the night sky. She reached out and took his hands in hers, and he couldn't help but flinch.

"Don't be afraid," she said, her voice as soft as velvet. She closed her eyes and took a deep breath. After a moment, her lips parted and her eyes flew open. The whites had completely disappeared, and her eyes were fully black beneath her eyelids. "You have to leave. You're running out of time," she said urgently, releasing his hands.

"I'm not sure what will happen when I go back," James said, fully trusting her in that moment despite his lifelong predisposition toward materialism and disregard for anything supernatural.

"Those people you brought with you." She shook her head. "You should have known better. They don't know how time works like we do. They can impact the natural order of things. The longer you're here, the more dangerous it becomes."

"I thought that was only a risk when traveling to the past."

"Time is not linear, James. The past is subjective. You of all people should know that."

"Who are you?"

"A traveler, much like yourself."

James was filled with confusion. "I came here tonight to retrieve my notebook. I need the coordinates to get back to the woods. Well, and to save one of the people I brought here. He's being held captive in this building somewhere."

"Forget about him," she said dismissively. "Find the notebook and get out of here. It's not safe."

"It's not that simple," James said. "He's my half-brother."

The whites of her eyes returned to normal and she stared at him for a moment. "Why take such a great risk?" she finally asked.

"I'll admit he was a diversion from my plan to traverse the wormhole. But he was going to be executed. I couldn't leave him in there."

She looked at him sympathetically and said, "Most things in life truly are out of our control. No matter how much free will we appear to have."

James stood to leave, but she grabbed his arm, her nails digging into his skin.

"You will need a faster way to track the coordinates," she said.

"Perhaps," James said.

In all his travels throughout the city, he'd seen no signs of the forest. Returning to the location they were taken from would be a difficult task.

"Find a member of the West District, a man called Rayne. He has a tracking device he intends to put up at the auction tonight."

The auction must be starting soon, James thought. Kendrick would be eager to get to the point of tonight's gathering. "Thank you," he said.

She nodded.

He turned to leave again but stopped. "You know about the device just by grabbing my hands?"

She smiled. "I overheard him talking to his friend about the new tracking technology he brought here tonight. It looks like you just got lucky."

James smiled back. "From my experience, luck has nothing to do with fate."

He exited the tent and paused for a moment, wondering if that encounter was a figment of his imagination. Then it hit him. She may have saved their lives with the information about the tracker. If they couldn't find the forest again, they might be stuck here.

James turned around to get another look at her, but she was gone.

5 2

Andre and Martina wandered the ballroom, marveling at the sights. He couldn't believe it. There was nothing to distinguish this party from a party in 2025. He questioned everything he'd seen over the past couple of days. He'd always thought the future would be filled with advanced technology his generation couldn't even imagine. Instead, it was filled with death, destruction, and a few rich assholes smart enough to hide in bunkers and preserve life as they knew it. "We should go look for Mason," he said to Martina.

"We will. I think we deserve to explore the party first, don't you? After all we've been through."

"It's risky. We could be seen."

She closed the distance between them. "Try to lighten up," she said, sliding her arms around his neck. She leaned in close. Her soft lips brushed against his ear as she whispered, "I know you wanna have fun."

The feeling of her breath on his neck sent tingles down his back. Andre grabbed her face and kissed her, giving in to temptation. What was he holding back for anyway? He'd been alone for long enough. Nothing felt as good as having human contact again.

Martina laughed and pulled him onto the dance floor. They danced, moving together to the beat. Neither of them could stop grinning. He watched in admiration at the way she moved her hips, how well she could dance in her tight, restricting dress. He was intrigued by how her smile lit up her face and the intense look in her eyes he only saw present when she was looking at him.

The song ended, and he pulled her close again. Andre kissed her hard, his tongue meeting hers. He didn't know if it was the energy in the room or what had gotten into them. They couldn't keep their hands off each other.

"I'm thirsty," Martina said. Her cheeks were flushed, and she was giving him that look again.

Andre glanced around the room until he located the bar.

"I'll go get us some drinks," he said.

"Want me to come with you?"

"It looks really crowded over there. I'll be right back."

"Okay." She smiled and kissed him again.

Making his way through the crowd, avoiding drunken party guests, Andre noticed there was one thing all these people had in common. Money. They all showed off their wealth. He thought back to the child labor he'd witnessed right before he escaped the Circle. Could that be going on in all the districts? Or was Kendrick the only one greedy enough to keep all the money to himself?

As he waited for the bartender to pour his drinks, something caught his eye. The woman sitting at the bar next to him was talking loudly, flailing her arms for emphasis. When she nearly smacked Andre with her hand, he saw she wore a white, diamond-studded Chanel watch.

He froze. His mouth dropped open in horror, and his mind was taken back to the worst night of his life. He was walking home from a bar that night, after celebrating his best friend's twenty-fifth birthday. The same city street he'd walked countless times, whether he was coming home from class or going out to eat. Sometimes he even jogged around these blocks when he didn't feel like going to the gym. Only this time, one misunderstanding would ruin his life forever.

He'd had more than a few drinks at the bar and was somewhere between buzzed and blackout drunk. Suddenly, a man rounded the corner and crashed into him, shoving something into his hands. Andre stumbled slightly, instinctively grabbing the object. He turned the corner where the man came from as he took a closer look at the hard metal object and realized what it was.

That's when he saw the woman lying on the ground. He rushed toward her and crouched down, dropping the gun, which was now covered in his fingerprints.

She was young, maybe nineteen or twenty years old. She wore a white, diamond-studded Chanel watch on her tiny wrist that seemed to glow under the streetlamps. A red stain was spreading on her sky-blue sweater.

Did she get mugged? If this was a robbery, wouldn't he have taken the watch? It must be worth thousands. He checked her for a pulse, but he felt nothing. His vision blurred as he started to panic. Andre stood and looked around. He was fumbling for the phone in his pocket when he heard shouting.

"That's him!" a man on the other side of the street yelled.

Before Andre could react, a police officer was charging toward him and tackling him to the ground. He came in and out of consciousness as the officer tasered him repeatedly. He had no motive to kill the woman, but they slapped that charge on him regardless.

Andre knew eyewitness testimony could be highly inaccurate. Studies had proven people's memories are unreliable, especially when it came to traumatic events. He'd learned that in school, but apparently the people on the jury hadn't, or reliability didn't matter when the defendant wasn't white.

Even with the lack of physical evidence, like blood splatter and gunshot residue, the eyewitness testimony and his fingerprints on the murder weapon sealed Andre's fate in the courtroom. What hurt the most was watching his dream of one day becoming successful enough to give his family a better life slip away. It wasn't that they were poor, but his parents worked hard, his mother as an English teacher and his father as a printing press operator, and Andre had always wanted to give them something more than they could afford on their salaries in high-priced Southern California. He'd expected to excel at the pharmaceutical sales job he'd finally landed just like he had at football. He had a whole career laid out in front of him.

In the end, none of that meant anything when the victim was from a rich, white family. Andre didn't have enough money to hire a good lawyer. He'd been happy with his life and proud of his accomplishments—until it was all ripped away from him like his word meant nothing. Although his family never gave up on him, no one else had believed him.

"Do you still want these?" the bartender asked in a harsh tone, failing to hide his irritation.

Andre wasn't sure how many times the man had asked or how long he'd zoned out. It didn't matter. His carefree mood had turned into something much darker. He accepted the drinks and chugged his in a single gulp. Then he stalked off to find Martina.

5 3

James set out to search for Hayden. His mind was spinning. Now he had to focus on acquiring not only the notebook, but also the tracking device. Winning the auction would be the easy part, but when it came time to exchange the money for the device, he had a feeling violence would ensue.

As James made his way through the crowd, he had a sudden urge to get another drink. He knew it was irresponsible, but it was an urge he couldn't shrug off. He chose a different bar this time, near the dance floor, and took a seat on a stool as the bartender filled a glass halfway and handed it to him. James chuckled to himself as a song he recognized came on.

"Having fun yet?" a soft voice beside him asked.

It took James a moment to realize she was talking to him. He turned to face the woman sitting beside him. She was attractive with kind eyes and olive skin. She wore a smile and a little black dress, and James had a feeling she was a few years older than him.

"It's like nothing I've ever experienced," he said, raising his glass.

"It's certainly improved over the years." She held his gaze, bit her bottom lip, and looked away.

A group of performers started a routine nearby, and the crowd formed a large circle around them. They danced, all perfectly in sync, and displayed their acrobatic skills. The women did front flips while the men did back flips. Then they gathered in a formation and threw each other into the air. James was mesmerized once again. Their moves were similar to a routine he'd seen a century ago. He couldn't comprehend how all this came to be after the world ended. But he was beginning to realize these people never changed their lifestyle. The rich, it appeared, had gone into hiding and carried on living like nothing had changed. They'd never had to fend for themselves or survive on the outside. They were more sheltered now than ever before.

"Where do you suppose they found the performers?" James asked.

A man and a woman climbed up thick ribbons of fabric connected to the ceiling. They wove their legs around the fabric and spun gracefully. Once they were at the very top, with the fabric woven tightly around them, they dropped simultaneously. Their bodies spun around and around, quickly unraveling the fabric, stopping just inches from the ground.

The crowd erupted in applause.

The woman smiled at James again. "The people all around you can have a limitless amount of talent. You just have to be willing to look for it."

"How are you able to let loose so easily," James asked, "with the dangers lurking right outside?"

"Even when they aren't ideal, we need to make the best of our circumstances. You're doing something wrong if you haven't learned to have fun during hard times. Each day we're alive is still a blessing," she said, running her fingers through her short dark hair. "What do you know about the outside anyway?"

"I've seen more than I care to share," he said, gulping down his drink. Just then, James noticed a man near the dance floor who towered above the rest of the guests. He wore slacks and a button-up shirt with no tie or jacket, and he looked out of place. The man kept staring in James's direction. It took James a while to realize he was the one being stared at.

"Maybe if you get out there, you'll loosen up." The woman motioned toward the dance floor and placed her hand on his arm.

James jerked his arm away and instantly regretted it.

Her eyebrows raised in surprise. "I didn't mean to—"

"It's fine. I'm sorry. I have to go." James stood and set his glass on the bar. He looked back at the dance floor, but the man was gone.

As tempting as it was to spend more time with the mysterious woman, he had to get back on track and find Hayden so they could search for the notebook and attend the auction—as if he needed any more on his plate. James turned to leave.

"Hey," the woman called after him.

James turned back to face her.

"All you have to do is allow yourself to be free."

James smiled and headed back into the crowd. As he made his way through a sea of people, he felt a hand on his arm.

"Are you James?" It was the man he'd caught staring.

"Who are you?"

"I'm Rayne, Camilla's partner."

They went to a far corner of the room to ensure they wouldn't be heard.

"I'm glad you found me," said James. "I hate to ask, but is there any way I could get my hands on the tracking device you brought here tonight?"

"Oh, I'm sorry, but we already entered it into the auction. What did you need it for?"

We'll have to win it then, James thought. "Never mind. I told Camilla I would try to help you. What is it that you need?"

"Well, I've been trying to get face to face with Kendrick. Maybe entice him to buy our technology somehow. But I haven't been able to."

"My suggestion would be to appeal to Kendrick's greed. When you're pitching the idea to him, make sure he knows your technology would make him richer. He'd no longer need to feed his working-class rations, or at least it would free them up to serve him in some other way."

"Thank you, truly. That's very helpful. I'll be waiting by those double doors before the auction starts." Rayne pointed at the back of the room.

James nodded and said, "I'll find you then."

5 4

This party reminded Hayden of one Jonathan took her to years ago on one of their weekend getaways to New York City. It took place in a ballroom much like this one. She was surrounded by the rich and famous, but her focus never left him. She was still buzzing from their walk through Central Park, the giant candy milkshake that reminded her of her childhood, and the romantic drinks they sipped as they watched the sun set over the skyline from a rooftop bar. If she'd known back then what Jonathan was up to, none of the following events would've happened. She was young and naïve, but she'd turned a blind eye to who he really was for far too long.

When Jonathan slipped away from the party to the hotel elevator, telling her he had to take a phone call and he'd be right back, she didn't have the guts to follow him. Maybe things would've turned out differently if she'd realized what kind of trouble the love of her life really was. Maybe she wouldn't have let him destroy her life, and she wouldn't have ended up in prison.

She still felt her stomach turn over when she thought about how he brainwashed her and then sold her out once the police were on to his schemes. How weak of a woman was she if she could be fooled by such a simple man? If she'd only opened her eyes to what was going on all around her then, she could have altered the course of her life. Instead, she stayed there all alone at the big party, waiting patiently. Just like she was now.

"Hey," James said, placing his hand on the small of her back.

Hayden jumped, spilling half her drink on the floor. "You can't just sneak up on people like that," she snapped. She was relieved to see him and annoyed all at once.

"I'm sorry. I thought you saw me." He looked concerned. "Are you okay?"

She sighed. "I'm fine."

A slow song started to play, and Hayden fidgeted uncomfortably and finished off her drink. "Did you figure out how we can get the notebook back?"

"I think so," James said, extending his hand to her. "But first, let's dance."

His suggestion surprised her, but Hayden accepted his hand and walked to the dance floor. She wrapped her arms around his neck and swayed to the music, to a song she didn't recognize, with a man she barely knew. As they moved together, she couldn't help the laughter that rolled off her tongue. For a moment, she felt carefree. She hadn't felt at ease with herself in years. There was something so peculiar about the shift from being confined to her cell every day to being free to do anything she wanted, especially in a world where she didn't belong.

Before she knew it, the song ended. She thought James was going to lean in and kiss her, but instead he pulled away.

"There's an auction going on here tonight," James told her. "I believe it's Kendrick's ploy to profit from all of this."

"I didn't see anything like that, and I've done a couple laps around the room."

"It's in a back room. I think it's supposed to be exclusive. A tracking device will be up for auction, and we need to win it. No matter the cost."

She stared into his eyes, wanting more explanation. "To get back to the woods?" she asked, shaking her head. "And you're just realizing this now?"

James rolled his eyes at her, and Hayden thought she might be rubbing off on him.

"I have a map and coordinates inside my notebook, which should be sufficient to get us back, but this could make the process a lot easier," James said. "There's one more thing. I told the West District we would help them in exchange for the help they offered us. We need to find the man I spoke to earlier."

"As if we didn't have enough to worry about already."

"Come on. I think it's this way."

She followed James toward the back of the ballroom where two double doors were hidden in plain sight. She thought of Noah as they passed the dance floor, where most of the guests danced like carefree children. She couldn't shake off the guilt. He didn't want to come back to the Circle. If they hadn't forced him to tag along, he would still be alive. It was clear to Hayden he had lost all purpose without his family. Now it was up to them to get the revenge he deserved.

Suddenly, James walked up to a tall, good-looking man standing against the wall. "Over there, Rayne," James said. "The middle-aged white man in the dark suit, I saw him with Kendrick."

James intertwined his arm with Hayden's, and as the man walked away, James quickly explained how he'd advised Rayne to get to Kendrick that night. He and Hayden walked down the dark hallway, and Hayden noticed the heavy presence of guards. *There must be a lot of valuable items here tonight*, she thought. They were escorted into an auditorium, with many of its seats filled, and handed a white bid paddle with the number twenty-seven on it.

Hayden was terrified of being recognized. Almost all eyes were on her as they walked along the back row of chairs and took a seat at the end. "They recognize us," she whispered to James.

"They've never seen us before in their lives."

"Then why are they staring?"

"Have you seen how incredible you look tonight?"

Hayden blushed and looked down, smoothing out her dress. She knew it was an eye-catcher. She'd felt the penetrating gaze of men and women alike all evening. She'd even caught herself gazing at the bottom of the gown, admiring the way the light bounced off the rhinestones.

A tall thin man with an overbearing presence walked onstage, and the room suddenly fell silent.

Hayden's heart raced. "Is that him?" she whispered.

James grabbed her hand. "That's him."

5 5

Zara took a seat at the blackjack table, and the dealer dealt her a hand. Kendrick really did think of everything. The guests were overwhelmed with entertainment, and the night was in full swing. The drinks were flowing, and everyone was dancing. Music and laughter enveloped her ears. She saw the intriguing stranger she'd talked to at the bar hurrying across the room, hand in hand with a beautiful blonde. *So that's why he got so jumpy when I asked him to dance*, she thought.

Kristal appeared out of nowhere and took a seat at the table, pulling her chair close to Zara's. She wore a bright blue dress, seemingly intended for someone much younger.

"What are you doing?" Zara asked.

"It's fine. Just act normal," Kristal said, accepting her two cards from the dealer.

Zara scanned the room and saw Kendrick in the corner, chatting and laughing with some of the guests she recognized from the North District. She looked down at her cards, a queen and an ace. "Stay," Zara said to the dealer.

"You were right. It's about time something's done about your husband," Kristal said as she glanced at her cards. "Hit me," she said to the dealer.

"Lower your voice," Zara said, looking around again. "I know. But it's not all his fault. I think Kendrick really believes he's doing what's right, that he's really helping people."

Zara thought about her time spent at the Circle. She was one of the lucky ones. She grew up poor with two parents who loved her more than anything in the world. During the Incident, the final stage of the war that caused humanity's near extinction in a few short weeks, she was able to link up with her wealthy aunt and uncle and tag along with them to this place. If it weren't for them, she wouldn't be alive today. Kendrick's father was the commander when she first arrived, until his death a few years later.

She didn't meet Kendrick until long after he became the commander. He told her his family had been killed outside the walls of the Circle, and he'd taken over at just eighteen years old. He never stepped foot outside the walls again after that day. He believed the outside was evil and no one stood a chance unless they lived inside the Circle, under his rule.

"How do you figure that?" Kristal asked.

"He believes that by taking people in he's providing them with a good life. A better life than they could've had outside the walls." Zara frowned. "He was so young when he lost his family, and he lacked the proper guidance he desperately needed." She sipped her drink. "Once he became commander, it was as if he forgot his values. He suppressed the good I know he has inside to project himself as a strong leader."

Kristal scoffed. "I don't think the people downstairs would agree with that. And for all we know, he's the one who killed his parents that day so he could take over."

Zara wanted to slap her. Kristal must have had too many drinks. "He was just a kid when it happened. He went through a traumatic experience that ultimately turned him into this. Do you really not take the threats seriously? When was the last time you were outside?"

"I've heard the rumors."

"Yeah, but you've never seen anything firsthand. Like Kendrick had to." Zara took a long swig from her glass. "He was always kind to me and to the kids. That's what makes this so hard. Lately things have just been . . . not the same anymore."

"I'm sorry. Maybe I'm being too hard on him. But you really got me thinking, Zara. Things need to change around here. We've let it go on for too long. It's just not right."

"I know. I just hope it's not too late."

"Too late for what?"

"Our salvation," Zara said, as she slapped her twenty-one on the table.

5 6

ndre found Martina sitting on a couch inside one of the curtained-off areas, smoking a cigar with a man who appeared to be in his seventies. Bewildered, Andre handed her the drink. "What's up?" he asked her, trying to keep his tone in check, but still reeling from seeing the Chanel watch.

"This man was just telling me about the districts. Explaining how it all happened, from his perspective," she said, shooting Andre a look.

The old man puffed his cigar and Andre watched the ember burn bright in the dimly lit room.

"As I was saying," the old man said, his voice rough and low, "the problems really started around the turn of the century. But the Incident didn't occur until 2109. All it took was one imbecile to be elected president for the world to go into a state of disagreement over dwindling resources, like oil and water. Well, that and the dispute over territories in Europe and Asia. There were problems for years before anything happened. But at the first threat of nuclear war from countries across the globe, the wealthiest families in the United States banded together to put protections in place. We prepared for the worst-case scenario, and we were right."

"So the result of political disagreement was nuclear war?" Andre asked.

The man nodded as he puffed on his cigar, slowly breathing out the smoke. "Nukes, biological weapons, you name it."

"Why would any nation want to risk wiping out all of humanity?" Andre asked. "It just doesn't make sense."

"China and Russia were only worried about wiping the United States off the map once we got hold of resources they desperately needed. What they didn't know is we could return fire at a much higher level." The old man shook his head. "These other countries didn't believe the US was capable of fighting back, not after we let them push us around for years under previous administrations."

Andre and Martina exchanged glances, and she blew a slow stream of smoke in his direction. Andre coughed.

"It's believed we're some of the last people left on Earth. Although, there were confirmed survivors in Russia. Tough bastards." The old man chuckled. "We established radio contact with some facilities over there just like this one. I'm sure there are other survivors out there in different parts of the world, but I doubt they live as well as we do."

A young man approached them, maybe the old man's personal assistant.

"Well, it looks like I'm being summoned to the auction." The old man stood to leave.

"Thank you for the history lesson," Martina said as she smiled and rested her cigar on the rim of an ashtray.

"Enjoy your evening," the old man said. He nodded to them and headed toward the back of the ballroom.

Martina grabbed Andre's hand, and they hurried away from the party and into the depths of the Circle.

The building was like a maze. Countless long corridors with an infinite number of doors on both sides just led to more of the same. It would be nearly impossible to find Mason. Walking around in their formalwear, they risked being noticed. It was impossible to blend, and anyone would know they shouldn't be here.

They searched hallway after hallway, exploring floors one through five. All they found were sleeping quarters and empty rooms. This whole side of the building looked deserted. Where was everybody? As they bounded up the stairs to the sixth floor, they heard voices. There they came across another cafeteria, different from the one through which they'd escaped. "Why do they need so many cafeterias when they're underfeeding half their people?" Andre whispered.

"Clearly, they're not underfeeding all of them," Martina replied.

"But you saw the people on the factory level."

Groups of people were casually seated around the room. Some of them appeared to be guards. It would be too risky to go this way; they couldn't get past the cafeteria without being spotted.

Suddenly, one of the guards got up and started walking in their direction.

"Shit," Andre said under his breath.

He and Martina turned and ran through the nearest door, into the men's restroom.

"Quick! Get in a stall!" Andre said.

They hid in a stall and pulled the door shut; their bodies pressed up against each other in the small space.

The bathroom door opened, and the man entered the room. He walked up the row of urinals and unzipped his pants.

Martina peered through the crack in the stall door as they waited for him to finish. As if he knew he was being watched, the man glanced in their direction. Martina stepped back quickly, inadvertently pushing Andre into the side of the stall.

"What the—?" Andre heard the guard mutter.

Footsteps approached the stall, and Andre motioned for Martina to get behind him. He opened the stall quickly, surprising the man. Before the guard could react, Andre swung hard, and his fist connected with the man's jaw. He dropped to the ground.

Martina let out a laugh.

"What? You've never seen someone get knocked out before?"

"Let's go before someone else comes in."

Andre dragged the man into the farthest stall.

Then they exited the restroom and started to walk down the hallway opposite the cafeteria.

"Mina!" Martina cried.

The little girl was walking away from them, her dark curly hair bouncing against her shoulders. She stopped and slowly turned around. She wore a guilty look on her face, like she was expecting to get reprimanded for being down there. Cautiously, she walked toward them. "What are you guys doing here?" she asked.

"Listen," Martina said, squatting to meet her height. "We just want to go home, but one of our friends is still here. We have to get him before we go."

"What happened to your shoulder?" Mina asked.

Martina covered the wound quickly with her hair. "Mina, we need your help right now. It's really important."

Mina looked at the floor and fidgeted with a bracelet on her wrist.

"I have a daughter around your age. Her name is Sofía," Martina explained. "And she needs me to come back to her. But I can't do that if I don't find my friend Mason. Do you know where he is?"

Andre watched with admiration as Martina convinced the little girl to help them.

Mina nodded and led them back to the stairwell. Martina grabbed Andre's hand, and they followed Mina up stairway after stairway.

"There couldn't have been an elevator," Andre said through gritted teeth.

"There is. It's broken," Mina said in a mousy voice.

"So, Mina, what's up with this party? Do your people have parties a lot?" Andre asked.

"No, this only happens once a year. The rest of the days, everyone has to work."

Andre and Martina exchanged a glance. He wondered what exactly they were working on.

As if the little girl had read his mind, she said, "Some people work on the floor where we create stuff, some people clean, and others do work outside of the walls. But a lot of those people don't come back."

They reached the twelfth floor, and Mina led them down a long hallway.

"Where do your parents work?" Andre asked her.

He couldn't shake the feeling he'd gotten after seeing the woman's watch. It felt like ancient history now, but it still dwelled on his mind. *What future can I have when we get back to our time?*

Mina was silent for a long time. Finally she said, "My mom doesn't work, except homeschooling me and my brother. My dad is the commander."

Andre was ripped from his thoughts. *Kendrick?*

"Where are your parents right now? Are they at the party?" Andre asked.

"Yes." She stopped in front of a steel door. "We're here." She stood on her toes and punched in a passcode with her tiny fingers.

Martina crouched beside her. "Thank you for helping us. It's very important that you don't tell your dad we were here, okay?"

Mina nodded, pushed open the door a crack, and then turned and walked away.

"How is she so mature at her age?" Andre asked.

"I think the better question is why does she know the code to a cell where a prisoner is being held?"

"I guess perks of being the commander's daughter."

"Do you think he has any idea what she's been up to?" Martina asked.

"I'm sure he's got his hands full tonight."

Inside the room, Mason was curled in a corner, badly beaten and bound to the wall. Andre rushed forward and quickly freed Mason's hands with the knife, helping him to his feet. Mason yelled in agony when he was able to fully stretch his limbs.

"You okay?" Andre asked, eyeing Mason's bruises.

Mason smiled. He seemed out of it. "You guys came back for me," he said. "I wasn't sure if you would."

"If it were up to me, we would've left you," Andre said half-jokingly.

Martina punched Andre's arm and then put an arm around Mason's shoulder. "Come on. Let's get you out of here."

5 7

"Going once, going twice, sold! To bidder number twenty-seven," the auctioneer bellowed.

Kendrick was pleased. The auction was well underway, and Marc had ensured everything was in place. They had many items to auction off, some of which were donated by the guests. There were ancient books, including history texts describing how life was before the Incident, Bibles, and various items of religious significance. They had relics, including archeological remains and treasures discovered from lost civilizations. There was even advanced technology from artificial intelligence to microchips. After the times of devastation, the extreme wealth gap increased, and the idle and ignorant rich liked nothing more than to boast about their wealth by buying things they didn't need.

At first, it was unclear if cash would ever be used again. But once the districts were formed, trade ensued, and both cash and goods were used in transactions. The four districts upheld the value of the previously used American dollar to buy and sell goods to each other. Some of the men and women in here tonight would be putting up large sums of cash as their bid. Others would bid valuable jewelry or solid gold.

The final auction required a payment of one million dollars in order to enter the secret bidding room, where Kendrick would present the notebook. They didn't tell the guests exactly what the notebook was. But they made it clear the item was priceless, containing the secrets to a technology they'd never dreamed of having.

With the profits from the entry fees alone, Kendrick believed he would be able to start any new venture he desired, including establishing trade with the South District. He estimated what they received for the actual notebook would at least triple what they received from the entry fees. It was only a matter of not revealing the scam.

Kendrick sat back, watching from backstage and sipping his drink, waiting in anticipation. To his surprise, five guests were eager to put up the money. He could barely contain his excitement.

A whopping profit of five million dollars just for the privilege of entering a room. *Idiots*, Kendrick thought, no longer trying to conceal his deceptive smile.

The rest of the guests from the auction were escorted back to the party in the ballroom, while the four lucky men and one lucky woman were separated and brought into the secondary room. Inside, they stepped into individual spaces divided by partitions so they couldn't see each other. The guests thought it was for their own protection, but really it was so Kendrick could take the winner aside and no one would know who they'd gotten rid of.

Kendrick addressed the group. "Thank you all for joining me this evening. This notebook is by far the most prized possession in the building tonight. It is truly priceless, for the individual who claims this prize will have the ability to journey through time. Containing equations, coordinates, and thorough research into the absolute possibility of time travel, this book is a door to the future and a key to the past."

He then started the bidding at twenty million and took a seat, letting Marc take the lead as the group fought for the notebook. Hearing the bids climb higher and higher made his heart race.

5 8

To avoid being seen, James and Hayden were the first to leave the auction room. He pulled her into the shadows of the corridor as they watched people meander out of the room and head back to the party. They'd won the tracking device for $100,000, an object he was sure would've sold for twenty bucks in their time. The winners were told to proceed to the next room and collect their items.

"What are we gonna do now? We don't have a hundred K," Hayden said.

"Improvise," James said confidently.

Hayden sighed.

James watched as the few people who paid for the secret auction were separated from the group and escorted into another room. "What could possibly be auctioned off down there?"

"What if it's your notebook?" Hayden asked, lacing her fingers between his and pulling him toward the room.

They entered a much smaller auditorium, where only the front-row seats were filled. There were five guests, each separated by a partition. The lighting was dim, except for the stage where Kendrick stood before them. James and Hayden crept into the back of the room and crouched down behind a row of high-back chairs.

"This is a technology that would advance you beyond civilizations that have come before you and ones that will come after you," Kendrick said to the group. "The ability to manipulate time itself."

"Oh, shit!" Hayden whispered loudly.

"We found it." James squeezed her hand. "Why is he trying to get rid of it?"

For the next few minutes, Kendrick continued to spew nonsense at the guests about a topic he clearly didn't understand. Then the auctioneer started rambling off numbers higher than James could ever imagine someone spending on a single auction item.

"Sold! To bidder number three."

Groans of disappointment erupted from the front of the room, and simultaneously, men in matching navy-blue suits emerged from a door next to the stage to escort the four unlucky losers from the room.

James practically tackled Hayden to the ground and pressed himself on top of her, getting the two of them as close to the row of chairs as he could and out of view. He could feel her heart beating wildly in her chest and her soft breathing on his neck. She felt warm, and he had the sudden urge to kiss her.

The guests walked to the top of the auditorium. James held his breath as they passed his row. Once the door closed behind them and he felt safe for the time being, he went for it. He kissed her, softly at first. Her lips parted, and she traced his bottom lip with her tongue. He heard her laugh quietly, and he smiled, sat up, and peeked over the top of a chair. Kendrick was bringing the winner to a door next to the stage.

"Come on," James said, helping Hayden stand.

Kendrick and a woman walked briskly, but quietly, down to the door, and James caught it before it closed. He and Hayden crept through and were suddenly in a curving hallway which led into a large open room where Kendrick, a man, and the woman gathered. James assumed the man was Kendrick's advisor. He'd figured this out as he observed the two of them throughout the evening because, despite seeming to grow more annoyed with him each time he spoke, Kendrick appeared to heed what the man had to say.

The woman was the notebook winner. She was young and attractive. Her hair was slicked back in a long ponytail, and she wore a black pencil skirt, matching blazer, and tall stiletto heels. In contrast to the many women at the party in colorful dresses, her only pop of color was on her lips.

The notebook was nowhere in sight, but James spotted the tracking device on a table next to them, along with some other items not yet claimed. He and Hayden backed up a few steps, staying out of sight, and watched as a man wheeled a giant cart next to the woman. The cart carried a stack of cash on it so large it looked like a crate. The woman nodded to him, and he turned and left the room. She looked eager to receive her prize.

"Can I talk to you for a minute?" the man asked Kendrick.

The two of them walked back toward the curved hallway and stopped about ten feet short of James and Hayden.

"I don't know if I can do it," the man whispered to Kendrick.

"What do you mean you can't do it, Marc?"

"I didn't expect her to win. I can't kill a woman, sir."

Kendrick's jaw clenched. "This was *your* idea. But as usual, I'll take care of it."

"I'm sorry, sir. I never should have suggested it."

Hayden squeezed James's arm. He could still see the highest bidder, looking abnormally small next to the largest amount of cash he'd ever seen. He could tell she was unable to hear what they were saying, but she looked confused as to why they were keeping her waiting.

Marc whispered something else to Kendrick, which infuriated him even more, and Kendrick walked briskly up to the woman. Marc trailed him, looking visibly upset.

"What's going on? Is there a problem?" the woman asked politely.

Marc opened his mouth to speak but Kendrick cut him off.

"Sorry. There's been a change of plans," Kendrick said flatly.

Her brow furrowed, but before she could get another word out, Kendrick withdrew a concealed handgun from under his jacket and shot her in the head.

5 9

James felt Hayden wince as the woman's body hit the floor. In one swift movement, he withdrew the revolver he was carrying under his jacket and cocked the hammer. The sound alerted Kendrick and Marc, and they turned in his direction. Before they could react, the men in matching suits barged through a back door. James thought this moment couldn't get any worse, but then he realized they were dragging Martina, Andre, and Mason behind them.

"Well, I have to say I'm impressed." Kendrick's tone was cold and held no amusement.

James stepped forward, closing the gap between them, and aimed the gun at Kendrick's head.

"Let's not get ahead of ourselves," Kendrick warned, his voice as calm as ever. He didn't even flinch. He just raised his gun to meet James.

"Don't you think you've alerted your party guests by now?" James asked through gritted teeth. He glanced at Andre and Martina, hoping they still had their gun. Thankfully, they weren't tied up.

"This room is soundproof." Kendrick smiled. It wasn't like the ear-to-ear grin on his face when he was out on the dance floor. His smile was cold, lifeless.

There were only three guards standing by the door, which made it five against five. Not bad odds, as long as the others could make their move at the right time. After watching Kendrick's extreme lack of remorse for the woman he'd just robbed and killed in cold blood, James had no doubt the man would pull the trigger.

Andre caught James's gaze, trying to indicate he was about to make a move. Kendrick faltered, just for an instant, and glanced at Marc, and James took his opportunity. He lunged, knocking Kendrick's gun to the floor, and tackled him. Hayden dashed in and picked up the gun, aiming it at Marc's head. James heard a struggle between the guards by the door and the others. He glanced over while he pinned Kendrick to the ground and saw Martina punch one of them in the face. At the same time, Andre withdrew the Glock from his waistband and forced a guard to kneel on the ground with his arms raised in surrender.

Mason was visibly hurt and wasn't much help, at least not until he used all his strength to knock one of the guards on his ass. He shakily climbed on top of him and withdrew something silver from his shoe. It looked like a scalpel. Mason cocked his arm back before shoving it cleanly through the man's eye socket.

"Let's get out of here!" Hayden yelled, grabbing the tracking device off the table, her gun still aimed at Marc.

"We can't leave without the book," James said to her.

"Let's go!" Hayden ran.

Martina ran after her, into the auditorium. Andre grabbed Mason's arm and led him to the door. James gave Kendrick one more punch in the jaw for good measure and sprinted down the winding hallway.

They almost made it out.

Mason struggled to climb the many steps of the auditorium, but Martina and Hayden went ahead and were already through the door. Just as James, Andre, and Mason reached the top of the stairs, a gunshot was fired behind them. Mason's legs buckled, and the two men barely caught him.

Kendrick stood on the stairs below them, holding the gun with a smile on his face.

If adrenaline hadn't kicked in for James yet, it did in that moment. He scooped Mason up in his arms, barely feeling his weight, and sprinted through the door into the ballroom. He scanned the room for Rayne, but he was nowhere in sight.

The music stopped and everyone stared, horrified, at the man covered in blood. It didn't matter. The group raced through the crowd toward the exit, and Andre did what he could to help support Mason's weight. Finally, they made it outside. They kept moving for minutes that felt like hours until the familiar vine-covered house came into sight, and James collapsed on the sidewalk with Mason still in his arms.

6 0

When James came to, he was surrounded by blackness. Hiding behind the cover of clouds, the moon no longer illuminated the street. His head was spinning, and it took him a few moments to remember where he was. Then memories of the night came flooding back. He managed to stand and walk toward the others, his blurry vision slowly subsiding. Martina and Hayden were trying to get the bullet out. Mason was screaming in agony. All James could think was his brother was losing too much blood. The bullet was lodged in Mason's chest, and the wound was hemorrhaging. James rushed toward them. "Wait! Don't take the bullet out," he said. "We need to stop the bleeding."

"You want to leave it in?" Martina asked.

"What should we do?" Hayden's voice was frantic and high-pitched.

"We needed you, Doc. You passed out in the street," Andre said from the corner of the room.

James found a towel and gave it to Martina to hold on the wound to try to stop the bleeding. He searched the house for Noah's alcohol to sterilize the wound and found it in the bathroom. He returned with the bottle and an old blanket and pillow to help make Mason more comfortable. He sat next to his half-brother on the couch, keeping pressure on the wound. "I'm so sorry," James repeated to him again and again. "I thought I was saving you all."

Mason faded in and out of sleep, murmuring, "Jane" and "Emily." Because he'd kept tabs on Mason over the years, James knew his wife and daughter's names. Now he regretted not reaching out sooner, before it was too late. They could have had a relationship, no matter how screwed up their family was. James had wanted to contact Mason countless times over the years, but he always changed his mind, figuring things were better off left alone.

James no longer knew how to help Mason. The blood loss was too severe. They'd probably made it worse by bringing him all the way back to the house. But what was the alternative? James couldn't just leave him there. Not with that worthless, vile human. His sadness turned to anger when he pictured Kendrick's face. *He can't get away with this*, James thought. He would make sure of it.

Not only had their plan to rescue Mason backfired, but they didn't get the notebook either. James felt trapped. Without the coordinates, they were stuck in this horrible place even longer. He couldn't accept his failure.

"Guys," Martina said, startling him. "He's not breathing."

"No. He can't be gone," Hayden said, a sob escaping her throat.

Next to the unlit fireplace, Martina consoled Hayden. Andre stormed into the bathroom.

James felt for a pulse on Mason's neck and then on his wrist, begging and pleading to find one. But he knew it was in vain. He let out a long sigh, feeling defeated and in shock, and he covered Mason with the blanket. James began to shiver, as if feeling the cold night breeze for the first time. How did this go so wrong? He thought the five of them were meant to be there. He believed fate had brought them together. But why bring Mason there just to die? James started to question everything.

He thought of what the fortune teller told him. She said he should leave Mason there in the Circle and just get the notebook. She must have known he wouldn't make it out. He thought of what she said about altering the future. And suddenly, he no longer cared.

He sprung to his feet and walked out the front door.

61

Hayden grabbed a flashlight and followed James out of the house. Her sneakers thudded along the pavement as she tried to keep up with him, her feet still aching from the heels she wore to the gathering. "Where are you going?" she asked.

"I'm going back," James said calmly. He quickened his pace, staying a few feet ahead of her.

"Are you crazy? You're gonna get yourself killed."

"I have to do this."

They kept walking, putting distance between themselves and the house.

"I know he meant a lot to you," Hayden said.

"Yeah, I have a funny way of showing it, right?"

"It's not your fault."

The moon reappeared from behind the clouds, making it easier to navigate the uneven pavement. Hayden followed James as he hurried through the streets leading away from their hideout.

"Maybe not," James said. "But all these years, I never reached out. He didn't even know I existed."

"I'm sure there's a reason for that," Hayden said softly.

"He didn't have an easy life. I just can't stop feeling like I could've helped him. Or at least been there for him." James's voice cracked. "Now I'll never get the chance."

Hayden fell silent. Nothing she could say would ease his pain. She was no stranger to grief, and she knew it manifested in different ways for everyone. But letting him go on a suicide mission wasn't the answer either. She reached out to touch his arm and James stopped walking. She pulled him close and rested her head against his shoulder, then closed her eyes for a moment and felt tears start to form.

A strange sound in the distance made Hayden's eyes fly open. "Not again."

"We need to get inside," James said, grabbing her by the hand and running down the street.

The buildings surrounding them were in poor shape, but many of them were still standing. James tried a door, but it was locked.

"Over here," Hayden said, pointing. "This looks like an old hotel."

James gave the door a hard nudge and it opened. They rushed inside, and James drew his gun from his waistband in case they weren't alone.

It was silent inside the hotel, and Hayden let out a sigh of relief. They were in the lobby, which was still exquisitely decorated. The old-fashioned paneling along the ceiling indicated this place might've been closed before the Incident, or at least it hadn't been fully remodeled like the rest of the modern architecture they'd come across. A grand piano stood out among plush armchairs. Hayden wondered why the residents at the Circle hadn't looted it. *Was it nailed to the floor?*

"We can barricade the door," Hayden said.

James nodded toward the piano and they pushed it, blocking the entrance. Hayden heard staggering footsteps approaching the door. She peered through the cracks of a boarded-up window and saw about a dozen creatures gathering outside.

"We better stay here until they move on," James said, taking a seat in a plush armchair.

Hayden nodded and sat on the piano bench. "We'll be safe in here for the night." *Anything to prevent you from going back to the Circle.*

"Do you know how to play?" James asked.

"I may have taken some lessons as a kid." Hayden slid open the lid, revealing the keys.

"Maybe you shouldn't. It'll only draw more of them here," James said. "They were attracted to the noise of the subway."

"Let's just see if it still works." Hayden played a few notes perfectly. "It's a shame I can't play you a full song." She could feel the intensity in his stare, and she was suddenly self-conscious of her appearance and ran her fingers through her hair.

"Come on. Let's explore this place. We're stuck in here anyway."

They wandered the halls with just a flashlight to illuminate the way. Hayden shivered; the air felt cool and damp. Most of the hotel was intact, but unforgiving cracks ran up the walls. Hayden looked in the guest rooms, which were identical, but at the end of the hall was a large suite full of luxurious furniture.

"A fireplace!" Hayden said, crouching in front of the large fireplace in the master bedroom. "And there's still wood in it and matches here. Someone must've been here recently."

James lit a fire and the room started to glow. Their shadows danced on the wall above the king-sized bed. The bedroom was still in perfect order; the only thing out of place was a lamp toppled over on its side in the corner of the room. James lay on the bed and stared at the wall with a blank expression on his face. Hayden curled up beside him and rested her head on his chest. Out of nowhere, the tears came. She cried like she hadn't since before she was locked up, and he wrapped his arms around her even tighter, comforting her. He held her for what felt like hours as she cried. She realized his support was exactly what she needed. Without it, she would be lost.

James leaned down and kissed her lips gently, which awoke something deep within her. She looked up into his green eyes and kissed him hard, parting his lips with her tongue. He ran his hand through her hair and kissed her back, seemingly surprised at her aggression. The room was beginning to fill with warmth from the fire, and she felt safe for the first time.

In her old life, Hayden was always too afraid to make the first move. But as she'd grown closer to James, everything had changed; her worries started to disappear. All she knew was she needed him more than she'd ever needed anyone in her life. She climbed on top of him and lifted her arms, allowing him to remove her shirt.

He paused for a moment. "Are you sure?"

"Yes," she said, running her hands over his chest.

He kissed her with an intensity she'd never experienced before, and he flipped her back over with ease, taking control. The fire crackled as she wrapped her legs around him, bringing them together. For the moment, she felt like they were the only two people in the world.

Hayden woke the next day to soft sunlight filtering through the curtains covering the windows in the executive suite. She felt James's warmth next to her and smiled, memories of the night before lingering on her mind. After realizing this was the first night she'd slept soundly without any help from her pills, she decided this thing with James might actually be something real. Her playful mood turned somber in an instant, however, when her thoughts turned to Noah and Mason. They didn't deserve to die. Not like this. *Not in prison either*, she thought.

"Good morning." James kissed the back of her neck.

She rolled over to face him, and he pulled her in close. She breathed in his scent, sweat mixed with a little alcohol, and closed her eyes. If only she could remain in this moment forever, safe and protected from the outside world.

"He's going to pay for what he did," James said.

And just like that, the moment was over. Hayden climbed out of bed and collected her clothes, which were strewn across the floor. She got dressed and turned to face him. "You can't bring them back. You can't undo what was done. No matter what you try to do now."

James got up and closed the distance between them. He brushed his hand against her cheek. "I know. But I can make it right."

"It's not worth putting yourself in danger."

His ambition both inspired and frightened her. She admired his drive to do what was right, but she feared he would take it too far with Kendrick. Could murder ever be the right thing to do?

They gathered their belongings and headed back to the lobby. Hayden felt tears threatening to stream down her face again, but she held them back. "What's our plan now?" she asked.

James appeared to be deep in thought.

"Shouldn't we go back and try to find the woods?" she asked.

"We will." James had a dangerous look in his eyes. "But not before I get my notebook back. And not before Kendrick is dead."

"You can't be serious." Hayden frowned. "I thought you were saying all this in the heat of the moment last night. I didn't realize you actually planned to go back there."

"I don't have a choice."

"Can't we just try to find the woods without the notebook?" Hayden asked. "This isn't our world, we don't belong here, and we have no business messing with the Circle that way. It's not safe here!"

"This isn't right! Don't you see that?" James raised his voice. "Kendrick is pure evil. He's enslaving his people while pocketing millions for himself. He doesn't deserve to be in charge. If we have the chance to help these people, can you really live with yourself if we don't even try? And we need the notebook. The woods could be twenty miles away for all we know."

"What if we fail? Is it really worth killing ourselves over?"

"It's worth it for Mason if for no other reason."

"I just don't think—"

"I need to make it right. If I'm not back by sunset, go ahead and search for the woods. Pack up the supplies and the weapons. Search an expanding perimeter around the Circle, and stay hidden as much as possible. If you find the tunnel, I don't know what you'll find on the other side. But it has to be better than here."

"Funny, I bet that's what you thought when we were still in prison."

James sighed. "Do you think you can make it back to the house to meet up with the others?" He rifled through his backpack and found a hefty wrench he'd taken from the store where he and Andre had hidden from the Remnants.

"I'll be fine," Hayden said, taking the wrench.

"You'll do whatever you have to do," James said.

James grabbed Hayden and kissed her forehead. He took the Glock out again as they cautiously headed outside.

6 2

Zara looked out her bedroom window at the gloomy morning, which perfectly matched her mood. The clouds rolled in and blocked out the sunlight, and rain tapped on their penthouse roof. Kendrick was beside himself over some incident at the party last night. He wouldn't tell her what it was. She didn't see what happened, but she knew many of the guests had left in a hurry.

The CB radio started to beep. It was the only method of communication the board members had with each other when they weren't face to face.

Kendrick stalked out of the master bathroom and answered the radio. "What is it?"

"Sorry to bother you, sir." Marc's voice came through the radio scratchy and difficult to make out. "I'm afraid it's urgent."

"What's urgent?" Kendrick's voice was low and harsh.

"It's, well, it's the notebook, sir. It's gone missing."

Kendrick dropped the receiver in shock, and it clattered against the nightstand, causing Zara to flinch. They both reached for it and Kendrick glared at her as he grabbed it. "It's gone missing? What the fuck does that mean? Did it grow legs in the night and wander away?"

Kendrick rarely ever cursed; Zara became worried.

"No, sir."

"Where the fuck is it?" Kendrick yelled.

"Keep your voice down. You'll wake the kids," Zara said.

Kendrick shot her a look of disgust.

"We think we know where it is. Late last night, at the end of the gathering, it appears members of the South District broke into the room below the auditorium and stole it."

Zara could practically see Kendrick's blood boiling.

"And the cash?"

"The cash she paid for the notebook is gone as well. Although all our other winnings were left untouched."

Kendrick pressed his fingers to his temples.

"And that's not the worst of it, sir," Marc continued. "We believe they were helped. By one of our guards."

"Fuck!" Kendrick punched the bedside table.

"Kendrick!" Zara couldn't believe he was acting like this.

"Marc, get one of the SUVs ready. We're going to get that book." Kendrick slammed down the handset of the CB radio. He walked frantically around the room, gathering items. He packed a bag full of weapons and cash. Sweat dripped down the sides of his face despite the cool temperature inside the room.

"Kendrick, what are you doing? You're not really going out there, are you?"

He ignored her.

"Talk to me. Please!" Zara followed him around the room. "This is insane. You know that, right? You never go outside."

He remained silent.

"All over some silly notebook?"

"Why did I marry such a half-wit?" he muttered, heading for the door.

Zara followed him. "You can't do this." She grabbed his arm.

Kendrick swung around and smacked her with the back of his hand, and Zara fell to the floor. She clutched the side of her face, which had already begun to ache, but it was nothing compared to the emotional pain she felt.

She looked up at him and saw a look of regret flash over his face. She waited for him to apologize, but instead, he let out an angry sigh and walked out the front door, slamming it behind him.

63

James set off toward the Circle, determination driving his tired legs forward with each step. He needed to get back inside unnoticed. If luck were on his side, Kendrick wouldn't be expecting him back so soon. Not only did he need to get inside, but he also needed to figure out where in this gigantic compound Kendrick lived and make his way there without alerting the guards. A seemingly impossible task.

As James approached the Circle, he gazed up at the building and debated his entrance carefully. As he stood there, rain poured down, soaking his clothes. It felt like a bad omen. He had to decide quickly which way to go. James figured a man like Kendrick liked to sit up on his throne and watch from above. His home was probably the penthouse, which appeared to be thirty stories high. He'd bet Kendrick had a great view out the wall of windows above the courtyard, where he could see danger coming from a mile away. *But he won't see this coming, not this time*, James thought.

He chose a different entrance this time, a utility door on the north side of the building. A guard was posted there, but

James waited nearby until the guard got a call on his radio and stepped inside. James took the opportunity and entered the building cautiously, his eyes peeled. While the guard had his back turned, heading in the opposite direction, James crept toward the stairwell door. Once safely inside, he ascended the stairs two at a time. The quicker he found Kendrick, the better, but something made him stop on the third floor.

A glass hallway allowed him to see into an industrial-sized room, where men, women, and children worked in what appeared to be a clothing factory. Some of the children on the assembly line looked as young as five years old, their gaunt faces expressionless. Their tattered clothing hung loosely on their thin, malnourished bodies. James was so caught up in what he was seeing, he barely noticed the man shuffling up behind him.

"What are you doing down here?" The man clearly knew James was an outsider.

James's hand instinctively went toward the gun in his waistband, but he realized the man wasn't a threat, as he was unarmed.

"Tell me what's going on here. Why are the children working?"

A confused look crossed the man's face.

"Please." James looked into the man's sad eyes.

"We have to work to stay here. All of us."

"Are the children paid wages too?" James asked, hoping to hear a different answer than the one he'd received from others.

"We work for food. For a roof over our heads. Otherwise, we take our chances on the outside."

Wouldn't that chance be better than this? These people were worked like slaves, denied their basic human rights. He thought about Noah, how he died for the rest of them, and whatever horrible fate his family must have suffered. *These people have no choice but to sell themselves into servitude if they can't survive outside the walls.* James knew he had to do something. He couldn't let it go on any longer, even if it meant interfering where he shouldn't.

The same five words repeated over and over in his mind. *Kendrick will pay for this.* "Can't you all find somewhere else to go?" James asked.

"I need to get back to work. The commander will know. He always knows." The man shuffled down the hallway away from him.

James fought back tears. He'd never been this emotional in his life. How could this happen? This should be a wealthy, thriving group of people. How could these people be eating scraps for meals when there were millions of dollars being carelessly thrown around just last night? He'd known the indentured servitude in the Circle was bad from what he heard from the others, but seeing it firsthand was almost too much to bear.

James made eye contact with a child across the room; he looked straight into the boy's big brown eyes. The boy held James's gaze for a moment, and then he lifted his tiny hand and waved. James waved back and pressed his hand against the glass. Then he stalked off to the stairwell and started to climb to the very top, vowing to make a difference. His mind raced, imagining all the different ways the confrontation with Kendrick could play out. Kendrick wasn't expecting him, and James would use that to his advantage.

After floor fifteen, the atmosphere of the building started to change. It was as if he could visualize the wealth increasing as he went skyward. He peered through a small window in the door leading to each ascending level. Each floor was slightly more elegant. Finally, he found what he was looking for. Floor thirty. There was a passcode to enter the door at the very top of the stairs.

Shit! James had no choice. He took out his gun, shot through the lock, and hurried through the door. The gunshot would alert someone unless Kendrick's penthouse also had soundproof walls. The floors were an immaculately clean white marble, and sleek gray paint coated the walls. There were open lounge areas on this floor, contrasting the long narrow corridors on the other levels. Floor-to-ceiling glass windows stood behind an array of couches, chairs, and even a pool table.

The thought of Kendrick playing games while his people suffered infuriated James even more.

Past the lounge, there were two double doors, which appeared to be the only ones of their kind up there. That must be it. The commander's home. James held his breath and gently knocked on the door.

A few moments later, two deadbolts disengaged, and a woman opened the door.

He recognized her short dark hair and big eyes. It was the woman from the party. He could see now, in the daylight, lines had started to form across her forehead and between her eyebrows. *She seems too young for wrinkles*, James thought. Maybe that's what being Kendrick's wife had done to her.

"Can I help you?" she asked politely.

James got the feeling she knew exactly why he was there. "Is Kendrick here?"

"No, he's out right now. Who are you?"

"James. I need to speak with your husband."

As James tried to determine if she was lying, she did the last thing he expected. She invited him in. He took a seat at her dining table, a sleek glass structure with its base distorted in a modern, angular way.

"Would you like something to drink?"

He wondered why she wasn't acknowledging that they'd already met. She must remember. "No, thank you. I'm here because . . . Do you even know what's going on downstairs?"

She maintained her composure. "I'm afraid I don't know what you mean."

Her eyes were kind, like he remembered. He couldn't find a hint of malice in them. James simply said, "On level three."

She looked down and away from him. "If you're referring to our class system, I am aware that it's . . . unfortunate. But it's just the way things are around here. I've found that it's better to learn to accept it than to dwell on things that can't be changed."

"Do you really believe that? I mean, did you ever think you might have the power to change that?"

"I—"

"Mommy, what's going on?" A young girl appeared in the hallway leading out of the kitchen.

"Everything's fine, honey. Please go to your room."

"Wait. This is your daughter, right?" James got to his feet. "Even a child, as young as she is, recognizes that what your husband is doing is wrong. She helped my friends."

The girl looked at the floor and retreated into herself.

"Jasmina, is this true?"

She was silent, clearly terrified of being reprimanded. She ran out of the room, likely to go hide in the safety of her luxurious bedroom.

"You seem so different now from the woman I met last night." James looked into Zara's eyes. "I'm sorry. I just feel compelled to do something. Your husband killed my friend, and I watched him kill a woman last night in cold blood. And frankly, it seemed like an ordinary Tuesday night for him." James thought she might slap him.

Instead, she looked like she was going to cry. "I've wanted to leave him for a long time," she said, her voice barely louder than a whisper. "But I can't."

"Because of the kids?"

She shook her head. "I don't know what he would do to me if I tried to leave."

"I'm going to help you get out of this. I'm going to make it right," James said, as he reached over and placed his hand on top of hers.

"Who are you?"

"I'm the owner of the notebook, and I'm telling you that you have the power to make a difference here." James proceeded cautiously. "I don't know exactly what happened here, and I don't know what you've been through. But I know for sure that we can put an end to this."

Zara dropped into a chair, appearing to be in deep thought, her gaze somewhere off in the distance. "Even if I wanted to make a change, I would never be able to. I have no real power. I'm technically a member of the board, but Kendrick has always dissuaded me from attending meetings, from any involvement in the decision-making process."

"You deserve more than that. I can tell you have compassion, and you're smart. Someone like you should be in charge."

It was the first time James had seen her smile since the night before, and he thought he was getting through to her. "I'm sorry to involve you in this, but I know Kendrick has possession of my notebook. I need it to get back home. Do you know where it is?"

Her smile disappeared.

"What is it?" James asked.

"I'm sorry. It's not here."

"Do you think Kendrick may have hidden it somewhere? I'm sure he would keep it close to home."

"You don't understand." Zara got to her feet and started pacing. "Kendrick doesn't have it. He's out looking for it."

"What do you mean he's out looking for it?"

"Apparently, it was stolen. By the South District."

"I need that book. It's our best chance of getting back home."

She frowned. "If you go now, you might catch him. Head down to the first level and follow the corridor around to the other side of the building. That's where our garage is."

"Thank you. I'll come back as soon as I find it," James said as he ran for the door.

6 4

The body in the center of the room made Andre feel claustrophobic, like the walls were narrowing. He kept glancing at the bulge under the blanket, the shell of skin and bone that used to be Mason. Andre had struggled to deal with death since he was a young boy. That's what made his homicide conviction so ironic, as if he could ever kill someone in cold blood.

How could James do this? The scientist had just left them at the house, expecting them to wait around with the dead body. He had no regard for anyone but himself, and now he'd set off on a revenge agenda, one likely to get him killed. If he didn't come back, they'd have to find their way to the tunnel without him. Just the thought of climbing through that small space again made Andre feel nauseous, but at this point, he would do anything to get back to his time.

"I think we should bury him," Martina said, as if she was reading his thoughts.

Hayden strode into the house looking disheveled and exhausted.

"That's a good idea," Hayden said. "Sorry I didn't come back sooner."

"Where's James?" Andre asked her before turning to Martina. "And how are we gonna bury a body?"

Hayden answered both questions. "We know a place. And James is headed for the Circle. I tried to stop him."

"Hold up," said Andre. "You want to move him? No way."

"It's the right thing to do. We can't leave him here to get eaten." Hayden said.

"How do you know what's right?" asked Andre. "We don't know what his religious beliefs were. And we don't know if the Remnants eat the dead."

"You grab his feet," Hayden said to Martina.

"Shit! Fine. I'll help." Andre moved to lift Mason's legs.

They wrapped Mason in the blanket and carried him out of the house, and Hayden grabbed the bottle, which was now almost empty, on her way out. They shuffled down the street. The body hadn't started to smell yet, thankfully, but it still made Andre uncomfortable. It felt like they were doing something wrong, even though he knew the women were right about Mason deserving a proper burial.

"Why's James acting more insane than usual?" Andre asked.

"I think Mason's death sent him over the edge," Hayden said.

"It was traumatic, so was losing Noah. But we all had to go through it, and we're keeping our shit together," Martina said.

"Mason was James's half-brother," Hayden said. "I overheard them arguing back at the cabin. Mason thought he was an only child until a few days ago."

"What the hell?" Andre stopped walking.

"How many secrets is he keeping from us?" Martina shook her head. "This is so screwed up."

Hayden shrugged. "I thought you should know."

"So many things make sense now," Andre said. "Even back at StormRidge, James sought him out when we could've easily found someone else to help us with the escape."

"I don't understand why he wouldn't just tell us," Martina said.

The two women led Andre up to a two-story brick home, which reminded him of the house he grew up in. The similarities were uncanny. Memories of his childhood flooded his head like water breaking through a dam. "What is this place?"

"Noah used to stay here," Hayden said. "You guys bring him around back. I'll be right there."

They set Mason on the ground, and Hayden came into the yard with a shovel a few moments later. She took a swig from the bottle and started digging.

"I can do it," Andre said, taking the shovel from her.

Martina and Hayden took a seat on the dirt and passed the bottle back and forth.

"How's your shoulder doing?" Hayden asked Martina.

Martina pulled down the collar of her shirt to reveal the wound, which was starting to turn yellow. "Still hurts." She took another sip.

"This should help," Hayden said, taking back the bottle. "Do you think that thing infected you or something?"

"She's not infected. The wound is," Andre said. The digging was almost therapeutic to him. The repetitive motions helped keep his mind at ease. After a few minutes passed, he looked up. Something felt so familiar about this small backyard.

"What if I turn into one of them?" Martina polished off the rest of the bottle, looking genuinely scared.

"You won't." Andre set down the shovel.

They were silent as they dragged Mason's body into the freshly dug hole in the ground. Hayden started to tear up, and Martina comforted her.

As Andre filled the hole with dirt, he looked around the yard. Memories flashed through his mind. He saw himself and his brothers running through the grass, playing tackle football, and getting yelled at by their mother. During the summer, they would play in the yard all day until she started cooking dinner and the scent wafted through the large kitchen windows, which always remained open, regardless of the weather. He looked up at the old brick house and dropped the shovel. Then Andre sprinted inside the house.

"Where are you going?" Martina called after him as she and Hayden got to their feet.

It was just like he remembered it. None of the belongings were his, but the bones of the house were the same. Tall archways connected the living room and the kitchen, making the house seem nicer than it really was. The same ugly tile he'd hated still lined the kitchen counters, though now it was cracked with pieces missing. He saw the back door that led out to the yard, and he remembered sneaking girls into the house when he was in high school. Sometimes, he missed those days more than he could bear—when his family was still together and he didn't have a care in the world. He ran his hand along the broken plaster walls, which revealed narrow strips of wood underneath. He closed his eyes and wished he could go back in time and do things differently.

Andre was already upstairs, in the second bedroom on the left, when he heard the women approaching. He was sitting in front of the broken window, looking down at the worn wood where he had rebelliously carved his initials many years ago. *AJW.* He fought back tears as he heard them enter the room.

"What are you doing up here?" Hayden asked.

After a moment of silence, he said, "I grew up here. This was my mom's house."

"How's that possible?" Martina closed the distance between them.

"I don't know." He turned to face them, and his eyes wandered around the room. Unfamiliar furniture surrounded him, but it appeared to still be a young boy's bedroom. A different boy, in a different time. He wondered how many families lived here after his, and if any of them were still alive.

"What part of the city did you grow up in?" Hayden asked.

"I grew up in West Covina. It looks so different."

"I guess it should. Technically, by now, none of us would be around," Hayden said.

"I should've known sooner," he said, shaking his head. "I didn't recognize the streets or anything."

Martina walked over and put her arm around Andre. "How could you have known? Most of the buildings are just piles of rubble. The city is unrecognizable."

He nodded. "I think I know how to get us out of here." Andre's mood suddenly improved. "I know how to get back to the woods."

Martina smiled.

"Back in high school, some of the kids would throw these crazy parties on the outskirts of the city. It was the perfect location because no city cops ever ventured out that far. It was basically the middle of nowhere. I bet it grew into a forest over the last hundred years. I think I can guide us back to the tunnel."

"Finally, some good news." Hayden put her arms around them. "We have to go get James."

65

Kendrick grabbed Marc by the shoulders and slammed him against the wall. "How could you let this happen?"

"I'm sorry, sir. I didn't know! We had it under surveillance all night with the rest of the valuable items."

"Useless!" Kendrick released Marc and headed back to the stairwell and down to the garage, where the SUVs were waiting.

Marc followed on his boss's heels. "I don't know how this happened. If we can't trust our own security, then we have nothing. Our protection is a lie." He scratched his head. "The board won't be happy about this."

"The board will not learn of this," Kendrick said through gritted teeth.

"Okay. No one has to know," Marc said reassuringly. "How are we going to get it back?"

"We'll burn the place to the ground if we have to."

"But if their compound withstood nuclear war, I'm not sure how much damage—"

"Oh, just shut up!" Kendrick wasn't sure if going after the book was the right decision, but he couldn't just let them steal his new prized possession. He wouldn't let them undermine him, not like that. What type of a leader would he be if his enemies could steal his belongings right out from under him?

Memories of his childhood rushed back to haunt him, images of his last day on the outside, when he had to watch those creatures so effortlessly kill his parents. He shut his eyes trying to block it out, but the images just kept coming. He imagined the horror his little brother experienced out there before he took his last breath. He recalled how the guard just drove off and left their bodies there with no burial to honor them. And how he was thrust into a position of power he never wanted, with no time to grieve the loss of his whole world, in one afternoon. It wasn't long before the power turned him cold. Responding with violence anytime his position was threatened turned out to be the only effective way to remain commander.

"I have a question," Marc said.

Kendrick let out a sigh.

"The winner last night. What district was she from?"

Kendrick's chest tightened. "Now that you mention it, I believe she was from the South," he said. "Trash." *This is all about revenge*, Kendrick thought. *The thieves must have known her. They must know we killed her.*

They arrived in the garage, where two guards stood beside one of the many blacked-out SUVs.

"Are you sure you don't want us to call for backup?" one of the guards asked.

Kendrick glared at him. "Would you like to keep your position of employment, or would you rather be thrown outside the walls? Do your fucking job and drive me where I need to go." He grew more furious by the minute.

"This is of the utmost importance," Marc explained. "We need to get there as quickly as possible."

Kendrick got in the back seat of the SUV, his hands shaking with rage and fear. This was his first time inside a car since that day. The memories flashed through his mind again and his head started to spin; he thought he was going to be sick.

"Is he getting carsick before we even leave the garage?" one guard asked the other as they climbed into the front seats.

"Just drive the goddamn car," Kendrick said through gritted teeth.

Marc slid into the back seat next to Kendrick. "Are you all right?"

"Fine." Kendrick leaned his head back against the soft leather headrest. "Let's take back what's ours."

66

James ran toward the garage. Fear and anticipation drove him forward. He had to beat Kendrick to the South District. But then what? How would he convince them to just hand the book over to a complete stranger, especially if they took it in retaliation for the woman's death?

Focus on one task at a time, he thought.

He heard an engine running. It might be too late. James stopped fast at the doorway to the garage. It was the size of an airport hangar, filled with armored cars and trucks that appeared to never get any use. In the distance, James saw Kendrick climb into the back of a vehicle. He watched as the SUV peeled out of the garage, tires squealing.

James got into an identical SUV. He was in luck. The keys were inside, and the battery was charged. He pulled out of the garage as Kendrick took a right turn. He could only keep a safe distance for so long until they realized he was following them.

Then he had an idea.

James stepped on the gas pedal and sped up until he caught up with them. He drove perfectly in line behind them, staying about three car lengths back. With any luck, they'd think the vehicle contained more guards, an extra security detail. Even the windshield was blacked out, so he doubted they could see him through the glass.

They kept going for miles. The other SUV didn't stop, which meant his plan must have worked and they had no idea he was following them.

Demolished buildings surrounded James, and he was grateful he hadn't witnessed what happened to cause the destruction. He thought about his beloved city, where he grew up and built his business. Ever since he was a boy, he'd known he wanted to create a laboratory. The inspiration came from his grandfather, a world-renowned astrophysicist with a leading career at NASA. From the age of twelve, James dreamt of having his name on a plaque, winning awards, and getting recognition for groundbreaking discoveries.

That city will one day turn into this. James shuddered at the thought.

He felt a sudden urge to get back there. To the safety of his glass office on the top floor. To the warming embrace of his wife. But he knew in his heart those things would never happen again. When he got back, things would be different in Avion. Depending on how much time had passed there, he would have to deal with whatever had become of his life's work. And he'd have to start searching for his wife. Chilling thoughts raced through his head. Had someone taken over his role at Avion? Was Isabella still alive?

The scenery started to change, bringing James back to the present. They were getting close to the destination.

This place looks even worse than the East District, James thought. The streets were filled with trash, and a heavy fog hung in the air. The road turned into a beaten-up dirt path. It looked like they were driving through what used to be a lush forest. But the trees had all been leveled, and there were no more vibrant shades of green.

Then he heard them, the creatures, all around them. The SUV in front of him continued at a steady pace. James kept in line with it, but his heartbeat quickened. He held the Glock in his lap like a safety blanket. After driving another ten miles, they approached a giant angular structure with a steel exterior, which James thought must be the heart of the South District. The building was covered in rust and the windows were boarded up. His hands started to sweat as he gripped the Glock tighter. He'd driven by hundreds of the soulless creatures at this point, and he didn't have an endless supply of bullets.

Kendrick's SUV came to an abrupt stop in front of the building, and two armed guards hopped out of the front seats.

What's Kendrick waiting for?

Finally, Kendrick stepped out of the vehicle with a man James recognized from the night before. If he wasn't mistaken, Kendrick looked terrified. James wondered if the commander was more afraid of the creatures lurking around the compound or what lay within it. The men glanced back at the SUV, waiting for the extra security they probably thought was driving it to step out.

The rusted metal front door to the compound swung open, saving James from having to reveal himself. The South District's armed guards, along with a tall man exuding authority, stepped outside. To James's disbelief, one of them was holding his book. He cracked the window and listened.

"Looking for this?" the tall man asked, taunting Kendrick.

"We've come to take back what's ours," Kendrick replied.

"Yours? I happen to recall my daughter paying for this in full last night."

Kendrick grimaced. "I don't know who your daughter is, but I can assure you—"

"We're not gonna play any more of your games, Kendrick. How 'bout you tell us what all this means, and we'll let you leave here alive." The man smiled.

Kendrick's guards raised their weapons, and James quietly opened the door, stepping out of the vehicle.

67

Kendrick started to panic. The tables had turned, and now his life was in danger. He'd expected to come down here and get the book back with ease. The South District was always known to be weak. But they were on to him. How the hell did they know?

"This doesn't have to be difficult," said Elijah, the South District's leader. His large build took up much of the doorway.

"Kill me, and you'll never find out what it means," Kendrick said.

"You sure about that?" Elijah asked.

Without hesitation, a Southern guard shot one of Kendrick's guards in the head. As his body dropped, so did Kendrick's mouth. He was in a state of disbelief; he had never been challenged by another district before. Instinctively, Kendrick's remaining guard shot back. It was the last thing he ever did.

Marc retreated, like a frightened child, until his back was up against the SUV.

"Now, are you ready to play on my terms?" Elijah asked.

Just then, Kendrick heard a familiar growl, and it sent a chill down his back. He was frozen in fear. His thoughts drifted back to that terrible day that changed the course of the rest of his life. And now they were coming for him too.

Suddenly, Kendrick felt himself being pulled from behind, an arm wrapping around him. He closed his eyes and prepared for the end. He didn't realize it was a human arm until the man spoke.

"I know what you did, Kendrick. And now, so do they."

It was the intruder. The man who'd broken into the Circle. Kendrick's rage returned, and he ripped himself away.

"Who the hell are you?" Elijah asked.

"My name is James Blackwell, and I'm here for Kendrick. Last night I watched him *murder* your daughter."

Kendrick turned to Marc for help, but he was nowhere to be seen. Everyone was against him. There was no way out of this. Then, out of the corner of his eye, Kendrick saw them coming. The creatures were headed straight for him—the way their skin peeled off from the radiation, their skeletal structures poking through, their unbearable stench, and their thirst for blood haunted his nightmares. His heart pounded inside his chest. He did the only thing he could think of. He reached for his waistband, but he was too late. Before he could draw his concealed handgun, a Southern guard aimed his gun at Kendrick and fired.

Kendrick collapsed to the ground, in shock, struggling to breathe. He heard Marc yell; he must have been nearby after all. It was only when he looked down that Kendrick realized the bullet had hit his shoulder. He clasped his hand over the wound, both terrified and relieved it wasn't a fatal shot.

The creatures were a mere twenty feet away now, and they had picked up speed, zeroing in on their kill. Kendrick's heart felt as if it were about to explode in his chest, and his vision blurred. *Is this what a heart attack feels like?*

The Southerners turned their weapons on the intruder, who now had his hands up in the air.

"We don't have time for this," one of the guards mumbled as he fired a few shots at the creatures.

The guards grabbed Kendrick and James and hauled them inside. Although he was surrounded by enemies, Kendrick finally felt safe and secure. Anything was better than being on the outside with those things. Kendrick looked back at the door to see Marc being dragged over the threshold. He watched as the metal doors slammed shut.

Kendrick felt betrayed. The closest thing he had to a friend had just sat by and watched as he was shot. He could have been killed, and there was no one there to help him. His blurry vision returned to normal, and the last thing he saw before his eyes fell shut was the man from the past sitting across from him—the man who came into Kendrick's life at random and might just cause his downfall.

6 8

They were taken down a dark hallway and into a large open room. James let himself relax, safe for the moment from the imminent danger outside. But a knot formed in his stomach again as the guard who was forcefully escorting him got in his face.

"I'm only going to ask once," the guard said, holding his hand out.

James eyed the gun, still gripped tightly in his hand. Reluctantly, he gave it to the guard. He was greatly outnumbered, and he had a feeling it was in his best interest to play nice with the Southerners.

This place was nothing like the Circle. It had an open architecture with dark floors and dark walls. They stepped inside a giant rec room filled with metal tables and chairs. People, young and old, talked throughout the room. James could feel a positive energy here, a sense of community. It was what he imagined the Circle should be like. He got a sense that the people had formed strong familial bonds. They trusted each other and relied on each other to survive.

There was nothing glamorous about it, however. From first impressions, a shabby place like this, with boarded-up windows and a deteriorating exterior, didn't seem capable of bidding millions in the auction.

As they walked through the room, the people stopped talking and stared straight at James. He jumped as a loud barking echoed throughout the room, rattling his eardrums. Embarrassed, he turned toward the corner of the room where four very large dogs resided. With thick gray and brown fur, sharp teeth, and glowing eyes, they resembled wolves. One snarled at him and licked its lips.

The man sitting beside the dogs chuckled and ran his hand over the one nearest him, stroking its fur. "Easy," he said to the pack.

James and Marc were separated from Kendrick and ushered down a hallway into a private room. It looked like an interrogation room with no windows, just a table and four chairs.

"Have a seat," Elijah said, gesturing to the table.

James sat, never taking his eyes off Elijah. Marc sat beside him, shaking. James almost felt bad for the guy as the guards tied Marc's wrists together with rope.

"What are you going to do with me? And with Kendrick?" Marc asked, his voice uneven and high-pitched.

"That depends," the taller of the two guards said.

A red-haired woman entered the room and took a seat next to the district leader. From their body language, James assumed they were together.

"What can you tell me about this book?" Elijah set the notebook on the table and looked directly at James.

"The notebook is mine," James said. "I mean, I wrote it. That's my research."

"What are you saying?" Elijah asked.

"I'm saying I need it back. But in exchange, I'll teach you what I've learned."

The district leader frowned. "To be honest, I'm not sure if I can do that. After all, we did pay for it in the worst way." He smiled, but it didn't reach his eyes.

"Where do you get all your money?" James blurted.

The district leader stared at James for a moment. "Kendrick's been running this auction scheme for years now, putting up worthless items at ridiculous costs. Now, we learn, with no intention of giving the winner their item at all. We thought it was time to catch him in the act and flip the script on him." He pointed his finger. "And that's his sidekick, sitting right next to you."

Marc sunk down in his chair as far as he could.

"He seems harmless," James said. "So you planned to win the auction this time?"

"We had a man on the inside. He was supposed to intercept Kendrick when he took Jen's money."

"Jen? She was your daughter?" Marc choked out.

"Not biologically. But everyone here is my family. And every loss hurts just as much."

"I'm sorry about that. What went wrong?" James asked.

"He got distracted from the mission. Apparently, there were some other intruders there last night." He glared at James.

"We did crash the party," said James, "but I can assure you we didn't interfere. She was killed before Kendrick and his men even knew we were there. Unfortunately, the night ended in failure for us too."

"What is it that you want?" Elijah asked.

"As I said, I need the book. I need the coordinates inside it to get back to a specific location."

The red-haired woman spoke for the first time. "You can take the page with the coordinates on it, no more, no less." Her voice was throaty to match her rugged look, dressed in all black, short, choppy hair hanging over deep-set eyes.

James sighed. "Okay. Fair enough. I'll do whatever it takes to get back home at this point." He spent the next hour attempting to explain his research to them, suspecting they would never have the resources to use any of it, at least not for a very long time. They seemed to appreciate it anyway.

"Why don't I show you around before you go?" Elijah asked when James was done.

James had unfinished business with Kendrick, and he wondered where they were keeping the East District's commander. If he had to, James would search the entire compound to find him.

The district leader led James through his compound, explaining the many things they excelled at. It was completely different than the Circle, but much more impressive. There was a school for all children under the age of eighteen and various occupations for the adults in the compound. He led James through an indoor greenhouse, where they grew their own food. They walked through a divider and James recognized marijuana plants, lined up by the dozens, under rows of lights.

"Recreational?" James chuckled.

"It's our modern medicine. We use the hemp plants for everything from clothing to lotion to food and pain relief. But we like to have some fun too." He smiled.

They walked into a different area, and the walls turned dark again. This place reminded James of an old industrial building, as if they'd remodeled a giant factory. They proceeded through two steel doors and James looked around in awe.

"This is the production room," Elijah said.

James was speechless.

They were manufacturing weapons. Machines churned out bullets while men and women assembled and modified guns. James thought about the workers at the Circle and noticed the men and women here appeared to be in better health and better spirits.

"How do you do all of this?"

"Honestly, we lucked out. When this compound was formed, we assembled a group of incredibly skilled and intelligent people. We have everything from medical professionals to manufacturing professionals. It's how we stay alive."

"So this is how you make all your money."

"We sell weapons and marijuana to the other districts."

"To tell you the truth, when I saw the outside of your complex, I would have never guessed you were this advanced."

"We rarely go outside. Well, the majority of us don't."

"Why aren't the other districts like this? I mean, the West seems pretty advanced, but the East seems to have gone backwards."

"I don't know. Greed? Corruption? Take your pick."

"Your people seem happy. And free. Unlike the people at the Circle."

"It looks like we may have helped them out. You cut out the cancer, the rest of the body might survive."

"Speaking of, I hate to ask, but can you take me to him? We have unfinished business."

6 9

Elijah seemed to think it over for a moment, debating whether to let James have his revenge.

"There's a bit more to the story," James said. "Kendrick didn't just kill Jen last night. He shot my brother too."

"I'm sorry."

"He didn't make it," James said, shaking his head. "That's why I need to see Kendrick. Make things right."

"Are you sure you know what you're doing?"

James nodded.

"Revenge is a funny thing," Elijah said. "It'll make you feel better for an instant. But once that instant is over, you're left with the same empty feeling as before. Only now you've lowered yourself to a place you can't come back from."

"I know what I'm doing," James said.

Elijah turned and led James into a part of the building he hadn't yet seen. They climbed a winding metal staircase up multiple stories until they came to a solid door at the top. Elijah unlocked the door and said, "He's all yours."

"Thank you."

"I trust you'll do what's right."

"That's all we can try to do."

"Amen to that." Elijah patted James on the back and turned to walk back down the staircase.

James took a deep breath and pushed open the door.

A rush of wind hit him as he stepped onto the roof. It looked like a rooftop lounge area. An empty bar, tables, and chairs dotted the cement floor. A low cement railing ran along the perimeter of the outdoor space. Solar panels lined the roof beyond the lounge. Kendrick was seated on the far corner of the rooftop. He didn't appear to be tied up.

James approached him, growing more nervous with each step he took. Although his rage had started to subside, he felt no sympathy for this man. He still believed Kendrick had to pay for what he'd done. And maybe this need for revenge reflected more on James and his own demons, but he'd deal with that later.

James thought back to when he first met Kendrick, the way the commander towered over him, exuding arrogance and making sure James knew who was in a position of power. "Looks like the tables have turned," James said, lightly.

The intense look in Kendrick's eyes indicated his mood was anything but light. He had a bullet lodged in his shoulder and he appeared to be in pain, but the bleeding was under control. He'd live. James approached the spot where Kendrick sat against the railing.

Kendrick got to his feet. "You think you've outsmarted me?" His eyes were wide. His clothes were disheveled, and he was covered in sweat despite the chill in the air. He no longer resembled the man who had interrogated James at the Circle. Although that man had evil deep within him, he'd maintained a façade of elegance and grace. Now he looked like the monster he really was. All the layers peeled back, his true nature exposed.

"I was never trying to outsmart you. I just wanted to do what was right."

"How do you claim to know what's right for this world? One that *my* family built. You don't belong here."

"Is this the world your family intended? A world of greed and oppression? If so, they're just as evil as you are."

The look in Kendrick's eyes turned to pure malice.

James continued. "You took my brother from me."

A look of confusion crossed Kendrick's face. "Ah, the bait you left behind. I knew it would be enough to lure you back in," he said.

"That was the last mistake you're ever going to make," James said. "Well, aside from coming all the way here on a wild-goose chase."

Kendrick chuckled.

"And in case you forgot," James continued. "*You* kidnapped *us*! If your people hadn't taken us from the cabin, I would never have stepped foot inside your compound. Never learned of the atrocities occurring inside your walls."

Kendrick was silent.

"Take a look around," James said, waving his hand, indicating the South compound. "There is another way."

"My way is the only way," Kendrick groaned.

Suddenly, a sharp pain shot up James's torso. He couldn't have anticipated Kendrick's move. He hadn't even seen the weapon, but James looked down to see a jagged piece of metal sticking out of his side. The pain was excruciating.

Kendrick grabbed James's shoulders and pushed him against the edge of the railing. The cement dug into his back, the sensation giving him an ounce of relief from the pain in his side. James gritted his teeth and fought back, using all his strength.

Kendrick was much taller than James, but he was thin. Although James had never learned to fight, he had a naturally muscular build and had used his recreation time at StormRidge to get stronger, giving him the upper hand. Kendrick kept pushing, trying to force him over the edge of the railing, but James had the commander's arms in a death grip. If James went over, he would take Kendrick with him.

James risked a glance over his shoulder at the steep drop. There was nothing but cement to break his fall, and the Remnants still gathered on the sidewalk below. They made the low growling noise he'd come to recognize.

Once Kendrick noticed them too, his demeanor changed. Pure fear flashed across his face, and James realized the creatures were what scared Kendrick the most. He'd found the commander's weakness.

Kendrick faltered for a moment, his grip on James's shoulders loosening, and James used all his strength to grab Kendrick by the torso and haul him up on the edge beside him. He pulled Kendrick into a bear hug, which caught him by surprise, and then flung his thin body onto the railing. Kendrick was balancing on the edge of the cement, barely holding on, and James saw a look of defeat in his eyes.

James hesitated for only an instant before giving Kendrick's legs a shove, which sent them sliding near the edge. Kendrick grabbed ahold of James's arm with his left hand and squeezed, digging his nails into his flesh. Then he used his right hand to grab the piece of metal sticking out of James's side.

James cried out in pain as Kendrick yanked down, digging the metal deeper. James felt the blood gushing out of the wound, and he used his last bit of strength to shove Kendrick as hard as he could. Kendrick let go, and James heard him let out an animal-like howl as he went over the edge, falling to a certain death.

James collapsed on the rooftop and yelled at the top of his lungs as the piece of metal twisted inside him again. His vision started to blur, and he knew he was going to pass out. Somehow, he mustered the strength to get to his feet and rest his weight on the railing. He looked over the edge and saw Kendrick's body, bruised and bloodied, his limbs twisted underneath him. And he saw the creatures surrounding the former commander, eager to clean up the mess.

7 0

James woke under bright fluorescent lights, his eyes blinking rapidly as he tried to recognize his surroundings. He was lying on a hospital bed. An attractive brunette woman dressed in all white was speaking to him, but he couldn't make out what she was saying. "I'll go get him," James heard her say before she walked out the door.

He sat up straight and felt a sharp pain in his side. The memories came rushing back. A bandage now covered the spot where Kendrick stabbed him. He got to his feet as the leader of the South District walked through the door.

"How are you feeling?" Elijah asked.

"I'm okay. I can't thank you enough."

He handed James the pages from his notebook that contained the coordinates.

"I guess I owe you now." James smiled.

"You owe me nothing." Elijah reached out his hand, and James shook it. "I almost forgot this," he said, setting James's Glock on the table next to the bed. "I'm sorry I didn't return it to you sooner, but it looks like you didn't need it."

"Thanks." James tucked the gun back into his waistband.

"Do you need anything else before you go?"

"No. I have everything I need." James folded up the pages and put them in his pocket.

"Good luck, James, with everything."

James headed back to the SUV, clutching his side. Despite the pain, he felt satisfied. Now he could finally get the group back home. As he exited the compound, he saw something out of the corner of his eye and spun around to realize Marc was following him.

"They let you go?" James asked, surprised.

Marc nodded; his hands were still bound.

"What do you want?" James asked.

"Take me with you," he pleaded.

"Why should I do that?"

"You did what no one else could. What no one else had the courage to do," Marc said, looking down. "You stood up to an evil man who treated people like his personal property. I'm so ashamed I was a part of everything he did."

"His wife should become the leader now," James said. "Your people need someone they can count on."

"Perhaps."

"If I take you with me, you'll do anything I ask?"

"Anything. Please. Just don't leave me here with them. They have no mercy for me."

Such a spineless man, James thought. "They let you go. What more can you ask for?"

"You're right. Can we go back to the Circle now?"

"Fine, but remember, this is your chance at redemption," James said, leading him outside. "If you don't do the right thing, I'll tell Zara everything. Including your role in Jen's murder."

As they walked to the truck, James looked up at the rooftop Kendrick had fallen from and then at the spot where he'd landed. Some of the creatures were still gathered where the body lay. James climbed in the SUV, started the ignition, and gripped the leather steering wheel. There was a single thought he couldn't get out of his head: *That could've been me splattered on the concrete.*

71

When James and Marc arrived back at the Circle, the garage door was still open. They returned the SUV to its spot, and James thought about what he should do next. His side throbbed, and he worried the medical personnel in the South District had missed some internal damage. He kept replaying what happened with Kendrick in his mind, but as he got out of the car, familiar voices interrupted his thoughts.

"James!" Hayden rushed toward him.

Martina and Andre were close behind.

"What are you doing here?" James asked.

"Andre figured out how to get us home, so we came to find you." Hayden said. "We saw the SUV pull in, and we waited and watched from right over there," she gestured outside the garage.

"How does Andre plan to get us home?" James glanced over at his former cellmate.

Hayden said, "It's a long story."

"Well, I got the coordinates," James said, showing them the pages.

Andre looked surprised. "Where's the rest of the notebook?"

"It's where it needs to be."

"Okay," Andre said. "As much fun as this has been, I think I'm ready to go home."

"Agreed." Martina nodded.

"I just need to do one last thing before we go," James said, glancing over his shoulder at Marc, who was listening to their conversation. "Wait here. I'll be right back." James pointed at Marc. "And keep an eye on him."

James headed up the stairs. He didn't know how to break the news to her. He could only hope she would feel like she had been set free.

James knocked on the door, once again.

Zara's head dropped into her hands as she sobbed. "What am I going to do now?"

"You can lead them. I know you'll be a better leader than he ever was." James tried to comfort her. "It will be tough at first, but the people will follow you." He worried he was pushing her too far.

"And raise my kids alone?" Tears streamed down her face.

"I'm sorry. But it's better this way."

"Who are you to tell me how my life should be?" Zara asked. "You don't know anything about me."

James wondered if she was right. No. What was he thinking? Kendrick was evil. He had to be removed from this place. His family would only suffer more in the long run if he were still alive. And his people, they would no longer suffer, if only Zara followed through for them.

"You said you've been afraid of your husband for a while," James said. "You've seen how he's mistreated his people. Now you can take over, and you can end their suffering. Offer them fair wages and food rations. Stop the child labor. I don't know if you're aware, but Kendrick must have made tens of millions of dollars in the auction last night."

"You make it sound so easy. And what do you know about the auction?"

James wondered if Kendrick really kept her in the dark about everything or if she intentionally turned a blind eye to her husband's wrongdoings. He explained to Zara what he'd learned from his brief time there. She claimed to have no knowledge of any of it, but James had a feeling she knew more than she let on, consciously or not.

"A woman from the South District won a bid for my notebook at the auction. I watched Kendrick kill her in cold blood as I tried to retrieve it," James said.

"Why should I believe any of this?"

"Ask Marc about it. The whole thing was orchestrated by him and Kendrick."

Zara appeared to think it over.

"I'll call an emergency board meeting," Zara said. "I know a few of them may agree with me about making some changes. But I don't think they'll just let me take over as commander. The second-in-command is Marc, so he's the logical choice."

"From what I've seen, Marc is a total pushover. You're much stronger than he is and certainly more powerful. Don't be afraid to use that to your advantage. And I've already spoken to him on your behalf."

"The East has never had a woman as commander," Zara explained. "How do you expect them to accept me as their leader?"

"Because this was meant to happen. You're meant to be their leader. I know it, and you know it. This all happened for a reason. Can't you see that?" James got closer to her. "I don't know if you've ever left this place. But the West District operates much differently. I think it would be beneficial for you to see it for yourself."

She thought for a moment. "I don't know if I can do it."

"Have a little faith in yourself."

A knock on the door interrupted their conversation.

"Are you expecting someone?" James asked.

"No." Zara walked to the door. "Who is it?"

"It's Jones, ma'am."

"It's the head guard," she whispered to James. "He only answers to Kendrick."

"I need to speak with Kendrick." Jones had a hint of urgency in his voice.

"He's not back yet," Zara mumbled, locking eyes with James.

"Please open the door."

"Zara, there's someone in the West District you need to meet. I guarantee she has a solution to all your problems," James said, knowing he would be apprehended the minute the guard came through the door.

"How will I contact her?"

"Have the guards drive you to the West District. Ask for Camilla. I promise it will be worth it."

Jones banged on the door again. "Last chance!"

"I'll try," Zara said softly. She unlocked the door and opened it, stepping aside.

It took a brief moment before one of the three guards recognized James. Then two of them barreled toward him, grabbing him by each arm. There was nothing he could do. He'd set his gun down on the table while he was talking to Zara, and he didn't intend on having a shoot-out in front of her children.

"Wait! Let him go," Zara pleaded as they escorted him out of the room.

"It's okay," James called back to her. "Don't forget what I told you. Now you have the power to make a change. And Zara, be careful."

The guards dragged James down countless stairs, the pain in his side returning. He let out a sigh of relief when they stopped on a familiar floor. Floor ten. It looked like he was headed back to the cell where they originally held him. It felt like ages ago. But this time, he was almost certain he was being taken there to be killed.

72

They dropped James on the hard floor, and he caught himself with his hands just inches before his face connected with the cement.

"You really thought you were going to get away with this?" one of the guards asked.

Another chuckled.

Although James didn't think they knew Kendrick was dead yet, they would find out soon enough. Then he wouldn't stand a chance.

"I've been waiting for this moment since we brought you in the first time," Jones said, raising a gun to meet James at eye level.

James shut his eyes and wondered if this was his karma for killing Kendrick.

Suddenly, one of the men by the door let out a grunt and fell to the floor. James craned his neck to look. It was Andre. Before Jones could react, Andre was upon him, knocking the gun out of his hand. James took down the man to his right. Then he climbed on the man's stomach and started punching him. Over and over. He couldn't stop. Something had come over him.

James snapped out of it when Andre pulled him off the man. The three men lay there, bruised and bloody. They would survive, probably. James and Andre stole the guns out of the guards' holsters and ran for the stairwell.

Hayden and Martina were waiting for them outside the Circle. Hayden put her arms around James again, pulling him close and burying her face in his chest. "Now are you ready to get out of here?" She looked up at him, visibly annoyed.

"Beyond ready." James managed a smile. "How did you know I needed help?"

"Marc's radio," Andre said. "He showed me how to find you."

"What happened?" Martina asked. "Kendrick?"

James looked down and then back up at her. "He's gone."

"What's going to happen to all the people? How do you know they'll be okay?" Hayden asked.

"I don't. It's in Kendrick's wife's hands now. But I believe she'll do the right thing. An opportunity to change things just fell into her lap."

James took one last look at the building towering above him. The fortune teller's words tugged at the farthest corners of his mind, but despite them, he hoped he'd made a difference here. Maybe he wasn't supposed to change anything, but this seemed like a place that had lost its way. He wanted to do everything in his power to make it right again. And he believed he had.

They took one of the SUVs and headed back toward the woods, carrying little more than the tracking device, their weapons, and a backpack full of the cash Martina had found. James entered the coordinates of the tunnel, which his team had discovered so long ago based on the electromagnetic field of the area just beyond StormRidge, into the tracking device.

They cruised through the city for miles. Exhaustion crept in, and the sun set quickly, turning a warm afternoon into a chilly night. When a light blinked on the dashboard, James guessed it indicated the car needed recharging.

"Shit," James muttered. "I think the car's about to die."

They continued on for a few more miles, and the car flashed the warning again before powering down.

"I guess we're on foot from here," James said, getting out of the SUV.

The group continued as far as they could as their legs grew tired.

"I need a break," Hayden finally said. "Just for a second."

They stopped to rest outside an old gas station. James knew they had to be approaching the outskirts of the city.

"What are we gonna do when we get back?" Hayden asked. "I don't know about you guys, but I can't go back to prison. Now that we've been out, I just don't think I can do it again."

"I'm with you on that," Martina said. "The way I see it, my only choice is to leave the country."

"What about your kids?" asked Hayden.

"I'm going to do everything in my power to get them back. But if I can't, I'll have to go away for a while. Try again in a year or so when the smoke clears."

"As the most high-profile person in this group, I can confidently say I have no fucking idea what to do," James said.

Andre put his arm on James's shoulders, and James realized how close the four of them had become, seemingly by chance. A part of him was grateful they all ended up in the medical room that night. His guilt hadn't yet subsided over what happened to Mason, but he had a feeling he'd been right about fate bringing the group together that night. He'd have to learn how to live with losing his brother before they got the chance to build a real relationship. It was no coincidence the two women also ended up with them during the riot. Some higher power wanted them to come here. James didn't know why yet. He figured he would find out when they got back to the other side.

"This place looks like it's still full of stuff," Andre said, wandering inside the store.

"You mean full of shit?" Hayden rolled her eyes at him. "Are you trying to take back a souvenir?"

Andre fake laughed. "No, but I know you could use something to drink. I can hear you wheezing from all the way over here."

Hayden shot Martina a look, but Martina threw her hands up.

"Let's take a quick look," James said, and he followed Andre inside.

James wondered how long the store had been abandoned. While some of the shelves were still stocked, the place was covered in dust. He looked behind the register to see if there was anything of value as Andre headed to the back of the store. James pulled open a drawer beneath the cash register and found an old pocket watch. It looked like it was made of gold. He opened it and realized there was a working compass inside. It reminded him of a similar compass his grandfather had owned. He closed it and held it tightly in his hand before slipping it into his pocket.

The creak of a door on old hinges was followed by Andre's voice. "Oh, shit!" Andre sprinted back toward the register and tripped over a rack of potato chips, his face smacking the floor.

James went to his side quickly, and just as he crouched down next to Andre, James felt a presence to his right. As he turned his head, he raised his arm instinctively to block the creature lurching at him. The Remnant sunk its teeth into James's forearm and a sharp pain shot up to his elbow. He lost his balance and fell next to Andre, still shielding his face with his arm, which was now gushing blood.

A loud crack rattled James's eardrums, and the creature collapsed, limp, on top of him. Disoriented, James pushed the body away and grabbed at the counter, pulling himself to his feet. Hayden was standing in the doorway, still aiming the gun.

James sank back to the floor and examined his wound. It was deep, and his arm was starting to go numb.

"What the fuck happened?" Martina's voice sounded distant even though she was standing just a foot away.

Andre looked at James. "I opened the door to the bathroom and that thing just came out."

"Your arm!" Hayden said as she knelt beside James and grabbed his hand.

"It'll be fine," James said. "I think."

Suddenly, more growling drifted into the gas station.

"Was that what I think it was?" Hayden asked with wide eyes as she gripped the gun tighter.

Still shaken, James couldn't answer.

The wind picked up and started to whistle, and the building rattled. Debris hit the last few panes in the gas station windows and smashed them to pieces. Glass shattering all around them.

73

"What are we gonna do?" Hayden asked, failing to hide the panic in her voice.

James crept to the front of the store and looked outside to see dozens of Remnants approaching. "They're coming from the city. We still have a clear path to make it to the woods."

"They'll be right behind us!" Martina said. "Do you really want to take your chances outrunning them?"

"There's gotta be a way we can hold them back," Hayden said to James. "Buy ourselves a little time."

James looked outside again; the horde was fast approaching. They were right, it would be too risky to make a run for it. He felt the compass in his pocket. *Think, goddammit.* He stared at the old gas pumps and a feeling of hope entered his mind. James ran back over to the counter and pulled open the drawer where he'd found the compass. An old Zippo lighter sat amongst pens and rusted keys and other useless items. He grabbed the lighter and headed to the door.

"What are you doing?" Andre asked.

"Do you think there's any gas left?" James asked, showing them the lighter.

"I don't know." Andre shrugged.

"There's still food in this store," James said. "We're in the middle of an apocalypse, and this place wasn't fully looted. I'd bet there's still gas in those pumps."

"Are you willing to bet your life on it?" Andre asked.

"You're right," Hayden said, nodding. "There's gotta be something left in there."

"I need something sharp." James looked around the store.

Hayden walked over to James and handed him Mason's scalpel. "It was the only thing he had on him," she said softly.

James accepted the scalpel and stared at it.

"We gave him a proper burial," Hayden said. "It was the least we could do."

"I should've been there for it."

Andre was watching the danger approaching through the window. "We don't have time for this."

James regained his composure. "On my signal, I want you guys to head out the door and run as fast as you can to the woods."

They nodded, all silently watching the creatures approaching them.

James gathered up the courage to run. "Now!" he yelled, launching himself through the double doors.

As they ran outside, Andre and the women turned right. James went straight ahead to the row of gas pumps. He flung the lighter open as he ran and flicked his thumb over the wheel. He stopped when he reached the center pump, said a silent prayer, and grabbed the hose. James squeezed the handle, but nothing came out. He ignored Hayden, who was yelling something to his right, and the creatures, dozens of them, approaching on his left. He carefully cut the hose with the knife until it broke free and the nozzle clattered to the ground. Gas spilled out and James quickly leapt back. He prayed it was enough and tossed the lighter on the wet ground.

As the flames flashed, James took off as fast as he could in the direction of his friends. "Run!" he screamed.

Fire rushed over the pavement, the flame traveling across the puddle toward the pump. James didn't risk looking back. He reached the group, and they sprinted away, dodging debris strewn across the once-bustling city street. James felt like he was going to be swept up by the wind.

The creatures' noises grew louder. They were closing in, walking across the gas station parking lot. Suddenly, the gas pump exploded with a deafening sound, the blast sending pieces of metal and asphalt flying in all directions.

James tackled Hayden to the ground to shield her. After a moment, they sat up and looked back to see a fire still burning and many of the creatures obliterated.

"Come on! I see the tree line!" Martina shouted.

James saw the thick forest up ahead, less than a quarter mile away. His feet pounded the ground as he pushed forward, struggling to breathe. The ground rumbled and shook beneath them; it felt like an earthquake. But somehow, he had a feeling this wasn't simply two tectonic plates shifting under their feet.

Andre ran ahead of the group, his athleticism coming in handy as he raced toward the edge of the woods. Finally, they crossed a field of tall dead grass, bridging the gap between the city and the trees. They were almost to the woods when Martina tripped and fell to the ground.

James stopped and turned back as Hayden and Andre were about to run into the line of trees. For a split second, his mind told him to keep moving, but his stubborn courage got the best of him. He raced through the tall grass back to where Martina lay. It looked like she'd twisted her ankle. Wind and dust swirled around her; the semblance of a tornado was threatening to form. James grabbed her arm and yanked her upright. She cried out in pain, trying to balance on her sprained ankle. They hobbled toward the woods as Andre rushed back to help.

"Hurry!" Hayden shouted.

James could feel the rotating wind surrounding him. Dirt and debris flew into his eyes, making it impossible to see. *We can do this*, James repeated in his head. They moved through the forest clumsily, crashing into trees, tiny branches creating little scrapes on their faces and arms. His legs felt like they were going to give out at any minute. But James continued to run; he knew they couldn't stop.

74

Andre struggled to run through the forest while supporting Martina's weight. It was a vast difference from his years as a football star, when he ran with ease. Back then he carried no more than a football.

The four of them kept running, trying to escape the elements, which were chasing them faster than the creatures could. Then it started to rain. And not just a shower, a torrential downpour. It was as if the elements were angry, as if something had set them off balance. The pouring rain made it increasingly harder to see through the thick woods.

Martina was between Andre and James, her arms around their shoulders. Out of nowhere, she tripped over a fallen branch and sent them all tumbling down a hill, bouncing on sticks and rocks all the way down. Hayden climbed carefully after them, stepping over fallen tree branches.

"Oh my God! Are you guys okay?" Hayden asked.

"Fine," James said as he got to his feet.

"Martina looks pretty beat up. We need to get her somewhere safe," Andre said.

James clasped his hand over his open wound, now covered with mud and tiny sticks. "Let me just see where we need to go from here." He patted his pocket. "Oh, shit!" He punched the ground with his good arm.

The tracking device lay on the ground next to them, shattered. Hayden picked up the pieces, but it was irreparable.

"Great. Now we're stuck out here in the dark with no idea where to go," Andre said.

"We'll be okay," said James. "I just need to get my bearings."

"Nah, Doc, it's not okay. If you weren't so stuck on getting revenge, we would've found our way back while there was still daylight."

"What he did was courageous," Hayden said, standing up for James. "He did it for Mason. And Noah. And everyone else who suffered at the hands of Kendrick."

"That's where you're wrong." Andre shot James a look of disgust. "He did it for himself."

Everyone started talking at once. Then the sound they all dreaded started again. The Remnants were there. An ever-growing horde surrounded them, a low growl escaping their throats. Their partially skeletal bodies appeared to glow under the moonlight.

The group withdrew their weapons, and Andre glanced at Martina. He worried she was too hurt to defend herself. Then as he looked around the ravine at the rocks and dried-up earth, he realized a river once ran here. Memories flooded his mind, taking him back to his teenage years. "Hold up! I know where we are!" Andre shouted to the group. "Follow me."

"Are you sure?" James asked.

"Yes, I've been here a hundred times. Let's go."

Then the Remnants attacked. One of them lurched at James and took him down. James struggled, trying to get a grip on the creature. As he grabbed its arm, James's fingers sunk into rotting flesh, peeling it away from the bone. The Remnant slashed James's face with ease, and blood dripped onto his shirt. James used all his force to flip it onto its back, pinning it there, crushing it under his weight. He searched the ground around him frantically, his eyes finally settling on a rock. James grabbed it and raised it above his head. In one swift motion, he brought it crashing down and crushed the Remnant's skull.

Andre and Hayden held the group of Remnants back, shooting each one in the head as it approached. They made every shot count. As the horde thinned, James helped Martina to her feet, and the group headed carefully down the ravine.

"If I'm right," said Andre, "the tunnel is somewhere up the hill to our left."

"How do you know?" James asked.

"The people from the Circle drove to the cabin we stayed in. The only road into the woods is straight ahead."

Andre helped Martina climb the hill as James and Hayden went ahead, the Remnants still close behind. Martina turned on the solar-powered lantern when they reached the top of the hill, and it illuminated the forest.

"Look!" Hayden shouted. "The stone house."

"The tunnel's close," James said. "This way."

The group followed James through the trees, and Andre thought of the first night they stumbled upon the cabin, where Mason made a fire. He thought about how they were returning with one less person than they came here with. What was going to happen on the other side? Was he walking himself right back into wrongful imprisonment? He'd sooner die. But they couldn't stay here, which left him just one option. Go on the run, and don't look back.

They approached the tunnel, and Andre's heart rate quickened. He didn't want to go back into that tiny space. But the creatures were gaining on them. He risked a glance over his shoulder and saw dozens of them moving quickly through the trees, trying to catch up, their thirst unquenched.

"Try not to get stuck this time." James gave Andre a pat on the back. "This tunnel is high in radiation. It's a miracle you made it out alive."

"Fuck you, Doc," Andre said, but the corners of his mouth twitched into a smile. "Okay. I guess I'll go first."

7 5

Zara's hands trembled as she stood in front of the long glass table filled with condescending, pitying stares. "In my husband's absence, I would like to discuss some changes we can make going forward," she said to the eighteen remaining board members, consisting of fifteen men and only three women. At least she had Kristal and Marc on her side.

"With all due respect, you're not the commander. No changes can be discussed until a new one is appointed," said John, the heavyset man at the table.

"That's the other thing I'd like to discuss. I believe I am fit to be the next commander," Zara said, straightening her shoulders.

John sat up in his seat and leaned in her direction. "That's preposterous. The second-in-command is Marc. He should be the one to take over duty."

"I think she's right—" Marc started.

"Yeah," a man named Charles said. "Marc will fulfill his duty as commander until your son, Ethan, comes of age."

"That's out of the question," said Zara.

"With all due respect, sir, you're an idiot," Marc said. "A child will never again have control over this district simply because his father was commander. Zara was at Kendrick's side for many years. She knows how things work around here, and she knows what's best for our people. She's more than capable of being our leader."

Zara heard whispers she couldn't quite make out. She felt vulnerable, having laid herself bare, with all eyes on her. "How about we put it to a vote?" she asked.

"We don't *vote*," one of the men said, becoming visibly enraged.

"Maybe it's about time we start." Kristal got up and walked over to stand with Zara. "I'm with her."

Voices murmured around the room, and a few other board members left their seats to join Kristal.

"See. I knew there were others who wanted change," Kristal said.

Zara waited for the room to quiet down. "For too long, we've gone on without change. Without democracy. My husband was once a good man. But greed got the best of him, and it caused him to become a bad leader. What I promise to all of you is equality. You will not lose your money or status, but you will gain a sense of community. I will end the suffering here at the Circle, offer fair wages to everyone, and create mobility among classes. This is a real chance for all of us to achieve honor and integrity."

More people came to the front of the room, silently vowing to stand behind Zara, but a few of the board members protested.

"You can't do this!" said Charles.

"We're the top of the food chain. Always have been. No one can take that away from us." John stood to leave.

"We made enough money last night to do just about anything," Zara said. "I propose that we use the money to not only secure our comfortable lives but also to make a change for the better." She cleared her throat and straightened her posture again. "I'm excited to present the newest technology granted to us by the West District. With this artificial intelligence, we will no longer need assembly-line workers on level three. I truly believe this new innovative solution will propel us forward as a district."

"That's great and all. But why?" Charles straightened out his suit jacket impatiently.

"Allowing others new opportunities and growth does not take anything away from you. If you can't see the difference between right and wrong, you have no place in the new and reformed Circle," Zara said. "Now, either you're with us or against us. And if you're against us, the guards will happily show you the door. It's your choice."

Zara felt more confident now than she had in her entire life. With Marc and Kristal by her side, she knew they would get the rest of the board to agree. She'd make changes to the Circle's politics immediately.

It wouldn't be easy, but she felt peace knowing there would no longer be unnecessary suffering in her district. She owed her people that and so much more. Although the outside world was dark, their future was bright. For the first time, she had something to look forward to, the promise of a world she could be proud to raise her children in.

76

Once again, the group was back inside the underground tunnel. They made it through the crawl space, one by one, and then they crept along the tunnel back toward the prison. James was terrified of what they would find. Memories of the months spent inside his cell washed over him. The smell, the loneliness, he knew he couldn't go back to that.

All James could think about was contacting his colleagues. After this experience, he felt prepared to continue his endless search for more traversable wormholes. He needed to get back to the lab unnoticed by the authorities so he could share this new information with his team.

Something felt different this time. The tunnel didn't look exactly as it had when they went in. And they never reached a fork. Instead, the tunnel suddenly stopped. It opened into a small underground room filled with old supplies and a stairway leading upward.

James turned to the group. "Maybe we should make a plan."

"What if we go up those stairs and there's an army of cops just waiting for us, ready to fire?" Andre asked.

"That's not going to happen. This tunnel is different than the one we went in," explained James. "That can only mean one thing. We're not coming back to the same day we left."

"What if this isn't even our time?" Martina's voice was filled with fear.

"Stop procrastinating already." Hayden said, pushing past James and climbing the staircase. She held her breath, pushed the door open, and walked outside.

This tunnel, unlike the one they entered just a handful of days earlier, let out in an open field. There were trees in the surrounding area, but it wasn't a thick forest like James remembered. The biggest difference, though, was instead of StormRidge with its barbed-wire fence and tall, windowless, concrete structures, a different building stood in front of them. It was still under construction, but a sign sticking out of the ground indicated it would become a school.

The sun was rising, and an early work crew was arriving.

James risked walking up to an old man wearing a hard hat. "Hey! What ever happened to the prison that was here?" he asked.

Confusion crossed the worker's face. "It burned down two years ago. There was a riot. A lot of inmates died." He seemed to take note of their disheveled appearance and blood-stained clothes. "What are you doing all the way out here?"

"Hiking, we ran into some trouble on the trail. Thanks for your time," James said. He walked away, hoping to evade any further questions.

Luckily, the man just shrugged and headed off to start the day's work.

James thought of the men at the mine and especially of Carlos. He wondered how their lives would change. Something told him Zara would come through and make a difference for her people. With any luck, there would be no more senseless, dangerous work done at the mine and no more unethical labor driven by greed. He had to believe she would bring about change. Otherwise, everything they went through would have been for nothing. Then he remembered none of those people in the Circle and the other districts had even been born yet. They wouldn't be for nearly a century.

77

One hand on the steering wheel, and the fingers of her other laced between Andre's, Martina drove southbound on I-5 toward the Mexican border.

"You feeling okay?" Andre asked.

Martina nodded. "I'll feel more at ease once we cross the border. How are you holding up?"

"Honestly, I feel fine," Andre said, never taking his eyes off the road. "Contacting my family would just cause problems for them right now. I don't want them to feel responsible for keeping my secrets, but sooner or later, I'll find a way to see them again."

Martina squeezed his hand tighter. "Maybe after more time passes."

Andre nodded. "After we leave the country, it's going to be a lot harder. Near impossible to come back. But if we can travel to the future and back, we can do just about anything."

"I don't want to leave if you still have unfinished business."

Andre shook his head. "This is the right move. We need to get away for now."

They'd decided it was too risky to stay in California, so they planned to head back to Martina's hometown, just outside of Tijuana. Andre negotiated a deal with a friend from college, who let Andre take his old Chevy Suburban. They planned to switch vehicles when they crossed the border, and thanks to the money she'd taken from the other timeline, Martina had acquired quality fake identification for them and the children to ensure they would get there smoothly.

The next task wasn't so easy. It took many favors and many strings pulled to locate the foster homes caring for the children. Luck was on Martina's side though. After a few short weeks, she discovered all four of them were in the same subsidized-housing development.

Martina found her daughter, Sofía, first, and she waited for the girl to get off the school bus one day. She'd learned Sofía's foster mother typically wasn't around when Sofía got home from school, so Martina waited in front of the apartment. Tears sprang up in her eyes when she saw her beautiful daughter, for the first time in years, jogging toward her.

"Mom?"

"Sofía!" Martina pulled her daughter into her arms and held her tightly against her chest. "I missed you so much." She ran her hands through Sofía's hair, which had grown much longer since she'd last seen her.

"Are you really back?" Sofía asked.

"Yes, of course I'm back. And I'll never leave you again." She looked into her daughter's eyes. "I promise."

Sofía looked unsure.

"Are you okay? Tell me everything that's been going on. How are your cousins?"

They talked for hours in a park around the corner from Sofía's apartment before Martina called Andre over to introduce them. Being reunited with her daughter was the truest happiness Martina had ever felt. And although she had a lot of missed time to make up for, Sofía already seemed to forgive her.

Martina told Sofía to round up her cousins and meet them the following day after school and not to tell anyone she'd seen her mother. Then they'd leave this place for good. It wasn't very difficult convincing the other kids to go. They'd gone from living with a poor family to an even poorer one, where they were largely neglected by a woman just out for government checks. It tore Martina up to think they spent even a day inside those places, let alone years. But they were all together again, which was the only thing that mattered. She felt an indescribable joy, and it showed no signs of fading.

Now she looked at Sofía sitting with her three cousins in the back of the Suburban, and their smiles and laughter warmed her heart. They had grown so much since Martina last saw them. Her heart rate increased as she thought about the fake identification for the six of them. She couldn't shake the onset of nerves as they neared the border. But she knew from experience, it was a lot easier getting out of the United States than getting in.

She thought of all the possibilities that lay ahead for them. It wouldn't be easy being on the run, always looking over her shoulder, while simultaneously trying to raise four kids. But they were finally free. Free from bad decisions and bad luck. The road was an open blessing, with the possibility to take them wherever they wanted to go.

78

One month later

James and Hayden were living together at the Motel 6 in a part of town dotted with strip clubs, liquor stores, and truck stops, trying to stay under the radar. They ate fast food and only left their room when necessary. Two years had passed here since they escaped StormRidge, but James didn't feel safe walking around in broad daylight. He was itching to get back to the lab. He needed to speak to his colleagues, those in his inner circle. He had to let them know he was alive and that he had made it back in one piece.

James had kept up frequent communication with his closest friends and most trusted colleagues while he was in prison. They must've assumed he made it out before StormRidge burned down. After all, they were the ones who'd made the calls to organize the riot.

The time spent with Hayden had been easy so far. They enjoyed each other's company, and James realized she had a much deeper side, which he had grown to like. They spent most of their time talking about ideas and making plans for the future. She asked tirelessly about Avion and his research, but he only disclosed enough to satisfy her initial questions. Although he'd grown to trust Hayden, he wanted to keep her separate from that part of his life. They'd dealt with the isolation well, until the past few days when she started to become anxious. Her anxiety led to his anxiety, and ultimately, they just couldn't take it anymore. Tonight, they wanted to go out.

James decided to make a stop first. He'd learned Hayden had no problem being lazy, and while she was taking her afternoon nap, he slipped away to flag down a cab. The sun was blinding as he stood out on the street corner. It was the middle of summer, and the heat was unforgiving. Sweat dripped down his side underneath his long-sleeve shirt.

A yellow Prius stopped in front of James, and cool air conditioning welcomed him as he slid into the backseat. The driver took off immediately before James could even give him Avion's address.

James leaned his head back against the headrest, the tension in his neck building. He was grateful for Martina. She'd been smart enough to collect some cash from the houses they searched for supplies in the East District. Once they got back and decided to split up, they'd divvied up the cash evenly. They would've been screwed without that money.

The Prius came to a hard stop and James tipped the driver well. He felt just as peculiar being here now, looking up at his building, as he had at the Circle. The silver sign reading "Avion" reflected the harsh sunlight into his eyes. He took a deep breath and went inside.

A receptionist he didn't recognize sent James to a waiting room on the twentieth floor near his old office. The floor-to-ceiling windows were once comforting. He would settle in behind his desk every day and look out over the city in admiration, full of ambition to achieve something better than they did the day before. But now they seemed obnoxious, and the bright sunlight hurt his eyes. All he could think about were the windows above the courtyard at the Circle, and how Kendrick would no longer be looking out of them, over his broken city.

Then a darker thought crossed his mind. *Did I stop him from ever being born?* No, he decided. He assumed something like that could only happen when traveling to the past.

"I can't believe you're here!" Tom threw his arms around James and pulled him into a tight hug.

James hugged back reluctantly, hiding his discomfort at their level of closeness. "Honestly, neither can I."

The rest of James's inner circle joined them in the conference room. Tom, his most qualified hire, Chris, his lifetime best friend, and Erin, arguably the most intelligent person in the entire company, all stared at him like a shiny new object they couldn't wait to pick apart.

"I want to start by thanking you all." James took the time to look directly at each person in the room. "Without your incitement of the riot at StormRidge, I wouldn't have been able to leave that awful place before the end of my sentence. Not only did you free me, but you allowed me to personally experience a time jump first-hand. This changes everything." His mouth twisted into a grin. Thoughts of all the deaths between the time of the riot and now lingered on his mind, but he pushed them aside.

"Tell us more about your experience," Erin said, inching closer to him.

"I'll get to that, anything you want to know. But first, I want you to start searching for more traversable wormholes. I know there are other locations out there just like the tunnel under the prison."

"I think we need to know more about what you just went through before we can start a new search," Chris said.

"Did I miss something while I was gone? This is still my company, and I will decide what direction to take." James clenched his jaw. "We should focus our efforts on this. I'm sure of it. We need to hit the ground running. Time is of the essence."

"With all due respect," Tom said, "it took us *years* to discover that StormRidge was even a potential—"

"You were right about StormRidge," said James. "That's why you're the people I trust."

"We can't even begin to understand what you've experienced. We have every intention of furthering our research. However, we do need your input to move forward," Erin said.

James looked at the clock hanging on the wall and realized it was getting late. Hayden would be wondering where he was. He only hoped his team would listen to his orders and get to work.

After proving humans could survive a time jump, there was no turning back. The possibilities were endless. James wanted to discover every wormhole that existed on Earth and go through them all. He needed to see what lay on the other side of them. He believed he'd made the greatest scientific discovery known to man, and his research couldn't stop until he'd pushed all boundaries and exceeded all limits.

"I have to go." James got out of his chair and headed for the door.

"Wait!" Chris stood and walked toward him. He handed him a prepaid cell phone. "James, there's something I need to talk to you about. Privately."

"Whatever it is, it can wait." James turned to Tom. "Assemble a team and start the search right away. I want them out in the field, investigating, finding all new possible locations. Expand the search to the entire Western Hemisphere."

"Yes, sir."

James addressed the room. "Nine a.m. tomorrow, let's meet here, and I'll tell you everything."

He felt them watching him intently as he ran out the door.

79

"Where were you?" Hayden glared at James when he got back to their tiny hotel room.

"I just went to get something from the vending machines," he said as he shut the door behind him.

Hayden looked at his empty hands. "Liar." She stepped in front of him to block his path.

"Why would I lie about that?"

She looked into his eyes, searching for some sort of truth.

James grabbed her face and kissed her hard. She took a few steps back until she was up against the wall. He pulled away, but Hayden pulled him close and ran her fingers through his hair, and her lips met his. He rested both of his palms on the wall behind her as he pressed himself up against her. For Hayden, all thoughts of a possible argument were quickly forgotten.

Hayden looked through the slats of the blinds on the single window in their room and watched for anyone suspicious. She noted a man in a blue sedan. He seemed to be staring in their direction.

After a few minutes, she returned to bed and relaxed.

"So I've been thinking about what I want for my future," she said.

James sat up on the bed beside her and waited for her to elaborate.

"We've been through more than most people have. I know everything will be different now that we have to keep a low profile, but I wanna do something meaningful with my life."

"I think that's admirable."

"If I've learned anything, it's that my entire life before prison was superficial. I think I was leaning on my ex as a way to escape my mundane, never-satisfying reality. I just let things go too far. By the time I knew I was in trouble, it was too late."

"But now you have the opportunity to do whatever you want."

Hayden nodded. "Even though you lied to us about the wormhole, I guess I have to thank you. You gave me a second chance."

"You don't need to thank me. I also could've gotten us all killed." James got to his feet and pulled on some pants and a T-shirt.

"I know you feel guilty about Mason. But you shouldn't. You still managed to save the rest of us."

"I can't take credit for that." James shook his head. "Still feels like I did something wrong."

"Maybe you should try to move forward. Plan your next move. What do you want for your future anyway?"

"I don't know. I guess first I'd like to try to get back to some semblance of normalcy. Whatever that means while we're on the run from the law. Honestly, I haven't given the future much thought."

"Well, hopefully I'm in it," Hayden said, smiling.

James raised his eyebrows. "Let's just see how things go."

Hayden threw a pillow at James, and he dodged it.

"Come on. Let's get ready to go out."

80

They decided to walk the short distance from their motel to the bar. The night was bright. A full moon illuminated their path as they wandered, hand in hand, down the street. They arrived at O'Reilly's, a quaint bar. It was the type of place busy enough to indicate it wasn't a total dive, but not popular enough that anyone might recognize them.

Lynyrd Skynyrd's "Free Bird" was playing on the jukebox when they went in. Dozens of tiny pictures plastered the interior brick walls. No one as much as glanced in their direction as they took their seats at the bar and ordered drinks.

"Are you sure you don't want to leave town?" Hayden's soft voice enveloped his ears. "It's risky staying here." She ran her hand up his arm, her soft skin still lingering on his mind from that afternoon.

"I told you I think we're safe for now. Two years have passed here since we've been gone. It's likely we were presumed dead in the fire, and they gave up looking for us a long time ago."

She frowned. "Come on. Don't you want to run away together? It would be romantic."

"You know I'd love that." James kissed her on the forehead. He couldn't leave town now, not until he figured out what was next with his company.

"Well, you can tell me where you wanna run away to when I get back from the bathroom." She grinned and got up from her barstool.

James swirled his glass and watched the bourbon dance on the rocks. He hadn't told her yet that he didn't want to leave. With the success of their journey and, more importantly, their return, his work was just beginning. Besides, his colleagues would hunt him down if he tried to leave. He'd never seen them more intrigued than they'd been in the meeting today.

Suddenly, a sweet aroma wafted over him, like roses, before he heard a familiar rhythm in the tapping of heels on the hardwood floor. His body tensed before he even heard her voice.

"James."

No. It can't be. James gripped his glass so hard it nearly broke and slowly turned around. "Isabella," he mouthed, but no sound came out.

James pulled his wife into an embrace, and the familiar feeling of her hands on his back sent chills down his spine. A sense of relief and confusion washed over him simultaneously.

She was the first to pull away.

"How did you find me here?" James looked into her eyes. "Were you having me followed?"

"You didn't think our colleagues would track you the minute you left Avion?"

James sighed. He should've been more careful. "Where did you go after you left the lab that day? We were supposed to meet back at the house, but you just vanished."

Patrons seated on either side of James turned to stare.

Isabella lowered her voice so only he could hear. "I was faking my death for you, remember?" She smirked. "It turns out you're not the only one with secrets, James. Did you ever stop and wonder why I would agree to such a thing?"

He stared at her, baffled.

"Let's go somewhere we can talk," she said, grabbing him by the arm.

James's head was spinning, and not from the alcohol. He followed her out to the street corner. She looked as beautiful as ever, her hair in dark loose curls, her skin radiant under the soft glow of the streetlights.

"I'm sorry I kept things from you. But I couldn't let you in on my plan to disappear. You had to believe it was your idea. That was the only way to keep you safe."

"What plan?" James asked in disbelief. "I don't understand." He realized he had no idea who his wife really was.

"All you need to know is that I've been on the run my entire life. Things were fine for so many years, ever since I came to America. But finally, they've caught up with me. And now I have to keep moving again."

"Who are you running from? I don't understand how you kept this from me." He grasped her arm, and a couple of kids who stepped out for a smoke watched to see what he would do next. "Why did you feel like you needed to hide this?"

Her lips parted, but no sound came out.

"I know I should've done better. I wasn't there for you when you needed me," James's voice cracked.

"You were consumed with your research. You did what you felt you had to."

He dropped her arm but took her hand.

She returned his grasp. "Chris told me you were back. I had to come see you in person."

"Where have you been all this time?"

"I've been in hiding, working on a plan of my own." She looked down. "I never fully explained to you where I come from. Or what happened to my family."

"Explain it to me. I want to be here for you now," James said earnestly.

"This is something I need to do on my own. You of all people should understand that."

"Even after everything, you're still my wife. I never wanted to put you in harm's way."

Isabella's smile was small. "I was willing to sacrifice everything to help you further your research. I hope you got what you needed out of all this, and I'd love to hear about your experience. But I only came back to let you know I'm okay. Now it's time for me to go on my own journey."

"Whatever you have planned," said James, "you shouldn't do it alone."

"I just want to know what was on the other side of the wormhole."

James thought for a moment. "The time jump was one hundred years into the future. And the place we ended up was, well, apocalyptic."

Isabella's eyes widened, then a look of confusion crossed her face. "We?"

The bar door swung open, and Hayden stepped outside. "Hey. What's going on?"

James dropped Isabella's hand. He felt his stomach turn over. He looked back and forth between the two women, and saw Isabella eyeing Hayden disapprovingly.

"Well, I'm glad we got to catch up. Goodbye, James," Isabella said, and she turned and walked off down the street. Her dress billowed behind her, leaving her scent lingering in the air, all the memories and turmoil lingering along with it.

As quickly as she'd arrived, she was gone. James was left with countless questions circling in his mind. He looked at Hayden, her brow furrowed and her hand on her hip.

"Who was that?" Hayden asked.

James opened his mouth to speak just as his pocket started ringing.

"Where did you get that?" Hayden became visibly upset. "Don't you know we can be tracked?"

James turned away from her and accepted the call. "Yeah?"

"James, it's Chris. Can we meet? There's some stuff I really need to talk to you about."

"Now's really not a good time. I told you I'd see you in the morning."

"There's something I have to tell you. Well, two things, but one's not work related," said Chris.

James said, "You have about five seconds before I hang up."

"The team didn't want you to know yet. They don't think you're ready," said Chris. "What you asked for, it's already done. About two months ago . . . we found another wormhole."

James felt a chill run through his body. *How could my team have kept this a secret?* It was even more of a reason for him to get back to the lab and resume his work. Right after he figured out what Isabella was up to. Despite all he'd been through, he had an unquenchable thirst to explore where any other wormholes might lead. What other times of significance could he visit? Could he change? He'd have a new challenge dodging Hayden and the authorities, but it didn't matter. He had the universe at his fingertips.

ACKNOWLEDGMENTS

I would like to thank everyone who made this project possible and allowed me to publish my first book. It was a long process, as I initially wrote this story years ago. However, I know I couldn't have done it alone. Through the help of others close to me, I am able to share my work with the world.

First, I would like to thank my parents, Ken and Marie Romanski. I appreciate your continued motivation and support throughout all my endeavors over the years. Publishing this book wouldn't have been possible without your encouragement. I will be forever grateful for all you have done for me.

I would also like to thank Anita Henderson, Candice L. Davis, and the team at Elite Online Publishing for helping me prepare my book for publishing by supporting me through several editing processes, marketing plans, and seeing the project through to its completion. I am happy to have worked with you all.

Finally, I'd like to thank my beta readers, who helped me improve my story in the final stages, Kristen Weppner, Kevin Burns, Nate Ament, Priscilla Marion, Siena Esha, Nat Cooper, and Helen Atwell.

ABOUT THE AUTHOR

Victoria Romanski's passion for writing science fiction evolved from early interests in time travel and social justice, resulting in a novel vision of what the future could hold for us all.

A diligent spectator of political discourse and current societal issues, she crafts stories with themes that explore familiar topics, but with a dystopian twist. Victoria considers these subjects valuable to engage with while expressing her craft in fresh and inventive ways.

A storyteller at heart, Victoria enjoys learning about other cultures through global travel. She uses her role as an observer of human behavior to explore avenues to make the world a better place.

www.ingramcontent.com/pod-product-compliance
Lightning Source LLC
Chambersburg PA
CBHW040513170726
48295CB00012B/184